Who Iced the Snowman?
(A Cisco Maloney Mystery)

by

D. Ray Pauwels

This book is fiction. All characters, events, and organizations portrayed in this novel are the product of the author's imagination or are used fictitiously. Any resemblance to actual persons—living or dead—is entirely coincidental.

Copyright 2016 by D. Ray Pauwels

All rights reserved. No parts of this book may be reproduced or transmitted in any form or by any means, electronic or mechanical, including photocopying, recording or by any information storage and retrieval system, without written permission from the author, except for the inclusion of brief quotations in a review.

For information, email **Cozy Cat Press**, cozycatpress@aol.com or visit our website at: www.cozycatpress.com

COZY CAT
PRESS

ISBN: 978-1-939816-94-8

Printed in the United States of America

Cover design by Paula Ellenberger
www.paulaellenberger.com

1 2 3 4 5 6 7 8 9 10

Dedication:
To Jacques and Danielle, who started me
To Natalie, who put up with me
To Christichka, who married me
To Chapelle, Lyra and Reed, who succeed me

Table of Contents

Chapter 1: The Office 5
Chapter 2: The Precinct 20
Chapter 3: The Reward 38
Chapter 4: The Penthouse 55
Chapter 5: The Sewer 73
Chapter 6: The Coroner's 86
Chapter 7: The Sporting Goods Store 101
Chapter 8: The Message 119
Chapter 9: The Warren 127
Chapter 10: The Kitchen 139
Chapter 11: The Warehouse 154
Chapter 12: The Cabaret 163
Chapter 13: The Fat Man 177
Chapter 14: The Alley 184
Chapter 15: The Lakeside 189
Chapter 16: The Parade 199
Chapter 17: The Dame 208
Chapter 18: The Chase 222
Chapter 19: The Squat 238
Chapter 20: The Wrap 255
Chapter 21: The Epilogue 263

Chapter 1: The Office

It all started on a cold winter's day: Christmas Eve, to be exact.

I remember it clearly, probably because the liquor stores were closed. This was not a nod to the Yuletide approaching, mind you, but as a hangover effect from back when every upstanding lady in the Temperance movement had a henpecked senator for a husband.

I was hanging around my office like a worn-out stocking on a burnt-out fireplace, dry as a Bedouin bachelor's bed sheet. It had been two weeks since I'd been last hired, but I couldn't even recall what I'd been hired to do.

I wondered why it was so dead quiet; then I remembered they'd repossessed my short-wave radio the day before.

That's right—a radio. This was back in the good old days, after the big war in Europe (no, not the one with trenches and spiked helmets and calliope music; the other one with tanks and bombers and swing bands). Everything was in black and white, which made laundry less complicated. A "cell phone" was what you used to call your lawyer from jail. And private eyes would mutter through clenched teeth about the good old days.

Yeah, that's me—Cisco Maloney, Private Eye. "No job's too small, no fee's too big." I'd been a cop once, but the paperwork wasn't my style. Kept the badge, though; I found it came in handy when dealing with a plus-sized palooka who didn't take a shine to the old please-and-thank-you approach.

Lucky for me, I was the only detective-for-hire in town. Unlucky for me, that town was Wurstburg. It wasn't a bad place, but that didn't help me much. Founded by 19th-century German butchers seeking to escape persecution under the strict Bavarian purity laws regarding the contents of sausages, it got a rather stuffy reputation. Like a calm eye in the hurricane of history, hardly anything of significance ever happened here, which didn't make it the best place to practice my profession.

My derelict Christmas tree stood sulking in the corner, on its last legs. Hauling it out of storage was getting more and more depressing each year, but at least it was cheaper than buying a new one every time. Of course, in those days we didn't have artificial trees; this one was real, and dropping needles faster than a clumsy junkie with the shakes. At least I remembered to use gloves when handling it this time around. The year before, I'd tried to add some tinsel and caught a decoratively transmitted disease off the thing. What a sap.

I was never big on Christmas, anyway. All the rush, the phony cheer, the slushy, dirty snow on the streets... Old Scrooge summed it up best with his "bah, humbug."

As for winter, it could go ride a bus for all I cared. Unlike some people, I wasn't a big fan of the seasons as a rule. Summer is too hot for my overactive sweat glands, and spring gives people that goofy sense of optimism that makes me want to stand in front of them and punch myself in the face just to shake up their rosy worldview.

If I had to single out the one season I disliked the least, I'd say it's autumn. Especially since I live in the city. Who doesn't enjoy taking a stroll through the park to watch the litter change colors? Plus, fall was the perfect time of year to wear a trench coat, and, as a detective, I owned seven of them. If you wear a trench coat in summer, people assume you intend to flash them your moon and sixpence.

But back to the office...

I sat down at my desk, took out my letter opener, and started going through the morning's mail: bill, bill, NSF check, collection notice, overdue notice, overdraft notice, overnight delivery of final notice, "We Mean It," "Don't Make Us Send Vito," et cetera. Man, the people who made those rubber ink stamps were getting specific.

Suddenly, I got a call.

"Hey, Mister Maloney!"

I snatched up the phone, and then realized it was coming from outside the building. I ran over to the window, lifted it open, and looked out.

The sky was overcast. Snow was drifting down gently, like it was in no big hurry to land.

Down on the sidewalk was a paperboy dressed in a tweed cap, duffel coat, knickerbockers with knee-high socks, and buckled shoes. *Who dressed this kid? Charlie Chaplin's wet nurse?*

I opened the window and hollered down at him:

"Don't ever call me at the office, you mangy munchkin! Now am-scray!"

He waved a rolled-up copy of the *Daily Tattler* over his head.

"But don'tcha want your paper?" he yelled back in a shrieky pre-pubescent voice.

"Not unless there's fish and chips in it, kid!"

I slammed the window shut. These damn kids had no idea what my heating bills cost. (Neither did I, since heat was included with the rent. But still, it's the principle of the thing.) Where did he get the idea I'd want to read that gossipy tabloid rag? It was mostly candid pictures of actresses sunbathing on the beach, and hunky actors getting led away in handcuffs by police for punching photographers for taking pictures of their wives sunbathing on the beach. Lurid nonsense.

I mostly ignored the press as a matter of professional pride; if you had to read the papers to get your information, you were way behind the game. Besides, if you really needed one, you could always find a newspaper on a park bench, lunch counter, subway train, or even the library if you were desperate enough, and I had a strict personal rule against paying for anything that I stood a chance of getting for free.

I turned my attention back to the pile of bills on the desk, trying to find one skinny enough for me to pay off...fat chance.

A minute later, there was a knock on my door. A short figure with a lump on its head cast a silhouette through the frosted glass pane, so I figured the rascally little newsboy was back for more abuse, unwilling to take tongue-lashing-and-window-slam for an answer.

I waited in ambush behind the door with a hardcover edition of *Lord Quigglebottom's Manners Makeover for Aspiring Gentlemen* held behind my back: I'd give the kid a manners makeover, alright.

"Come iiiii-in!" I sang in a rich, mellifluous baritone. (One benefit of being the narrator is getting to write your own reviews.)

The door cracked open as I got ready to swing the heavy tome at the impish intruder's herringboned dome.

The shadowy head poked through the doorway. It belonged to a little old lady, her hair done up in a big grey bun that looked as though a chinchilla had decided to ball up and park on her melon. I put the brakes to the book-bashing, shelved *Lord Quigglebottom*, and courteously swung the door open the rest of the way.

"Uh, come on in, ma'am," I said. "Can I help you?"

She squinted up at me through her inch-thick bifocals, which may well have been made by Ben Franklin himself. Her voice cracked the air like a dried-out bullwhip.

"You were *supposed* to help me! You're that Costco Baloney, aren't you?"

Close enough. I'd been called a lot worse.

"Cisco Maloney, ma'am, like it says on the door."

I doffed my fedora as she shouldered her way past me and into my office.

She was dressed in some kind of alpaca wool petticoat, the kind of thing you might knit for yourself if you were marooned on a deserted island and forced to tailor your own duds from goat hide, Robinson Crusoe-style.

She turned clockwise on her clogs, planted her feet square in front of me, and pointed a bony index finger almost straight up my nose.

"And you call yourself a private detective?" she rasped.

I threw my caboose into reverse and took a step backaways, putting a more comfortable distance between her index and my nostril.

"That's what it says on the sign, madam."

"Then you need to get your sign fixed," she croaked as she jabbed her walking stick into my solar plexus.

As I clutched my chest, gasping for breath, she paced around the room, a palpable ring of displeasure with every step. I noticed that she didn't use the walking stick to walk so much as to poke at things that looked foreign to her, which meant anything built since the dawn of the steam engine.

"Back in my day," she raved, "we had real private eyes who could find a giblet in a gizzard pile! You paid them in bullets and they'd spit out lead for change! There was a work ethic you just don't see anymore, thanks to those no-good Existentialists and all their *acte gratuit* nonsense..."

Clearly, I wasn't the only bee in her bonnet. I caught my breath while she opened her steam valve full-throttle.

"Irish were considered ethnic! They weren't allowed in the good clubs! And don't even get me started on that Pablo Picasso character. He paints a house with two noses and they hang it in a museum. My canary does better than that on the newspaper! Speaking of which, they don't make good newsprint anymore, either. That *Tatler*'s ink rubs off on your fingertips, and it takes half a bar of carbolic soap just to wash it off..."

She continued raving, which gives me a little time to explain my business tactics to you, dear reader.

Keeping one's cool is Private Eye 101, a lesson that applied in all aspects of this line of work; not least of which was dealing with dissatisfied customers. (If you think about it, they started out dissatisfied in the first place, so you can't say I left them worse off than I found them.)

When dealing with an unhappy client, the important thing is to show them you're not rattled. If they've gotten desperate enough to hire you, their world is likely falling to pieces all around them, and they need the reassurance of having someone calm nearby to take it out on. It's all part of the job.

While the old bat flapped around the office, venting and poking at things, I pulled a slug from my pocket (the kind you use to trick slot machines, not the slimy cephalopod) and started rolling it over my knuckles like a poker player does with chips. It was a good way to appear nonchalant.

The old lady wasn't having it.

"Pay attention!" she snapped as she smacked the metal disc out of my hand with her stick and almost fractured a bone.

Ouch! It was a palpable hit, and dead accurate, too; she must have done a tour of duty as a nun at some point. The slug flew out of my hand and whizzed across the room, slicing a branch off the balding Christmas tree. More needles rained down.

"So?" she fumed.

"So what?" I replied.

"Have you been listening to a word I said?"

"Sorry, ma'am. I was in the middle of a narration."

"I hired you to find my lost kitty-cat, Smitty!"

"You did?"

When the unrattled front failed me, my backup plan was to play dumb and get clients to repeat themselves. That usually bought me some time to think up excuses.

"I did!" she replied. "You wanted payment in advance."

"I did?"

She raised the walking stick in my direction.

"You did! I gave you fifty dollars two weeks ago."

"Was it cash?"

"You insisted on it."

"Did you get a receipt? 'Cause if you did, it probably wasn't me."

She stepped closer, the walking stick clutched in both hands as though she were holding a samurai sword. She gave the impression of a raving ronin who'd just found an errant pube in his miso soup.

"Oh, it was you, alright," she said, her nostrils flaring. "I recognize the smug look on your face."

I racked my brains like they were billiard balls, but for the life of me, I couldn't remember having doings with the chinchilla-headed Gorgon before. Maybe I'd have remembered her if she'd been forty years younger, back before gravity bent her over and yanked her cheeks down to her collarbones. (I must admit, when it comes to women, I'm better at remembering the young, pretty ones, probably because I don't come across very many of them.)

"Well?" she asked. "Are you just going to stand there daydreaming? Or am I going to have to start playing a bit of whack-a-mole?"

She twirled her walking stick in the air like a batter at the plate and then wound 'er up, getting ready to knock my block into the bleachers.

I smacked myself on the forehead a couple times to get the old brain-brine circulating.

"Smitty...Smitty..." Then the light bulb lit up. "Now I remember! I checked every bar in town."

"And?"

"Well, you see, ma'am, results aren't necessarily guaranteed."

I shrugged for emphasis. (Mind you, I shrugged with a lot of style in those days, back when my shoulder blades were still sharp.)

"Then why does it say *that* on the door?" she asked, pointing to the words "RESULTS GUARANTEED" stenciled on the glass pane, just below my misspelled name.

Dang it, the old harridan was quick. I launched into a well-rehearsed disclaimer.

"Ah, I can see how that statement might have caused a slight misunderstanding..."

"What do you mean, buster?" she growled, shooting daggers at me though her coke-bottle specs.

"Beneath those words, there's some fine print that cost me a small fortune in legal fees: 'Terms and conditions apply. Guarantee void where prohibited by law. This offer only applicable at participating locations.' In addition, I should add those words are a guarantee that there will be *a* result; nowhere does it warranty that it has to be a *successful* result."

I should've been a lawyer.

She squinted, trying to read the tiny text backwards through the glass.

"Poppycock!" she concluded. "There's been no result, so I want my money back."

I trotted over to the other side of my desk to avoid getting jabbed or smacked by her stick again.

"Lady, the 'result' is that your kitty has flown the coop. Who knows why cats do these things...dodging unpaid debts is my guess. Oh, by the way, I also ran up a couple of bar tabs. Expenses are extra."

Ah, my favorite part of the job: billing for expenses. I'd usually tack on a few grocery bills, a full tank of gas, some cushioned insoles, and anything else I thought I could get away with.

I rummaged around in the drawers, trying to find a few receipts to fob off on the old crone, but I guess I overplayed my hand: as I bent down, something whizzed over my head and went "crash!" against the wall behind me.

Sharp shards of glazed ceramic cascaded over my head and shoulders. The septuagenarian serpent had pitched a vase! Lord knows where she'd been keeping it; her purse was tinier than my wallet, and my wallet was empty nine days out of ten.

"Hey!" I shouted as I shielded my head with my arms. "What the Maltese-Falcon-hell are you trying to do, lady?"

"Put my vase collection to good use," she replied as she swung her purse over her shoulder. "I'll be back in a week for my money, Malorkey. Maybe my son-in-law Vito can help you with your refund policy...or else do a renovation on that ugly face of yours. He knows karate personally."

She spat on the floor, then stormed out in her army-grade heels and slammed the door behind her so hard, she knocked my framed private investigator diploma right off the wall.

I guess little old ladies weren't as meek back then as they get painted out to be.

As I swept up the shards of vase into a manila file folder with an old toothbrush, I contemplated early retirement. The problem with that plan was that I had nothing to retire on except a vast collection of rare parking tickets. Any savings I'd managed to squirrel away usually got eaten up by the lean times when work was scarce, and this particular Christmas was the leanest one yet.

I knew when I'd gotten started as a freelancer that private investigation would be a tough racket, but I was champing at the bit to be my own boss. As I gathered up the bits of vase, it became clear that I was my own janitor, too. I chucked the broken pieces into the trash, hung my diploma back on the wall, and sat down at my desk to watch the phone mock me with its obstinate silence.

There was a knock at the door again, and another short shadow appeared through the frosted glass. For a minute I was worried that the old harpy had found more earthenware in her purse and was coming back to practice her fast-pitch.

But I was wrong.

It was worse.

The door burst open and in walked my landlady, a spiky little battle-axe with hair like a cluster of vampire bats, a nose like a can opener, and a thick accent that came straight from the seventh circle of Dante's *Inferno*.

"Malonno!" she hollered like a banshee on a butane bender. "Latey-monny, dice embers pinch an hour if ease a tree weakling!"

These weren't her exact words, but more of a loose transcription based on my admittedly wrecked recollection. I had absolutely no idea what lingo she was speaking, but managed to decipher her meaning by body language, tone of voice, logical abduction, and sheer force of will.

I was fairly certain that she was trying to remind me that December's rent was overdue by more than three weeks. Bracing myself for the onslaught, I turned the charm-o-meter up to ten.

"Missus DeSoutamianoguasalingam, what a nice surprise! Have you gained weight? You look so plump and chewy, like a Rubens model. Or the 'before' picture of a dieting ad."

(Actually, she looked more like a rat terrier that had gotten tossed into a tugboat's bilge, but telling massive lies is just part of my charm.)

She stared hard at me, probably trying to figure out if what I'd just said had anything to do with the rent money I owed her.

I tried to steamroll over the subject and flatten it with flattery.

"Is that a new coat? I was just talking to a client with the exact same one. I love the way it enhances your figure. *Très au courant*."

(Seriously, she and the little old lady must have raided the same bargain bin at the Andean shag rug store. When they call clothes "duds," this must be the fashion they're referring to.)

Mrs. DeSoutamianoguasalingam marched up to the desk and gave me a series of machine-gun taps on the shoulder.

"Spin a cuppa pita, tell sit tuba marinos! Rentboy raffle ticket! A selenium Dion!"

"Okay, okay!" I pleaded as I blocked her tapping with one hand and reached for my pen and checkbook with the other. "How about a post-dated check? Just fill in your name here..."

Her eyes caught fire at the sight of my checks. She smacked the pen clean out of my hand, flinging it across the room where it embedded itself into the wall.

"No no no! Dribble, bouncy, shoot–a-miss! Banquet shea 'UNICEF'! Hairy canary! Take-a-cash! Chuck-a-check!"

I looked her square in the eye.

"Listen, Missus DeSoutamianoguasalingam, I'm expecting payment any day now from a few clients who owe me big-time fees. As soon as the money comes in, I'll bring the rent straight to you in unmarked fivers. You'll have it by new year."

She stormed towards the door, trembling and shaking her fist.

"Gamble trot alpha bravo, dinghy caftan Novotel!"

(Even if I could translate it, I'm pretty sure that last bit wouldn't get past the Postmaster General.)

She slammed the door behind her so hard, it almost fell off the hinges. You'd think she'd be more careful with her own property.

My diploma fell off the wall again. I hung it back up.

If I'd thought pleading would do me any good, I might have tried to explain to her that I'd already been evicted from my apartment, and had been living in the office for almost a month (it wasn't all that comfortable, but at least the commute was quick).

If I'd thought threats would do me any good, I could have pointed out that she was in contravention of the Landlord and Tenant Act for having a resident living in a building zoned for commercial and retail use. But somehow, I got the feeling that she wouldn't flinch either way.

So I moped around the office instead. After two hours and three ham-on-ryes, I was starting to gather moss (or maybe it was a foot fungus). For the department stores, business was doing flat-out gangbusters this time of year, but for the private investigation racket, things only picked up *after* the holiday hubbub. That's when presents went missing, elderly relatives got lost in the snow, and daddy divorced mommy for locking lips with Santa Claus. Not the most exciting jobs in the world, but a private eye's gotta eat.

I suppose I could have closed up shop for the day and taken time off to do some Christmas shopping, but I had no one to buy presents for except my sidekick, and the only thing I ever gave him was a kick in the backside. What else is a sidekick for?

I decided to head on down to the police station. On my slow days, if things got really desperate, I'd hang around the old Wurstburg precinct and try to drum up some business.

People usually go to the cops first when they have a problem, but once they find out the Long Arm of the Law won't reach out to help them spy on their cheating wife or find their missing sock (unless they're the mayor), they tend to become more amenable to my fee structure. This makes the cop-shop a good place to troll for clientele. Besides, the fuzz always had some rum cake lying around, so it was never a complete waste of time.

I locked up the office, wondering how much longer my key would work, and how much longer Missus DeSoutamianoguasalingam would wait before she changed the locks and gave me the boot. I'd been there for a couple of years, but landladies don't generally take customer loyalty into consideration.

It wasn't the best building in the nicest neighborhood, but I knew from experience how much worse it could be. My first "office" had been a luggage locker at the train station, which I'd shared with a backpacker who'd gotten stranded when the company that issued his traveler's checks went bankrupt. His name was Jimmy. Actually, that was the nickname I'd given him; he used to jimmy open the locker whenever the key got stuck and wouldn't turn. For all I knew, poor Jimmy was still there, waiting for me to come back with lunch.

I stepped outside into the cool air of the afternoon. The sky was overcast: a hazy, gunmetal grey, typical of the shortest days of the year. The snow was still falling (in case you needed a weather update).

I hopped into the slagheap I called my car, a 1932 International Harvester combine chassis that was salvaged from a barn, converted into a hot-rod dragster, then downgraded to little more than a motorized shopping cart after a few too many crashes 'round hairpin turns.

The car was what you might call a "work in progress"; I kept it together with matchsticks, freezer tape, and chewing gum, and it usually needed a bump start when the engine was cold. Luckily, thanks to the neighborhood geography, it was downhill everywhere I went. (Metaphorically speaking, it wasn't much different.) The car might not have looked like much, but when push came to shove (and neighbors came to push), the engine usually fired up after a couple of tries.

Traffic was light. The suckers who still had to work nine-to-five on Christmas Eve weren't on the roads yet, although it wouldn't be long before the rush-hour lemming run got underway. I made it to the police station without even having to stop once, which is good because my brake pads were about as thin as a dime that got left on the railroad tracks.

There was only one small spot available outside the precinct, so I found myself attempting a parallel parking job that would have given Euclid some mighty geometrical nightmares. Still, with a bit of bumper grease, I managed to squeeze the car into the tiny space.

I climbed out and headed for the front door of the police station.

Chapter 2: The Precinct

The precinct was one of those stately old brownstone buildings typical from back in the days when cops still walked the beat, twirled their nightsticks behind their backs, and whistled Wagner's Greatest Hits as they strolled beneath the streetlamps. There was none of this antiseptic glass-and-steel nonsense you get nowadays; architecture seems to be a lost art, like dowsing, spoon bending, and macramé.

I pushed my way through the heavy oak entrance doors, polished to the bare wood by the countless callused hands of street-weary police officers and their delinquent charges, and instantly caught the warm, sweet whiff of nostalgia—sweat, blood, and black mold providing body notes, faint traces of vomit and urine in the bouquet, and a crisp disinfectant finish (pine scent...or could it have been Douglas fir?).

The smell brought back memories of my days as a fresh-faced recruit, eager to take on the bad guys, bring justice to the city, and tap into a modest stream of steady graft that would fly just under the taxman's radar. Ah, to be young and idealistic again.

It wasn't long before police work made me cynical, though. When crime rates were down, politicians would happily take the credit, or people would say it was thanks to a strong economy; nobody gave a nod to the cops. Then the crime rate started to climb like a rat up a drainpipe, and suddenly it was all our fault.

For every bad guy taken off the streets, two seemed to take his place, as though there were some kind of criminal-breeding pyramid scheme going on. We were damned by the press if we didn't solve the latest sensational felony to hit the headlines, and damned by the human rights kooks if we hauled someone in and connected their body bits to a car battery to get their talk-taps flowing. We couldn't win.

Everyone freaked out in different directions: some wanted the cops to have more power, others thought we had too much. There was no moral compass, let alone a fancy moral GPS like they have nowadays. The system was headed for a breakdown: a conflict of too many interests that were only interested in conflict. To add to the confusion, that was when they started coming out with twin-bladed shaving razors (I didn't get it: did the second blade put the stubble back in?) Society was changing, and I didn't want to be around when it asked if the new dress it was trying on made it look fat.

But what slowly sucked me dry of my motivation for police work was writing those confounded reports. I didn't join the force to hone my secretarial skills; I joined because I wanted to be part of the action, out there kicking ass and taking names in a way that would inspire folks to come up with new names for me kicking ass. Not to mention that I was deemed unfit to serve in the Red Cross, Salvation Army, or Rotary Club. But I digress...where was I?

Oh yeah: the precinct. Every time I visited the place, I was reminded that my own run-down office building didn't quite hold up in comparison. Whoever designed the station paid attention to the details; it had marble-tiled floors, switchblade-carved banisters, blood-stained-glass windows, and delicate wrought-iron bars. Most importantly, it had a cleaning staff to do the dirty work. Sometimes I missed working in a place with class, but the thought of having to change another typewriter ribbon soon cured me of that.

As I walked into the main entrance hall, I immediately spotted a few familiar, spotted faces: good old Officer Reilly was standing in front of the station desk, a beacon of Celtic pastiness with his flame-orange hair and galaxy of freckles, and sitting behind the desk was Sarge, our creatively nicknamed desk sergeant, roosting at his usual post, occasionally rubbing mail-order hair-growth formula into that cue-ball scalp of his.

Reilly was keen, but not likely to get any medals for bravery. His arrest policy was "women and children first," because they were least likely to put up a fight.

As for Sarge, no matter what time of day or night it was, he was always sitting at that desk, and I mean *always*; I never even saw him take a bathroom break (not that I'd want to watch, mind you).

Next to Reilly was a woman, and I mean that in the fullest sense of the word. She was wearing a dress fit for an Italian funeral: black, short, and so tight, I could barely breathe. She was tapping her stiletto heels impatiently, as if she were trying to chisel her way to China.

It looked like Reilly had pinched another miscreant of the fairer sex.

"Got a live one for ya, Sarge," he said in his Irish brogue. "Her name's Frieda. Frieda Rome."

Sarge heaved a sigh and reached for his fountain pen.

"What's the charge, Reilly?"

"She's a woman of pleasure, Sarge."

Sarge gave Reilly a blank stare.

"Let's put it down as 'living off the avails of indecent behavior.' You got evidence, right?"

"I'm still saving up so's I can afford some."

The streetwalker nudged her captor.

"I don't take pennies, hopalong."

I took an instant shine to the cut of her jib.

Sarge tried to write in his notebook, but his fountain pen was dry. He dipped it in an inkpot and filled it up.

"Come on, Reilly. The prosecutor's going to want something more substantial than that."

"Well, ya see, Sarge," Reilly explained, "she's a stenographer by day and types forty words per minute. But she's been moonlighting on the Dictaphone™ and charging forty dollars per hour...if ya know what I mean."

He tapped the side of his nose with his forefinger.

"I don't," Sarge replied, "but it sounds filthy enough. Let's book her."

The call girl landed both elbows on Sarge's desk, rested her chin on her interlocked fingers, and purred at him like a Cheshire cheetah that just ate the world's biggest canary.

"Good luck, officer. I'm already booked for the rest of the month."

"See?" said Reilly. "She's a brazen hussy, no two ways about it. Absolute dearth of scruples."

The way she batted her false eyelashes, she was obviously swinging for the fences. She turned to Reilly and stroked the buttons on his uniform.

"Why, is that *me* you're talking about with those big fancy words?"

Reilly stammered as steam rose from under his collar and his orange hue turned to red.

"That is, I, uh...Ya know, Sarge, about that evidence? Maybe I'd best give her a quick pat-down, just to be on the safe side."

The call girl's tone took a testy turn.

"Hey, I know my rights, buster, and there's no way I'm gonna let some low-rank flatfoot *habeas* my *corpus*." Then she leaned over to Sarge and tapped the desk impatiently. "Just hurry up and put me in jail, would ya? I got customers in there, too."

I decided to join the fray with a bit of flair; I flung my fedora towards the hat rack, giving it a bit of a flip.

Missed. My flip turned to flop.

I picked up the fedora and put it on a hook. To cover up my gaffe, I tried to muster up some of that phony cheer I mentioned earlier.

"Evening, fellas! Merry Christmas, and all that jazz."

Sarge folded his arms into an origami of disapproval.

"Well, well. Look what the cat coughed up."

It seemed my welcome at the station was starting to wear out. Maybe Sarge was still sore at me from the time I'd filled his tube of muscle rub with hair remover. Can't see why, as he didn't have very much to lose in the first place.

I ignored him.

"What'cha got there, Reilly?" I asked in reference to his attractive arrestee. "Early Christmas present?"

"She's being charged with soliciting, Cisco," Sarge interrupted.

I looked the lady up and down, this time from close range. From where I stood, it was like getting a bird's-eye view over the French Alps...if the French Alps were getting pushed up by a French bustier, that is.

"Soliciting, eh? And I bet she wasn't selling Fuller brushes."

I noticed that she and Reilly had their wrists cuffed together. I gave him a sly poke in the ribs.

"Say, Reilly, I didn't take you for the kinky kind."

"He'll be getting my invoice in the mail," cooed the call girl. She gripped Reilly's chin between her finger and thumb and cracked a smile for the first time.

Reilly blushed.

"But I'm on duty!"

"So am I," she countered, "and the meter's running."

Impressed with her moxie, I handed the plucky miss one of my business cards.

"Here, honey, take my peculiars."

She let go of Reilly and pinched my card like it was a dead bug.

"Who are you?" she asked, wrinkling her nose.

"Cisco Maloney, private investigator. Let me know if you need your priva—uh, something private investigated."

She read the card.

"Private investigator, huh? That's a relief. For a second there, I though you were the public defender."

Sarge butted in.

"Cisco, what makes you think a call girl would hire you?"

"I dunno. Maybe she needs me to find her virginity."

That got her dander up. She dropped the card and grabbed my tie by the double Windsor.

"Make wise again, buster, and you'll need to hire somebody to find your teeth."

"Cute," I answered. "They teach you that line in concubine college?"

"Smart aleck!"

Smacko. She walloped me right in the jowl with an open hand, each finger tipped with a red-painted talon that she could have used to shuck oysters.

It was my first slap that day, and talk about a left hook! Good thing, she only hit the face, but still...she practically knocked my neck out of joint.

Reilly restrained her from dishing out some more.

"Alright, miss, that's enough," he said. "Come along."

He dragged her away as she painted the air blue.

"You creep! You BLEEP with me again and I'll hoof your BLEEP with a size-ten boot so far up your BLEEPing BLEEP, they're gonna need forceps to get it out!"

(Sorry about the bleeps, but I'm sure the Postmaster General goes through my mail, and I don't need him going postal on my lowly self over a few excessively Anglo-Saxon words.)

I straightened my necktie in the hopes that it would hold my vertebrae together while they healed.

It was obvious that Sarge got an extra helping of kicks watching me get whacked by a sawbuck streetwalker. He chuckled to himself as he unwrapped an enormous hero sandwich, dripping with mayonnaise and extra pickles.

"So what brings you here, Cisco?" he asked between chomps on the footlong. "Jonesing for some rum cake, or is business slow again?"

"Slower than a sandpaper toboggan, Sarge."

"Why don't you rejoin the force? We could use some more chuckles 'n' yuks around here."

"Because I refuse to shower with other men, that's why. I only slather the lather solo."

"But you work with Carmine."

"That's different. We take baths."

A pickle slice shot out Sarge's nose.

"Separately!" I clarified.

As every cop within earshot burst out laughing, I remembered another reason why I'd quit the force. Good-old-days notwithstanding, being a cop was like working with every gridiron goon you hated in high school, except they were all grown up, grown fat, armed to the gills, and itching for an excuse to shoot first and ask questions *maybe*. People often asked me if I missed being part of a team, but I told them most of the cops I knew bore all the camaraderie of a pack of jackals.

"Listen up for once and get it straight," I said to Sarge, loud, so everyone else could hear me. "I only keep Carmine around so dames think I look good by comparison."

I didn't like to badmouth my sidekick, but it flowed so naturally off the tongue...

Sarge pulled a toothpick out of an olive and poked it in my direction.

"I hear you only keep him around 'cause you can't read," he said.

"That's a lie!"

I admit that Sarge's slander left me a bit flummoxed.

"I'm not...he doesn't...it's just that..."

You know those times when you can't think of a good retort, so you let your mouth off the reins and it flaps in the wind like the mainsail of a loony schooner, while you buy time until your brain can cook up a decent comeback?

"What I meant was.... Hey, is it hot in here? Who won the fights last night? Hoo boy, how about those ice hockey teams, huh?"

I was having one of those times.

Luckily, my hyperactive word-hole was plugged up by a gust of cold air from outside as the precinct doors opened.

Speak of the devilled egg: in walked Carmine himself.

As you might have gathered, Carmine Appelbaum was my sidekick. I can't remember when he'd first started working with me, but it felt like he'd been hanging off my coattails since forever.

Carmine was so short, he had to reach up to tie his own shoelaces and stand on a stool to brush his teeth. He dressed the same as me (heck, back then everyone dressed the same), but did his shopping in the children's department. The advantage of his lack of stature was that on the few occasions when we had to fly together, he fit in the overhead compartment—anything to keep expenses down.

Carmine strolled up to the station desk, his hands behind his back.

"Hey, Cisco. Hey, Sarge. Merry Christmas."

"What brings you here, shortstop?" I asked.

"I've been lookin' all over for you," he replied.

There was a definite squeak to his voice, like air being let out of a party balloon.

"Why didn't you call my office?" I asked. "It would have been nice to hear the phone ring for a change."

"Sorry, boss. I'm down to my last nickel."

"So what do you want?"

"To give you your second Christmas gift."

"Second gift? I don't remember getting a first."

"I got you a subscription to the *Daily Tattler*. Didn't they deliver it?"

"Uh, no... Why would I want the *Tattler*?"

"You're always staring at the front page when we're waiting in line at the grocery store. There's not many words, and it has loads of pictures."

I stitched my eyebrows together and fired him a look.

"I thought I said no gifts this year."

Carmine took a paper shopping bag from behind his back.

"I know, boss. It's just that I saw something in the store and couldn't resist."

That Carmine: always a sucker for fancy retail displays. He stuffed his hand into the bag and pulled out a little package wrapped in newsprint; the kind you get free when Jehovah's Witnesses come knocking.

I got over my disapproval, took the package, and tore it open. Inside was a box with a label that read: "Barkley's Soap-On-A-Rope. Now with 10% more musk."

I admit I was moved by the gesture.

"Gee, that's swell of you, kid. I can use this if I ever wind up in prison."

"Why's that?"

"Cause you never want to drop soap in the Big House. Believe me, it's bad for your...uh, never mind. I'll explain when you're older."

"But I'm thirty-two!"

Poor kid. So innocent. *Ignorant* mostly, but innocent too. Not to mention naïve. (Well, okay, I just mentioned it.) Carmine was something of a man-child, if you will, although he had a big heart, which might come in useful if I ever need a transplant.

He cast his eyes to the ground and fidgeted a little.

"You know, Cisco, I might have to take my old job back at the carnival. Things have sure been quiet lately."

Sarge butted in with a smirk.

"You could try for a job as an elf at the department store."

"Hardy-har, Sarge," Carmine rebutted. "You couldn't even get a job as a security guard at the department store."

Sarge had no comeback. I had to admit: sometimes the mouse could roar.

I leaned over Sarge's desk and tried to peek at his notebook.

"Anything interesting on the blotter, desk jockey?"

Sarge cocked an eyebrow at me and pulled the notebook closer to his chest. Then he cocked his other eyebrow.

"Not if you civvies are going to talk to me like that."

Sheesh, who knew the crusty old bureaucrat was so thin-skinned?

"Aw, lighten up, Sarge, and help out an old buddy," I said. "You don't want Carmine to wind up selling matches on the street again, do you?"

Sarge looked down at Carmine's mopey face and rolled his eyes.

"Okay, okay. You can cut the violin music."

He flipped through his notes.

"We just got the usual Christmas antics," he explained. "Kids chucking snowballs, caroling without a permit, transporting mistletoe across county lines, snowicides..."

"Snowicides?"

"Section 11-38: It's when someone murders a snowman."

"Ah, gotcha," I replied. "I don't remember that one being on the books."

"It's new," Sarge said. "Some bleeding-heart do-gooder at City Hall managed to get it passed."

Carmine piped in.

"They call it 'bonhomicide' in Quebec. That's French."

"Try learning English first," I advised him. "You don't go from training wheels to unicycle just like that."

Sarge flipped through his notes some more.

"Come to think of it, looks like we've had quite a few snowicides lately," he mumbled.

That got me interested.

"You don't say? Give me the scoop, Sarge, with nuts on top."

"Here, read the reports for yourself."

He handed me his notebook with a grin. I fobbed it off on my young apprentice.

"Uh, you read it, Carmine. The left hook that hooker landed blurred my vision a bit."

"What's a hooker?" he asked.

"Never mind. Read."

Carmine pored over the notes, silently mouthing the words with his lips as he went along.

"I mean *out loud*, nimrod!"

"Five victims," he read. "All of them white snowmales of average build, three snowballs tall. Each dressed in a top hat, plaid scarf, and wool mitts. Found melted in various locations: the first one inside a garage, the second in the trunk of a car, the third at the soda fountain at Pilkington's Department Store, the fourth on someone's front lawn, and the fifth in a public restroom. Cause of death in each case determined to be acute melting, followed by dehydration through evaporation."

"Sounds like these could have all been accidental," I said to Sarge. "Why are they being treated as snowicides?"

Sarge shrugged again.

"That's how they were described when they were phoned in, but when we tried to find witnesses, nobody would make a statement."

"Figures," I said.

Carmine handed the notebook back to Sarge.

"Think there's a connection between all of these, boss?"

"Do ten dimes make a buck? I *always* think there's a connection. But *we* need a connection to a case we can make some money on. This isn't it."

"I never read about any of this in the papers," Carmine said to Sarge.

Sarge shifted back in his seat as he picked at his teeth.

"Melted snowmen don't exactly make the front page," he said. "It's just as well; we don't have the budget to set up a snowicide squad. And if we did, people would just complain that we're wasting resources."

Sarge had a point, and not just at the tip of his pen. Back then, snowmen were what you might call an underclass; people could barely tolerate them, especially in Wurstburg where their appearance was a relatively new phenomenon. They weren't exactly my cup of tea either (I prefer coffee, black, with a shot of whatever's hot 'n' handy), but I went by the philosophy of live-and-let-live. So long as nobody's trying to stab, shoot, or subpoena me, they're okay in my book.

I could stand the snowmen one-on-one, but put a group of them all together and I had to admit, they could be a downright unsavory bunch. (Now don't get me wrong; I have snowman friends. Well, more like one snowman friend. Okay, he's this snowman living in a refrigerator box outside the five-and-dime where my bookie does his loitering. Whenever I go in, he asks me for spare change and I do a slight hunch of my shoulders to make it clear that I'd give him some money if I could, but don't have any to spare, since I already had to search the couch cushions all morning to scrape together enough to pay off my bookie. That counts as a friend, right?)

Though snowmen were mainly loners, every once in a while you'd come across a pack of them gathered on someone's front lawn, littering the place with stray buttons and lumps of coal, or dropping the occasional corn-cob pipe. Some said that snowmen hanging around on your property was a sign of good luck—a superstition that was likely started by the cheeky buggers themselves. But people mainly thought of them in the same terms as bubonic plague, root canals, or fanged bedbugs. In other words, if I haven't made myself clear yet, they were for definite certainty almost universally regarded as *personae non grata*.

Snowmen traveled around like gypsies back when it was okay to call them gypsies. Given their tendency to melt in warm weather (the snowmen, not the gypsies), it was natural that they'd migrate according to the seasons.

In warmer months, they headed up to the Arctic. Word on the street was that most made a beeline for the North Pole; apparently Santa Claus hired them to do the dirty jobs his elf syndicate refused to do, like scooping up after reindeer or finishing off the half-eaten candy canes. I'd heard it claimed that snowmen who could read and write were tasked with answering letters from children. (Apparently, some of the sprats who'd been good all year would develop a sense of entitlement and get cocky, presenting Santa with long lists of their expectations that required sophisticated rebuffing). And I heard Claus had an entire department dedicated to answering appeals from kids who complained about the presents they'd gotten the previous year. If anything grated on my nerves, it was ingrates.

As winter approached, the snowmen would migrate south, picking up odd jobs here and there. In rural areas, cross-country skiing clubs would hire them to pick up trash along the trails. Ice fishermen hired them as gophers to shuttle beer and vittles to their huts out on the frozen lakes. Long-haul truckers would pack a few dozen of them in their refrigerated cargo holds in case the cooling unit broke down. There was plenty of work to keep them busy in the country. But in the cities, people had very little use for snowmen, at least not anymore, and they mostly loitered around the streets, making a nuisance of themselves.

One thing's for sure: whether or not they worked for a living, snowmen were scavengers to the core. I guess in the frozen wastes of their homeland there wasn't much in the way of knick-knacks, so down in the city they went positively ape collecting all manner of crap. (Pardon my language, but it's the technical term.)

This was often the root of human-snowman friction: snowmen didn't observe the same boundaries that regular folks did in their relentless quest for tat. Every once in a while, one of them would get trapped in a heated garage while rooting around in a coal bin or rummaging through the garbage for buttons or a spare carrot. The result was a big puddle on the floor, to be mopped up and wrung out by a peeved proprietor.

I guess that's why I'd never heard of the term "snowicide" before: when a snowman melted, it was considered just another thing that happened, no more newsworthy than a squirrel getting squashed under your car tire. It's not like there'd be much to report: you couldn't tell any of them apart, and they didn't seem to have any names.

Except for Plotzky, of course.

One winter's day, long ago, who knows why, Plotzky the Snowman blew into town. Despite his commie-sounding name and an accent as thick as the Iron Curtain, he managed to wrangle an audition for a talent show and wowed the kids with his "holly-jolly-Christmas" routine. (I guess he had more personality than most snowmen, but that's like saying he was fatter than a toothpick.) He got signed up with a contract and instantly became the star of his very own Saturday-morning kiddie radio program, which then made the move over to the new medium of television. All of this was too much to bear for the Decency League, which saw him as the wrong kind of triple-threat: snowman, foreigner, and a suspected communist agitator going after the hearts and minds of our most impressionable and gullible demographic. I heard that threats of bodily harm were a regular concern for the public relations team that answered Plotzky's fan mail.

I get why the Decency Leaguers were so paranoid. For some reason that no parent in the world could understand, kids just ate up Plotzky's act. (I never had kids of my own, mind you, but as a private eye, I had to keep up with whatever the culture was up to, regardless of how ridiculable it got.) By the time his original contract came up for renewal, he was in a position to write his own meal ticket.

To call him "the richest and most famous snowman ever" seems like an understatement, given that most snowmen lived approximately 20,000 leagues below the poverty line and were an anonymous, homogeneous mass, all seemingly identical. Plotzky was probably the only one to have a bank account, let alone a personal fortune.

And he took to the high life like a duck to champagne. Word on the street was that he had set himself up with a deep-freeze penthouse in a chichi part of Wurtzburg so he'd be cozy-cold all year round. During the warmer months, he was chauffeured about in a refrigerated limousine, custom-crafted by a luxury German automaker that normally built parade cars for dictators, despots, plutocrats, and pontiffs. He had expensive tastes: his scarves were cashmere, his carrots were organic, and he'd had his coal-lump eyes pressure-treated to form diamond pupils in the middle of each one. It was clear that he didn't exactly embrace the lumpenproletariat lifestyle, let alone champion their cause, and suspicions about his communist sympathies eventually melted away.

With endorsements up the yang, his own chain of ice-cream and slush-drink stands, and his face and logo on paper cups and waffle-cone napkins scattered around gutters and bus shelters all over the city, Plotzky was here and he was here to stay. If there was one snowman that people might talk about in grudgingly respectful terms, it was him, and he was it.

But let's go back to the station desk...

"Maybe snowmen getting melted isn't good enough to make the news," said Carmine, "but it still sounds like somebody should investigate."

Sarge scoffed and put away his notebook.

"It's just your garden-variety snowmen, sprout. It's not like Plotzky got melted."

Hasty footsteps echoed from down the hall. Officer Reilly ran up to the station desk all a-fluster, screeched to a stop on his heels, and wheezed for breath.

"Hey Sarge, did'ja hear?" he asked between gasps. "Plotzky got melted!"

Like a bunch of first-class doofuses, we all said "What?" at the same time. From a nearby hallway, I heard what sounded like a brass band playing a not-so-in-tune musical stinger: Dunh-dunh-dunh-DUUUUNH.

Reilly caught his breath.

"No foolin,' or me name's not Porick! It happened late last night."

"Where?" asked Sarge.

"In his penthouse, 43rd and Main. Right next to the poinsettia shop."

That was the only cue I needed. I gave my sidekick a kick in the backside.

"Ow!" Carmine wailed. "What was *that* for?"

"Motivation. What's more, I kinda like it. Let's go."

As I headed out, I noticed a shabby-looking brass band huddled in the hallway, poring over a batch of sheet music that looked like a butcher had used it to smack a cloud of flies.

Along with the more familiar combination of trumpet, trombone, and bugle were a French horn (I guess like vanilla ice cream, it was just a regular horn, only slightly off-white and with the word "French" in it), a flugelhorn (is *flugel* how you say "French" in German?), a tuba (the Fatty Arbuckle of the orchestra), a euphonium (think *tuba-lite*), and what looked an awful lot like a bazooka (the guy playing that one must have taken himself for top brass—he was probably suffering from bandshell-shock).

I turned back to the desk.

"Hey, Sarge, what's with the band?"

"They're playing our Christmas party tonight," he replied.

The boys in brass attempted a New Orleans-style chorus of "Jingle Bells" in a brief flourish, which should have gotten them immediately arrested for attempted impersonation of the Perspiration Hall Jazz Band. Forget the rockin' pneumonia and the boogie-woogie flu: these guys could have caused a raging epidemic of tin-ear tinnitus and the hearing-aid skronk.

"Eh. To each their own," I muttered to Sarge.

"Don't you like music?" he asked.

"Sure, I do," I answered. "I just hate the way it sounds."

I grabbed my hat off the rack and made for the exit, calling out to my sidekick:

"You coming, kiddo?"

From behind me, I could hear Carmine's voice and shoes squeaking in tandem.

"I'm with ya, Cisco! Wait f'me!"

Chapter 3: The Reward

You might be wondering why I was so keen to check out the crime scene, so I'll tell you.

When I first started out, I assumed people would be banging down my door, begging for my help, but I soon discovered that finding clients was no cakewalk in the park.

The people who sought me out tended to be those with the most to lose: friends and relatives of moribund aristocrats engaged my services to dig up dirt on each other while they jockeyed for pole position in the Last Will and Testament race; sometimes a hotshot journalist working on a breaking story got paranoid about getting scooped, and needed my help to flush out the dirty details before the competition did, or to find out how much the competition knew, or to feed the competition false information; and I'll never forget the time a Saudi prince hired me to find out which wife he was currently cheating on (his rug was a few weaves short of a thick pile, if you know what I mean).

Their motives weren't always pure, and the only thing they really had in common (besides loads of money) was deep-seated mistrust; so the tough part was convincing them to take me into their confidence and lay their crooked cards on the table. That could be a tough hump to get over, which I learned the hard way, but at least the rich and desperate types knew they needed me.

Most of the others didn't. It doesn't occur to the average upstanding citizen who's been wronged that they can buy themselves a bit of justice if they know where to shop, so they rarely came knocking on my door.

I realized early in my career that the cheese doesn't come to the mouse...I'd have to follow the trail of breadcrumbs if I wanted to locate the loaf. Jumbled metaphors notwithstanding, what I'm getting at is that if you're not proactive in this line of work, you're dust.

Private investigation thrives on paranoia, suspicion, jealousy and mistrust, and in my experience, nothing stirred up those murky waters more than money, fame, death, and sex. It was obvious that the Plotsky case involved at least three of those, and the fourth was likely to be mixed in as well. This meant there was a good chance that somewhere, someone with a stake in the affair might want to hire a guy like me. So there I was, chasing after a melted snowman on Christmas Eve.

Carmine followed me to my old bucket of bolts, still parked outside the precinct. The windshield was covered in the white flaky stuff, and I don't mean canned tuna. I didn't have a fancy snow-removal brush (what am I, a millionaire?), and my wipers were worn down to the bare metal, so I had to brush off the snow with my tie. I didn't mind; the tie had been a tablecloth in a previous life, and if it had good karma, it would get reincarnated into a nice pair of shoelaces one day. What I *did* mind was the parking ticket buried under the layer of powder—another one to add to my collection.

We hopped into the car. As the engine was still a bit warm, I managed to start it with nothing more than a turn of the ignition key and a selection of Italian threats and curse words my mother taught me.

Carmine, big fan of simplistic entertainment that he was, turned on the dashboard Victrola™ as soon as we pulled out of the parking spot. The radio hissed a symphony of white noise until he finally landed on a station.

A horrible warbling sound howled from the speaker. At first I thought it was the car's engine giving up the ghost, or maybe I'd run over a set of bagpipes, but it turned out to be something the show's host referred to as "contemporary opera."

"Will you turn that damn thing off?" I ordered. "It's like headache fertilizer."

"Can I at least try to find my program?" he asked.

"I'd prefer you try to find another hobby."

"But it's almost time for the Big Band Swing Hour with Hyman Moyleskin and his Real Gone Baton," he whined.

"Fine, fine. Just turn down the volume."

Carmine twiddled the tuner to a new frequency. A crackly cacophony sputtered out of the speakers.

"Give me a few seconds to tune it in," he said.

"I'm having trouble tuning it out."

"Gee whiz, boss, you should learn to appreciate modern music."

"Modern music? All I hear is static and non-copyrighted snap, crackle and pop."

"Just wait," he said. "I'll see if I can get a better signal."

He fiddled with the radio while my ears burned.

"I think it's time to replace the coat hanger we put in when your antenna broke," he added.

"You mean when *you* broke it," I said. "You're the one who forgot to put it down last time we went through the car wash, remember? That was my last hanger."

"I thought you kept a spare?"

"I had to use it to unclog the toilet."

"Ugh. No further questions, boss."

He turned the radio dial like a safecracker breaking into Fort Knox.

Back then we didn't have sophisticated diagnoses for these things, but if I were to make a list of Carmine's personality peccadilloes, it would include obsessive-compulsive disorder, attention deficit disorder, inferiority complex, and omniphobia.

"You kids and your loony tunes these days," I grumbled. "Whatever happened to the classics? Like silence?"

"Who are you calling 'kid'?" he replied in his peeved voice. "I'm almost middle-aged."

"It's a miracle you made it that far."

I didn't mean to be so grouchy, but those ham-on-ryes I'd scarfed down earlier weren't sitting so kosher.

Carmine finally homed in on the signal, without the static. An eruption of jazz blasted forth from my tinny car speakers, which made it sound as if the orchestra were playing from the bottom of a can of pineapple juice.

"Listen to that band," said Carmine with revolting enthusiasm as he snapped and popped his fingers along to the epileptic meter.

"What's the point?" I asked. "I can't even hear a downbeat."

"It's polyrhythmic syncopation," he said. "FIVE-one-two-THREE-four-FIVE-and-six-bits-SHAVE-and-a-HAIR-cut, RINSE, lather, RE-peat, TAKE your MO-ther to the BAR-ber-SHOP..."

"Turn it!" I demanded.

Carmine cringed and spun the tuner again. He dialed past a newscast for a split-second.

"Hang on," I said. "Turn it back."

Though I only caught a few quick words, one of them sounded like it could have been "Plotzky" (or maybe it was "plots quay" or "blots gee," but let's not split hairs or we'll be here all night).

He swiveled the dial back to the news program.

The announcer spoke in that typically reassuring baritone that helped everyone forget we were in the middle of the worst economic nosedive since the Great Bathtub Bubble had burst at the close of the 1920s. He was just wrapping up a hot story.

"...a housekeeper discovered the melted puddle of the beloved children's entertainer on the living room carpet and called the city's finest. Police are promising a thorough investigation and expect to have the mystery solved by Boxing Day. Plotzky's exact age was unknown. No next of kin have been named. We'll have more on this story after a minute of respectful silence."

Carmine broke the respectful silence.

"Hey, boss, he's talking about the...the whatchamacallit. You know—that thingymadoodle we're going over to investimagate!"

"It's called a 'snowicide,' remember?"

"Yeah, that's it! 'Bonhomicides' in Quebec!"

"Just shut up so I can listen."

There was a quick rustle of papers, and then the newsman continued, his voice punctuated by intermittent static and the irregular murmur of the car's timing belt.

"And in breaking news, this station, Kay-Oh-El-Dee twelve ninety on your AM dial, has just received word that an anonymous figure has posted a thousand-dollar reward for any information that will explain the mysterious circumstances of Plotzky's demise. We will return with more well-timed news items after these messages from our sponsor: Olson's Orthopedic Truss Fabrication Corporation."

An all-too-familiar, insufferably perky melody started up. I almost upchucked my ham-on-ryes in a reaction that would have given Pavlov plenty of satisfaction.

"Ugh, turn it off!" I moaned. "If I have to hear that damned orthopedic truss jingle one more time, I'll get rid of the radio and learn harmonica."

Carmine killed the radio, suddenly as excited as a teething puppy with a brand new pair of slippers.

"Copulatin' clams, Cisco! Did you hear that? A thousand dollars!"

I had a brief daydream about how many harmonicas I could buy with that kind of money.

Carmine smacked me in the arm, waking me from my woolgathering.

"Are you listening, boss? A thousand dollars!"

My daydream changed to one of how many harmonicas I could shove down my sidekick's throat. I resisted the urge to throttle the living Shinola™ out of him as the number of zeros slowly sank into my brain.

"*Comprende*, kiddo," I muttered. "That's a boatload of gravy, alright."

Hey, don't laugh; back then that *was* a lot of money; enough to cause delusions of lucre so powerful that I almost hit the curb.

"Look out!" Carmine yelled.

I swerved back into the middle of my lane, with cars behind us honking their klaxons off.

I couldn't help it. You know those cartoons where two characters are in a boat at sea, and one of them gets so hungry he hallucinates that the other has turned into a T-bone steak? I was getting that way from starvation of the monetary kind. Just the mention of any amount over three figures made my brain start doing cartwheels.

When Opportunity knocked, I wasn't going to keep her waiting on the doorstep: I'd pick her up and carry her through the threshold like a freshly minted bride.

(Or at least try to. Usually I tripped and fell flat on my face, and then the bride wanted an annulment—I always pictured Opportunity as being Catholic, by the way.)

I stepped on the gas, not wanting to spare the horses. The engine reacted like a dog getting smacked with a rolled-up newspaper, so I spared the horses a little bit. The old buggy took her taillight out from between her legs and motored on. Boy, was I overdue for a new car.

Not that I couldn't handle a smattering of engine trouble, seeing as I used to work as an apprentice grease monkey in an auto garage back when I was a young whippersnapper (when I wasn't busy snapping whippers). But the route from the police station to Plotzky's apartment took us through a rough part of town—not exactly an ideal spot to pop the hood, bend over the engine, and "present" one's most vulnerable assets to Wurstburg's sketchiest denizens.

Like everything else downtown, they've cleaned up that neighborhood a lot since then, what with the shiny glass condominium complexes, fancy multi-grain donut chains, and gourmet Italian coffee made by a machine the size of a truck engine. But at that time it was roach-infested tenements and low-rent donut chains serving burnt coffee that customers would throw in each others' faces when the dope deal went sour.

(On the plus side, they used to allow smoking; if you could survive long enough to catch lung cancer in *that* part of town, you'd be considered exceptionally lucky.)

I don't know what you call the stuff that rust turns into when it gets old, but this neighborhood was covered in it. The leftover chassis of stripped-down cars took up most of the parking spaces, and bicycles with flat tires or missing wheels sat chained to lampposts with dead bulbs. Businesses were mostly boarded up, with the exception of gun stores, liquor stores, tattoo parlors, pawn shops, and, worst of all, those check-cashing places that shave off the last bit of your wages that the taxman didn't get.

Some of the signs were still there from the mom-and-pop businesses of the neighborhood's more wholesome past. Their faded paint sketched a picture of happier times: Greta's Floral, Thom, Thompson and Thompsonson's Plumbing, Vito's Martial Arts and Ballroom Dancing, and so on. But as the cookie crumbled, the moms and pops must have read the signs, seen the writing on the wall, gotten the picture, and peeled it for the 'burbs long ago. The place was strictly no-man's-land; there wasn't a yes-man for miles.

We pulled to a stop at the intersection of Skeezy Street and Crookit Crescent. Carmine started yanking at my sleeve like the little paw-monkey he was.

"Look, boss! Snowmen!"

Sure enough, under the awning of a donut joint, a couple of snowmen were up to their usual hustle, selling snowballs to a clutch of pre-teen pubescents. These blizzard-birthed bastards were even filthier than most, looking like the grimy old roadside snow banks of early spring, when the thaw finally starts. And the snowballs they were selling didn't look any cleaner.

A snowman grinned as he handed one of the kids a half-dozen filthy freezerchuckers in exchange for a mitt-full of nickels. The kid wasted no time and scarpered around the corner followed by his buddies, no doubt on their way to launch a little mischief through some poor shopkeeper's window.

The snowball trade was the only entrepreneurial activity that snowmen actively engaged in. It was technically a misdemeanor, though law enforcement turned a blind eye to it most of the time. The chattering classes debated it endlessly, with the equal-rights camp saying snowmen shouldn't be denied their traditional means of subsistence, and the us-versus-them side arguing for more enforcement, increased penalties, longer sentences, extradition, and forty lashes.

I'd always wondered why kids would rather buy filthy snowballs made by itinerant petty criminals instead of getting outside in the fresh air, scooping up the nice clean powdery stuff themselves, and rolling their own for some good healthy fun.

(Then again, I think I just answered my own question. At least these kids were still spending time outside; nowadays they waste endless hours on those newfangled pinball machines they play on their miniature televisions.)

Carmine interrupted my editorializing.

"Hey, boss, they're buying snowballs on the corner! Ya think we oughta tell the police?"

I gave him a gentle smack.

"You're yanking my chain, right? Why should we rat out a bunch of young scamps just looking for a little harmless fun?"

The light turned green. I had barely taken my foot off the brake when a thundering stampede of thuds sounded from the windshield and bodywork of the back of the car, like a hundred wild horses trampling a hundred dead hobos.

"Holy Hail Marys!" Carmine shouted, even though he wouldn't recognize a rosary if it landed in his bowl of fettuccini.

We turned around to see the car's back windshield smothered in dirty snow. I checked my side-view mirror and spotted a gaggle of street urchins laughing their mugs off.

I rolled down my window to have a good holler.

"If I ever catch you little bastards, I'll string you up by your pinochles!"

I tended to lose coherence when I got mad.

Traffic behind me started getting honky, so I had little choice but to roll up the window, make with the gas foot, and continue on our way. But I swore that if I ever saw those little faces again, someone was going to end up with a sore spanking hand. (Just to be clear, that someone was me.)

Carmine inspected the damage behind us.

"Looks like they put a crack in the windshield," he said.

"Aw, you gotta be kidding me," I moaned. "I just had it replaced nine years ago."

"Them snowballs musta had rocks in 'em or something. That must be why the kids buy 'em."

"Nice deducing, deduce-bag; of course that's why the kids buy them."

Carmine stroked an invisible goatee.

"I've always wondered why kids would rather buy dirty old snowballs made by itinerant petty criminals instead of gettin' outside in the fresh air, scooping up the nice clean..."

"Damn it," I interrupted. "Have I been thinking out loud again?"

"Ever since we left the police station, boss."

"Well, that doesn't mean you can plagiarize. Hands off."

"Aw, shucksicles."

That was an irritating habit of mine, especially when narrating: I'd be sitting there thinking, thinking that I was just thinking, when in reality I'd been yakking away like a Tibetan cowboy.

"Cisco, what does 'Tibetan' mean?"

Damn it, I was doing it again!

"It means you need to go look it up in an atlas," I said. "Now keep quiet and stay on the lookout for more snowball chuckers."

The car rolled along through the maze of streets. Gangs of young vandals loitered around, taking down traffic signs to decorate their bedrooms and spray-painting their illegible graffiti on every available surface. The scene was practically a diorama of delinquency.

"Kids these days," I griped.

"You were young once," said Carmine.

"Back then, it was different," I replied. "We had a sense of pride in our home turf. We didn't deface buildings with spray paint; it was all brushes and oils. There was an art to it."

"You were in a gang?"

"I was a prospect of the Tedesco Boys when I was eleven. They would send me around to the shopkeepers to collect money."

"Money for what?"

"To make sure no one else shoplifted from their stores."

"Sounds kind of like a protection racket."

"Well, yeah, when you put it that way, I guess it kinda does."

I don't think the Tedesco Boys ever really explained their business model to me properly, but at the time I knew nothing about leveraging market incentives in order to maximalize amortization of revenueutical...uh, streams?

Obviously, I still know nothing about it. But I was naïve back then: I just wanted to hang out with the cool kids who carried switch-combs.

I looked out the window at the juvies as they committed their petty misdemeanors. Seeing them put me in the mood for another editorial.

"Kids don't belong in the city," I said. "They're better off growing up in the countryside, learning the value of an honest day's hard work, and giving something back to the community. Besides, nothing builds character like accidental dismemberment by farm machinery."

"What kind of farm work could they be doing at this time of year?" Carmine asked.

"What am I, the Jolly Green Giant?"

Carmine arched a brow and aimed his B.S. detector at me.

"Have you ever *been* to a farm, boss?"

"How is that relevant?"

"So the answer is 'no' then..."

"Look, all I'm saying is, these kids need the fixed routine of a steady job if they're ever going to fit in with decent society."

Carmine looked out the window at the blight of urban decay surrounding us.

"You call this 'decent' society?"

"You got a point, kid."

We saw more snowmen loitering among the misspent youths. Some peddled snowballs, while others just milled about, sticking their carrot beaks into garbage containers and newspaper boxes.

Now I don't want to sound prejudiced or bigoted or small-minded, but in those days that was common currency, so here goes: you could tell by taking one look out the window that snowmen didn't belong in the city. (There, I said it.) They rooted around in the trash, lived in old cardboard boxes, and scrounged up a pretty miserable existence as it was, without everyone hating on them just for being 'round.

Pundits of all stripes liked to wring their hands over the "snowman problem," and there were always editorials in the newspapers and gab on the radio about what should be done to fix it. The more hawkish solutions were mass deportation back to the North Pole and building a mile-high fence around the Arctic Circle.

One politician got his name in the papers after he made a big stink in front of the city council, saying we ought to fill the atmosphere with chlorofluorocarbons, methane, and CO_2 gas, and raise the atmospheric temperature high enough so that the polar ice caps would melt, taking all the snowmen with them. Crazy idea, I know; it seemed like cutting off your scalp to spite your skull.

Of course, there were anti-snowman extremists: vigilante gangs of uptight citizens with armbands who would patrol their gated communities and keep all the snowmen out. Some of them formed powerful lobby groups that claimed to be grassroots organizations, but their financial backing was rumored to come from a small cadre of extremely wealthy sympathizers. The conspiracy crowd named lots of possible funding sources: the Rothschilds, Illuminati, Freemasons, Bilderberg Group, Cosa Nostra, Jesuits, lizard aliens, grassy knolls, and anyone who didn't land on the moon.

I wasn't a big fan of snowmen and wouldn't be thrilled if the daughter I never had married one, but this issue was so complicated, even politicians, xenophobia, race war, conspiracy theories, and atmospheric pollution couldn't fix it.

Lots of people treated the snowmen like an invasive species, but conveniently forgot that *we* were the ones who'd first encouraged them to come this far south. You see, long ago, when Christmas was just another extra-long church service, snowmen mainly stayed north. Families would have a nice dinner and sing some songs, good kids would get a few oranges, the bad ones would get coal, and all the adults would get drunk. But then businesses realized that Christmas was the perfect vehicle to boost their year-end sales figures, and the holiday started to gain traction. As things got more and more commercialized, everyone decided each

Christmas should be bigger and better than the last, and people started going a little bit bonkers towards the end of December.

Before you could whistle a few bars of *Pop Goes the Weasel*, we had Christmas advertisements and window displays popping up right after Halloween, riots in department stores over gifts that cost a month's pay, and entire houses decorated to the last square inch in holiday tat. What was supposed to be a time of solstice celebration to get ourselves through the darkest days of the year turned into a festival of one-upmanship, a competition to see who could buy the most expensive gifts or run up the highest electric bill with all those lights.

Of course, everything remotely related to Christmas and winter got turned into a mascot or decoration or gimmick you could purchase. People weren't happy doing the same thing each year, so they were prone to latch on to passing fads. One year it was elves; another year, fairies. Stores were flooded with knitted tea cozies shaped like dwarfs, Styrofoam snow banks, dancing plastic feet for your stockings, and aerosol snow-in-a-can for moustaches and beards.

Then one year, a new craze caught fire like Dutch tulips doused in kerosene: everyone just had to have a snowman on their front lawn. And before you could say "overkill," pretty soon one snowman just wasn't enough: people needed snow-couples, snow-families, snow-choruses singing Christmas carols, even complete snowman villages.

An entire industry popped up just to bring snowmen in from the north, so that people could show the Joneses who had the biggest snowballs on the block.

The "agents" who ran this racket made a killing. They lured snowmen to town with promises of quick and easy cash, but then nickel-and-dimed them with "immigration" and "processing" fees, taking advantage of their lack of legal and financial acumen. What's more, the snowmen were often paid in scrip that could only be spent in the agents' stores, and because those blizzardy bumpkins didn't know what things should cost, they had no clue that they were being fleeced.

The snowmen were rounded up in camps, mainly in the parking lots of Swedish furniture stores, right next to the Christmas trees. People would pick out the ones they wanted and rent them from the agents at ridiculous rates. The snowmen seemed quite happy at first, but maybe that was the bliss of ignorance. They were excited at the prospect of getting paid to stand around, something they normally did for free anyways.

But all good things must come to an end, and the same goes for the not-so-good. Artificial snowmen hit the market at a fraction of the cost of the real thing, and without the hassle. Inevitably, the snowman trend peaked and started to wane as other corny fads popped up. More and more snowmen went unpicked each year. Of course, even those who found work at Christmastime were out of a job once the New Year rolled around.

Inevitably, the locomotive of a booming economy that once bore the load of such conspicuous consumption jumped off the rails, crashed into the ditch, and skidded to a halt, putting the brakes on most types of extravagance, with the exception of overwrought metaphors. (If you wonder why I use so many, it's mainly because they're free.)

The snowman craze died, but the snowmen didn't. They'd had it up to their head-balls with the Arctic, and who could blame them? It was three months of solid darkness up there during the winter. Not to mention that every time they lay down for a nap, they ran the risk of getting mistaken for a baby seal and clubbed to death by a snow-blind Canadian hunter drunk on maple-syrup moonshine.

Down here, they acquired a taste for our cast-off clutter, and carved out a niche market with the snowball trade, from which they could eke out a living. They kept coming back to Wurstburg and other cities, showing up earlier and earlier each winter, and staying later and later, despite the fact that people had stopped rolling out the welcome wagon and regarded them more as detritus than décor.

But back to my story...

At last, Carmine and I reached Plotzky's neighborhood, which was in the posh part of town. Here, the boulevards were fat and wide, the women were tall and shiny, and the buildings had long legs. The sidewalks were so clean you could eat off them, although the Maître D's wouldn't let you without a reservation.

And there were no snowmen about.

Along the so-called "Mink Mile," they had the kinds of fancy clothing boutiques with just a logo and a single mannequin in the window, wearing an outfit that probably cost as much as a used car. You wouldn't know for sure, though, because there was never a price tag on anything. What is it with rich people and price tags? Is it a phobia? Or do they already know how much everything costs through some kind of retail telepathy?

I didn't get these hoity-toity boutiques: if you wanted to know if you could afford it, you had to go in and ask, and if you had to go in and ask, you couldn't afford it, in which case they didn't want you coming in to ask. Even if you told them you were just doing a bit of casual browsing, you still got pinched looks from a bird-like blueblood broad who told you to stop sleeping in her storefront or she'd call the police. Not that I know from experience or anything...

Plotzky lived at the corner where a short residential street met the main drag, in one of those trendy condo buildings where "every suite is a penthouse suite." You know the kind: red velvet awnings and revolving doors, with doormen who dress up like they're about to get decorated by the Grand Poobah of their brotherly lodge.

We pulled up in front of the building and saw a couple of uniformed police officers exit and get into their squad car. Their casual demeanor told me the investigation was wrapping up, so I knew I had to hurry.

Chapter 4: The Penthouse

There was a small parking area in front of Plotzky's building, so I snagged a prime spot. Then Carmine spotted a notice that read "Visitors Only: Tow-Away Zone," so I pulled my favorite free-parking stunt: the old "Exterminator on Duty" sign placed on the dashboard. Never got bothered with that one.

Well, almost never. A bone-dry Limey accent spoke up behind me as soon as I stepped out of the car.

"The tradesman's entrance is around back, sir."

It was a doorman, who summed up everything he thought of me with one disdainful twitch of his freshly trimmed moustache.

At first I was put off by the intrusion of uniformed authority, but then I got a load of his Captain Kangaroo costume and almost busted a giggle-gut: the epaulettes on his shoulders looked like a shoeshine boy's buffing brushes, and his bright red jacket had a trail of shiny metal buttons that led all the way from his collarbone down to his nether-bone. Give this fellow a sword and a horse costume, and he could re-enact *The Charge of the Light Brigade* single-handed. What's more, his thick glasses magnified his eyeballs so I could see every vein.

He eyed me with a strange blend of curiosity and disregard. (Now I know what it's like to be a germ on a microscope slide and look up to see a giant scientist's pupil staring down.)

"Don't sweat it, Colonel Huffandpuff," I said as I patted the belligerent bellhop on the shoulder, "I'll be in and out in a jiffy."

But his upper lip stayed stiff.

"Normally our head office informs me of these matters. Were you called by one of our tenants, sir?"

"Sure, Igor," I answered. "Tell Doctor Frankenstein we're here. He's got an infestation of plug-necked monsters."

He frowned and tuned his head away slightly, as though he might catch the cooties by inhaling too closely to me.

"Doctor Frank N. Stein is on vacation in the Bahamas. There must be some mistake."

"I see they bred the sense of humor right out of you, *Cuthbert*," I said, reading his nametag as I locked my car door. "That was supposed to be a joke."

"Duly noted, sir."

Talk about rigid: he must have been a Beefeater back in Merrie Olde England. Either way, it looked like he was determined to have a beef with yours truly.

"Unless you provide me with the name of the tenant who made the call, I cannot let you in," he said.

"Sorry, your lordship," I replied. "Customer confidentiality is a sacred trust. Infestation can be very embarrassing, you understand."

He frowned and peered inside my car, putting his nose to the grimy windows.

"I don't see any spray equipment or pesticides."

"These are all I need," I said, pulling my tweezers and magnifying glass from my pockets. "My methods are all-natural."

"How so?"

"You're looking at the only exterminator in the city who still practices manual castration. If pests can't breed, they can't feed."

Maybe that slogan was supposed to be the other way around. Hey, I had to make this stuff up as I went along.

"In any case," I continued, "these things have to be dealt with quick, before they spread to other units. You could have a full-scale plague on your hands."

The doorman cringed. I could tell I was pushing his pommy little panic button. He took a furtive look around, and lowered his voice.

"Well, we can't have that sign in plain view. You people are supposed to be discreet."

"Maybe, but parking enforcement isn't," I said.

"I'll watch the car," he replied. "Just *please* take down the sign."

"Alright, but only because you used the magic word," I said. "Just know that if I get towed, you're on the hook for it."

I opened the door and took the sign off the dash.

"Thank you, sir," he said with relief. Then a question occurred to him. "I expect you're fully licensed and bonded?"

I pinched my tweezers in the direction of his moustache.

"Bonded, certified, licensed, blessed, anointed, and baptized," I said. "You're talking to the Termite Terminator... Raccoon Eradicator... Bedbug Obliterator... Cockroach Corpse-Maker... Doormouse Destroyer..."

"He also finds lost cats," Carmine added.

The doorman stepped back towards the entrance of the building as I stalked him like a Bengal tiger hunting down a Bangalore bunny rabbit. Carmine followed close behind.

The doorman bumped into the revolving door.

"If I could just see your license from the city..." he stammered.

"It's at home in a frame, Cuthbert," I said, using the pushy tone I learned in assertiveness training. "Now step aside and let me do my job. I'm in a castrating mood today."

"Yes, sir. Was just about to do that, sir."

He started spinning the revolving door, which I guess was his way of holding it open for us. As I trotted inside, trying not to let it slam my rear on the way in, Carmine jumped in behind me. We were stuck in the same section.

"Hey, one at a time, dummy!" I said.

"Sorry, boss! I was just trying to stay close."

"Well, not *that* close, unless you're going to give me a prostate exam. And even then, you're not wearing the right gloves."

We shuffled our intertwined feet until the revolving doors spat us out into the lobby.

For the first time, I took a close look at the gloves Carmine was wearing. They looked like they were made from mangy gorilla hair, shaved from the last part of a gorilla that you'd ever want to touch.

"What's with the hairy hand-socks, anyways?" I asked him. "I thought you were against fur."

"They're not fur," he said. "I dunked a pair of old dishwashing gloves in horse glue and ran 'em along the floor at the barbershop."

"Yech! Remind me to give you a raise sometime. I recommend waiting until I'm good and drunk."

I took a look around and noticed we were fetching hard stares from the passing socialites who lived in the building. No doubt we stuck out like two sore thumbs; I wasn't exactly dressed for snobby company, since I didn't think to change clothes for this job. After all, Plotzky was too busy pushing up daisies to judge my appearance. But I hadn't reckoned on his neighbors.

If I need to blend in with the yacht crowd, I always wear my good suit, inherited from my crazy Uncle Louie. Uncle Louie made a quick fortune inventing a disposable, single-use zeppelin. Then the Hindenburg went kablooey and his stock plummeted with it, taking Uncle Louie to the cleaners. Once the creditors stripped him down to the bare essentials, he only had one suit left to be buried in. Luckily, it was just my size; equally luckily, the undertaker at the funeral home was looking the other way. I managed to slip the suit off Uncle Louie's cold corpse and sneak it out through the coal chute. You might be horrified at that story, but don't worry; the suit was a charcoal color to begin with, so the trip through the coal chute didn't ruin it. With a squirt of cologne to mask the formaldehyde smell, it was good as new again.

Uncle Louie's suit might have helped me get past ol' Cuthbert Killjoy and mix with the moneyed classes more easily, but I had to save it for special circumstances, and never wore it for my day-to-day prowling. So there I was, standing in a fancy lobby looking just slightly better dressed than a tramp on his wedding day.

One thing I can say: Plotzky's lobby sure was posh. I was accustomed to the tastes and trappings of the well-to-do, seeing as how they were the ones who could afford my fees. Carmine, on the other hand, never got over a face-to-face encounter with the finer things in life.

"Look, Cisco: brass doorknobs!"

"I think those are gold-plated, kid."

"And real glass chandeliers!"

"Those are crystal."

"Genuine velour drapes!"

"That's velvet."

"Wow," he gushed as he looked around, "Plotzky must have been rakin' in the greenbacks. Did you know his Christmas special was on TV last night? They say it had over a million viewers!"

"You have a television?" I asked, surprised but skeptical.

"The neighbor does."

"You peep though your neighbor's window to watch their TV?"

"Naw, I listen though the walls."

"I suppose that's only half as creepy. Now come on, let's go find the elevators."

Carmine froze. His upper lip started to twitch.

"Can't we take the stairs instead?"

I forgot that Carmine had an irrational fear of elevators. No matter how often I explained to him that he was far more likely to injure himself while climbing a staircase, it always took some cajoling to get him to ride in one. Normally, I wouldn't tolerate his verticular hang-ups, but knowing how lazy the cops were in this burg, I figured the stairs would be more discreet anyways; we'd be less likely to run interference from the Donut Brigade if we hoofed it.

We snuck through a door marked "Fire Exit" and climbed the emergency stairwell all the way up. The only fire was the burning in our thighs from the workout.

The top-floor hallway was empty, except for Christmas decorations and some bright yellow police tape blocking one of the suites. I could smell money and hooker-grade perfume as we approached the taped-off doorway, which was obviously the scene of the crime.

Call me old-fashioned, but I consider it impolite to knock, especially at a dead man's door. Besides, it wasn't locked, so we went ahead and tiptoed inside.

The penthouse interior was pitch black and freezing cold. Carmine and I were searching around for a light switch when we bumped smack into a body: a live one, belonging to officer Dutch Blinsky.

"Durr, who goes there?" asked Dutch, his teeth chattering like castanets.

Invisible in his midnight-blue uniform, Dutch stood in the foyer, blocking the way to the rest of the apartment. I could barely see him, but I'd recognize that donkey bray anywhere.

"Dutch, is that you?" I whispered. "It's me, Cisco."

The fog cleared from around his lighthouse.

"Oh. Merry Christmas, Cisco."

"Merry Christmas, Dutch," I replied, relieved that he greeted me with his tongue and not his nightstick. "How come it's so dark in here?"

"The Chief says to leave everything exactly how we found it."

"Did you find it?"

"Uh, no."

"Then we can turn the lights on, right?"

He thought about that for a full minute.

"Err, okay!"

Dutch wasn't exactly the sharpest tooth in the jaw, but that's exactly how I liked 'em.

I felt around on the wall for a light switch and flicked it on. A string of dangling icicle-shaped Christmas lights illuminated the foyer, casting a dim glow on the dead man's digs.

It was so cold in Plotzky's apartment, I could see Dutch's breath. (Smell it, too: did he gargle with onion juice that morning?) I shook his hand. In return, he shook my entire body with his vise grip. Dutch might not have been bright, but he was built like a cinderblock with arteries.

"Good to see you, big fella," I said, shaking out my hand to get the blood circulating again. "How's the wife?"

"House the wife? I do more than house the wife," he answered. "I house her, feed her, clothe her, and still she takes off on me."

"Oh. Sorry to hear it, buddy."

"That's okay," he said with a shrug. "She'll come back when she deflates."

I thought about that image a bit longer than I wanted to. Then I slapped Dutch on the shoulder by way of encouragement.

"It's a natural law of attraction, old pal: what goes up must come down. So where's the body?"

"No body here."

"No body? What about Plotzky?"

"He's not a body. He's a corpse."

Dutch did his best to stifle a titter. It wasn't very hard to tell when he was trying to be a wiseguy.

"Okay," I said, "are we splitting hairs for a reason?"

"Because he melted," the big oaf continued. "Know what that makes him?"

"I'll bet I'm about to find out."

"A marine corpse!"

Dutch let out a guffaw that sounded like a water buffalo with whooping cough skiing down a mogul run.

"Geddit? Marine corpse?"

Carmine rolled his eyes and crossed his arms.

"What a dumb joke," he said.

That crossed Dutch.

"Shut up, shrimp."

I stepped in quickly between them.

"How about you let us guess where Plotzky's at?" I asked. "We can make it a game, like twenty questions, or Battleship™."

Dutch shook his head.

"I'm not supposed to let anybody in. Chief's orders."

"Fair enough," I said. "Say, do you hear that dripping water sound?"

"No. What does it sound like?"

"Drip, drip, drip, drip, drip..."

His knees started to tremble.

"Uh, I gotta go see a man about a mule, fellas. Don't touch anything I wouldn't."

"I wouldn't even touch most things you *would*, big guy," I said. "Don't fall in."

Dutch loped off to find the convenience.

"It worked!" said Carmine once he was out of earshot.

"Always does," I said. "And it'll take him at least ten minutes just to figure out his zipper. Now let's go get a gander while the going's good."

We hustled into the living room, which bore all the decorative details New Money could buy. Obviously, Plotzky had the scratch to pony up for the best decorators in the city, and the rugs, drapes and furniture were all impeccable, even though I tried my best to pecc them. From here, I could see where all the cold was coming from: customized refrigeration units were built into all the windows, blasting chilly air into the condo. The dead guy was a big fan of old Jack Frost.

A gas fireplace made to look like real burning logs flickered behind a brass screen that covered a carved stone mantelpiece. Right in front of it was a big wet stain on the carpet.

"Zowie," Carmine said. "Is that all that's left of him?"

"Guess so, kid. Let's get a closer look."

We bent down to check out the broadloom. There was a top hat, a pair of wool mitts, black leather boots, a carrot, buttons, and two lumps of coal in the middle of the water stain. A chalk outline was traced around it.

"You take the low road," I said. "Get down and inspect the body. I'll take the high road."

Carmine whined.

"Why do I always gotta take the low road?"

"Because for you, it's less travel. After Nature made your head and feet, she must not have had enough left for the parts in between."

"Very funny, boss."

"You think so? Maybe I should write that one down."

I scanned the room with my trusty magnifying glass.

"Try not to disturb anything," I said. "If anyone else has been here, they would have left clues."

I passed the magnifying glass along the mantelpiece and could have sworn I saw a crowd of dust mites doing the Mexican wave at me, with rude gestures thrown in.

Carmine got down on all fours and sniffed the carpet like a dog trying to look up one of its friends in the "yellow" pages.

"You think it was murder, Cisco?" he asked.

"Normally, that's my first, second, and third guess."

"I can't imagine who'd want Plotzky dead. He seemed like such a jolly fellow."

"Everyone who's anyone's got enemies, kiddo."

"I s'pose it could've been one of the usual suspects," he mused. "Like maybe a mark."

"No dice."

"A fence?"

"You're barely out of the gate."

"A stool pigeon?"

"This job was too cool for a stool."

"A punk?"

"Not exactly a piercing observation."

"A web-footed, boxing chimpanzee with a nervous tic coming down off a tetra-ethylene jag?"

"Now that's just crazy talk."

"What if it was a kid?"

"A kid?"

Carmine pointed at a section of carpet.

"Look! Little footy-prints. Sneakers, it looks like."

I bent down to get a closer look. Sure enough, there were faint sneaker prints in the carpet fibers.

"Well spotted, kemosabe. Are they fresh?"

Carmine lowered his nose and sniffed again.

"Yup, and look how crisp they are. Those sneakers were brand new, right outta the box."

I weighed the possibility.

"A kid, eh? I thought kids loved Plotzky."

"Everyone did," said Carmine. "But especially those aged nine and under."

He thought for a second and then snapped his fingers.

"I know! Maybe one of his fans loved him too much. Broke in here for an autograph. Plotzky tries to kick him out, they tussle, things get heated, and he melts. Realizing what happened, the kid runs all the way home for his Christmas cookies 'n' milk and doesn't say a word."

"Not bad for a first conjecture. Did the wizard finally give you a brain?"

"I signed up for those night courses," he said indignantly. "And you said they wouldn't do me any good."

"Fine, let's say you're on to something. How could some little kid get the better of Plotzky?"

"I dunno. Maybe he ate a lot of Wheaty Flakes."

"You've been eavesdropping on too many TV commercials."

Carmine scratched his head. Either he was trying to think, or it was time I checked him for lice.

"Maybe it wasn't just one kid," he said, "but a bunch of 'em wearing the same footwear. You know how they follow the trends."

"Now you're multiplying entities," I answered. "Okay, let's pretend for a minute that Occam's Razor is dull, and you're not."

"Who's Occam?"

"A medieval philosopher."

"A philosopher? How could he afford a razor?"

"He made a fortune when he founded Occam's Rocc'em, Socc'em Boxing League. The lucky bugger never had to think another thought for the rest of his life."

"Oh."

"So anyways, if it was kids, how'd they do it?"

"Simple," said Carmine. "Four or five of them run in, home-invasion style. They gang up on Plotzky and pin him near the fireplace 'til he melts."

"You're spinning your wheels so fast, I can smell the rubber burn. Either that, or you've been smoking elastic bands again."

"You don't think it coulda been kids?"

"Not for a Cincinnati second. For one thing, it would take at least a half-dozen kids to hold him down. Now a single deranged fan is one thing, but *that* many? Not likely, unless they're putting cuckoo-chemicals in the candy canes. And then there's the problem with the fireplace. Check out Plotzky's vital stats: he was six-foot-two, all ice and snow, and must have weighed at least 250 pounds. If I know anything about the laws of thermodynamics..."

"Which you don't."

"...I'd say the fireplace would take too long to melt that much snow and ice. Look at this thing: it's purely ornamental. I bet it barely puts out more than a few thousand BTUs."

Carmine stepped close to the fireplace.

"You're right," he said. "I'm still freezing cold."

I reached out and put my hand over the air vent of one of the refrigeration units.

"No surprise," I said. "The cooling system is maxed, for crying out loud."

"I suppose it's back to the drawing board?"

I paced the room to get a little warm blood flowing up my neck to where it was needed.

"Time to think like a killer," I said. "If you wanted to turn a big lump of snow to water quick, how would you do it?"

"If it was me, I s'pose I'd use a blowtorch," Carmine mused. "It's portable, concealable...all you need is a flick of the flint. Oxy-acetylene would probably do the job in a jiffy, and you can buy it wherever flammable gases are sold."

"Good gravy, Stroganoff, that's using your noodle. It's also a decent sales pitch."

"See?" said Carmine, beaming. "I told you night school would pay off."

"But we still don't have a motive."

He snapped his fingers again.

"I got an idea," he said. "How about we picture the killer getting executed for his crime and work our way backwards from there?"

"Too straightforward. Think laterally."

"What if we write all the facts we know and turn it into a book?"

"Don't take 'laterally' too literally."

"How about we visualize the clues as puzzle pieces and start with the corners?"

"You can't solve a crime like it was a paint-by-numbers set: you have to think outside the crayon box."

"You mean draw outside the lines?"

"Sure, mix in all the metaphors. Now let's dust the place for fingerprints before Dutch gets back or—uh oh."

With perfect timing, like the sulfurous eruption of a hot geyser at Yellowstone Park, Inspector Murray walked in.

"What the hell are you doing here?" he asked with a scowl.

Murray was your typical veteran cop, a lifer who slogged through the routine and toed the line, moving up through the ranks the hard way (i.e. without marrying the commissioner's daughter). His overcoat was tan and his face pale as a newborn mole rat, though he wasn't nearly as cute and lovable. He always had a chaw of tobacco in his cheek, which made his breath smell like cancer's gym locker. But something was different about him that day: the knot in his tie was done up properly for once.

"Inspector Murray!" I said. "What a nice surprise."

"That's *Chief* Murray," he huffed. "And I can't say likewise."

"You made Chief? When did that happen?"

He narrowed his beady rodent eyes.

"Can't remember. Time flies when you're always busy combing nits out of your hair."

That dig hit me square in the dignity.

"I'm just trying to get to the bottom of this caper, Murray."

"Hah. You couldn't get to the bottom of a birdbath."

He spat down at the carpet for emphasis, then realized he was about to contaminate a crime scene, and caught the loogie in midair with his hand. He cursed as he wiped his palm with a handkerchief.

Murray and I had been partners way back when, before I swapped my flatfoot for a gumshoe. After that, he rose to the rank of Inspector, and I figured that's where he'd stay, but I must have misunderestimated him. He was sore at me for going freelance, but that's okay: I only need to be popular with Mr. Long Green.

"I suppose that thousand-dollar reward has nothing to do with your interest in this case?" he asked.

"Until they discover a cure for hunger, I'm not in it for philanthropy," I said.

"Well, go starve somewhere else. No private dick's getting in my way just to make a buck off someone's tragedy."

"Tragedy? Don't tell me you're crying crocodile ice cubes for ol' Plotzky here."

I could sense Murray bristling like a porcupine in a barrel full of toothbrushes.

"My daughter's a fan," he said.

"So this isn't exactly an impartial investigation," I replied with a wink.

"You're in no place to judge, Maloney," he sneered. "You're just after quick cash."

"As opposed to slow cash? Whoever said 'crime doesn't pay' never saw a cop's salary, Murray. My conscience doesn't exactly keep me up at night."

"Hah. You treat your conscience like it was trying to sell you a vacuum cleaner."

If Murray's eyes had been a donkey's hind hooves, they would have kicked me clean out onto the sidewalk. I don't know why he was so resentful—it's not like I'd been raking in the bucks since I'd hung up my billy club. In fact, sticking with the force would have brought more rewards: steady pay, benefits, a pension, and the respect of people who are intimidated by a uniform. Plus there's the recognition: cops get heaps of praise by the trashy tabloid press, and if they actually do something brave, they're handed a medal and maybe even the key to the city (in Wurstburg, it's a brass-plated crowbar). And when they retire, they can start a cushy paralegal business helping crummy drivers get off the hook for their traffic tickets. Yep, all that could have been mine if I'd only played by the book. Instead,

I got treated like a crossbred cur and kicked out of all the good crime scenes.

Seeing how Murray held all the cards, I fought against my fighting instincts and tried to persuade him with reason.

"It's not like you and your men can claim that thousand," I said. "Why let a nice fat reward go to waste?"

"Reward, my tightly-clenched ass," he snapped. "It's a bounty, Cisco. We don't need bounty hunters in this town."

"You should see this as a win-win situation: if I fail, you can have a good laugh at my expense. And if I succeed, it'll free up some of your manpower. Plus I'd get the reward, which would make it win-win-win."

Murray took another wad of tobacco from a tin and popped it into his gob.

"You don't even know who put up that money," he said as he chewed away.

Carmine piped up.

"We heard it was a ay-nonymous benny factor."

"You should know better than to take money from strangers," Murray replied. "You don't know where it's been."

"Thanks," I said, "but if I want advice, I'll crack open a fortune cookie."

That got his goat. He stepped up and grabbed the lapels of my coat.

"Just don't cross me, Cisco," he hissed, "or I'll crack open your head. You hear?"

I nodded. His breath hit me in the face like a hurricane of halitosis and almost blew me down.

"You might flash your badge all over town," he continued, "but you aren't the law, and you sure as hell aren't above the law."

"I'm on the up-and-up," I said, fighting back tears from the stench.

"He's a stand-up guy," said Carmine.

"On the level," I added.

"Straight as an arrow," Carmine concluded.

Murray slowly released his grip. My coat was already wrinkled from a thousand fingers doing the same thing, so it didn't make much difference.

"Yeah, yeah, whatever," Murray growled, brushing his hands as if he'd just touched a smallpox blanket. "Just stay out of trouble and stay out of my way. Do I make myself clear?"

"As a bell, Chief. But tell me one thing: have your boys figured out what killed Plotzky yet?"

"We mopped up most of the puddle and sent it to forensics. If you want to know more, buy a newspaper."

"But Cisco can't..."

"Shut up, Carmine!"

I gave my sidekick a hoof in the heinie.

"Ow!" he yelped.

"Time to go," I said, dragging him towards the door. "Good luck with the investigation, Murray, and may the best man win."

"Wish the luck on yourself," he replied. "You look like you need it."

As we headed for the door, Dutch returned from the privy in his polka-dot boxer shorts, his pants having apparently taken a sabbatical.

Murray barked at him.

"You're relieved, Dutch!"

The big lout grinned from ear to ear.

"I sure am!"

"Next time, keep the riffraff out of here."

"Yes, sir," he said with a grand salute.

"And what happened to your pants?"

"I was trying to pull up my zipper...turns out it was a button fly."

He held up his damaged trousers in his non-saluting hand.

"Well, put them back on with a safety pin," said Murray. "It isn't casual Friday yet."

"Okay, Chief."

Carmine and I couldn't help but laugh as Dutch raced back to the powder room.

I noticed Murray staring at me, fists on his hips.

"I thought you were leaving, Maloney."

"Sure thing," I said. "Oh, I almost forgot: congrats on the promotion, Chief."

"Ah, stuff it in a gym sock," came his reply.

What a curmudgeon.

Chapter 5: The Sewer

It seemed like the higher Murray climbed up the ladder, the more he looked down on me.

It was a shame, really, because I thought we were a pretty good team back in the day: our "good cop, bad cop" routine always brought down the house at the Policemen's Revue. Of all the men on the force (not to exclude you, ladies, but back then it was strictly Sausage City P.D.), Murray was the one guy who had my back. I even trusted him with my grandmother's secret crêpe recipe, and he swore he would never make them with margarine instead of butter. We'd have taken a bullet for each other, if there were some kind of scenario in which doing so would make a shred of sense.

Murray and I were a study in opposites: I was a hothead, while he always kept his cool; I bent the rules while he straightened them; he was analytical and stoic, while I leaned more towards empirical Pyrrhonism (although I didn't care much for the didactic side). It was a good balance, but the complementing strengths and weaknesses that made us good partners also sent us on different career paths.

What he had going for him was that he could tolerate the minutiae of police work. I always felt like I was being run over by the procedural steamroller, but Murray could let it roll right off his back. He didn't mind the paperwork, the red tape, or the petty rules. While my grapes gradually soured as they got crushed under the leaden feet of police bureaucracy, Murray fit right into the law enforcement machinery like a greasy palm in a latex glove. So naturally, he rose through the ranks.

It's not that he was bucking for promotion or kissing caboose to get ahead, like a lot of cops I could name. Often it's the scum that rises to the top, but at his core, Murray wasn't a bad egg, just a hard-boiled one.

It shouldn't have surprised me that he made chief. In the world of law enforcement, those who play by the rules get squeezed up, while those who chafe at them get squeezed out (I was aiming for a toothpaste image there, but let's just brush it aside). That's the natural order of things, so I bore no bitterness, and didn't begrudge Murray his promotion. I was genuinely happy for him, but it bothered me that he wouldn't cut me some slack, especially when I needed this case so badly.

As you might have gathered, the biggest thorn in Murray's side was the fact that I still carried my old police badge around. Of course, nowadays I'd get arrested for impersonating a police officer if I used it, but back then it was still technically legal.

Actually, it was technically in limbo. There was a case being dragged through the courts where a disgraced ex-cop's lawyers were arguing that since his badge had his name stamped on it, it should be considered his property (as precedent, they referred to Finders-Keepers vs. Losers-Weepers, and millions of pairs of men's underwear with names sewn in by their mothers). Preposterous, I know, but until that case settled, I wasn't going to give up using the badge if I didn't have to, and there wasn't a thing Murray could do about it except badger me.

But back to the story...

We left Plotzky's penthouse suite and headed back to the stairs. As an indulgent nod to my sidekick's elevator phobia, Carmine and I marched all the way down the stairwell of Plotzky's building to the ground floor and made our way back to the lobby.

It was a zoo in there. In the short time since we'd first arrived, the place had become jam-packed with Plotzky's upset fans, who'd come pouring in to pay tribute to their dead idol.

"I knew this would happen," said Carmine.

"You realize predictions are more impressive when delivered before the fact?" I asked.

Many of the fans were weeping openly, clutching photos and other mementos of the celebrated stiff. One thing was certain: there wouldn't be any autographs that day.

Along with the throng in mourning, there was the usual mix of opportunity seekers and street entrepreneurs who just couldn't resist the urge to start milking when presented with a herd of cash cows. There were hustlers selling all kinds of knockoff Plotzky-branded commemorative goods, like T-shirts, coffee mugs, flags, and pencil sharpeners. I have no idea how they got the products manufactured and shipped on such short notice, especially when most of it was stamped "Made in Taiwan."

Cuthbert the doorman was overwhelmed by the mob and having a hell of a time trying to sort out which ones were residents of the building and which were the hoi polloi. Cops were guarding the elevators and checking ID's to make sure only legit tenants were allowed up, and doing their best to convince the crowd to go somewhere else and maybe get a life.

Carmine and I pushed and shoved our way to the exit, stepping on plenty of toes in the process. As we spun through the revolving doors, I noticed a small group of snowmen gathered outside on the sidewalk, all wearing black armbands. It was hard to read a snowman's mood, what with the coal eyes and everything, but it was obvious that these ones were mighty ticked off. Their gathering was one part vigil, two parts protest.

"Justice for Plotzky!" they shouted. "Sub-Zero Tolerance!"

That last bit was the slogan of the snowmen's equal rights movement, identifying this bunch as a group of Arctic activists. There was a lot more of them than I'd have expected, seeing how most snowmen were too preoccupied with scrounging out an existence to bother with political affairs. But boy, the ones who spoke out sure had a big axe to grind.

Not that I like to nitpick, but I could have pointed out to them that Plotzky was already getting more attention from the cops than most regular people do when they kick the bucket, and certainly more than any dead snowman ever got before. (If you want your death investigated with gusto, folks, make sure that you're famous or have an upscale address and matching bank account.)

There was a tall snowman at the front of the crowd. He must have been the leader of the protest, since he was carrying a bullhorn and prompting their chants.

"What do we want?" he asked.

"SUB-ZERO TOLERANCE!" the crowd answered.

"When do we want it?"

"BY CHRISTMAS!"

Although I could understand why they'd demand a full investigation into the death of their most famous son, one might also point out that the snowmen's protest was diverting police resources away from the inquest: namely, in the form of a line of beefy cops descending on them in full riot gear.

With their black helmets, shields, and truncheons, it was clear these cops weren't here to get someone's kitty down from a tree. The protesting snowmen saw them marching towards them in formation from the opposite side of the street and must have realized what was coming. So did I...as both a former juvenile delinquent and former officer, I've been on both sides of police brutality, and consider myself something of a qualified expert.

With nowhere else to go, the snowmen retreated towards the condo building, but it was impossible for them to get in; the police inside were starting to force the crowd of mourners out of the lobby and through the front doors, and the flow was strictly one-way. The joint was reaching a critical mass of humanity and snowmanity, and there was going to be a meltdown.

"What are we gonna do, boss?" asked Carmine.

"Act first and think about it later," I replied.

The mixed mob of bereaved Plotzky fans and peeved snowmen activists was now blocking the way back to my car. On top of that, the riot police were marching towards us, eagerly smacking their batons into their palms. I looked around for an escape route, as we were in imminent danger of becoming the corned beef in a crowd-control sandwich. Then I spotted a manhole cover on the pavement under our feet. I used the handle of my magnifying glass to pry it open, lifted it up with my fingers, and shouted at my sidekick.

"Jump in if you don't want an extra helping of lumps on the head!"

I slid the manhole cover off to one side, exposing the dank, dark hole.

Carmine sniffed at it.

"Is that for rainwater or sewage?" he asked.

"*You'll* be sewage if we don't get out of here! Now get in!"

He scuttled down the rung ladder, followed by yours truly. When I climbed down far enough, I heaved the heavy pig-iron cover over the hole above me, but my morbidly curious side couldn't resist leaving it partly open to watch the coming train wreck.

The riot squad closed in on the crowd.

"Stand your ground!" yelled the snowman leader through his megaphone.

The snowmen scattered like a bunch of scaredy cue balls, but the line of cops was already crashing into them. They were applying the textbook crowd-control methods a little harder than they needed to, which was *not at all* since the protest had been completely peaceful up to that point.

Even I was shocked at the selective way the beatdown was being meted out: it was pretty obvious that the police were targeting the snowmen and ignoring the humans in the crowd. It was as though every cop involved had just found out that his wife was cheating, and his shrink had prescribed taking it out on something cold, white and round with a truncheon.

But I didn't expect what happened next: the mourning Plotzky fans became angry Plotzky fans, and started fighting back alongside their cold comrades, shoulder to shoulder. They dug up cobblestones and lobbed them at the police, and used their mementos and souvenirs as weapons of mass obstruction (of justice, get it?). The cops sure weren't ready for that, and started doling out the donnybrooks more equitably.

The powder keg ignited, but I didn't get much of a chance to witness the fireworks. Police jackboots tromped over the manhole cover, slamming it shut a mere split second after I pulled my fingers out of the way. Had I withdrawn them any later, I'd be speaking American Sign Language with a bad stutter.

It was pitch black in that manhole.

"How long do we have to stay here, boss?" Carmine asked from somewhere beneath me, his voice echoing off unseen walls. "My feet are getting wet. At least, I hope it's water."

"Shush," I said as I tried to listen to the sounds of the riot going on above us, now muffled by a solid inch of cold metal.

"Uh, Cisco? There's something creeping around my leg."

"So brush it off, Carmine. It's probably just a salamander."

"Aren't they poisonous?"

"I don't know, I've never eaten one. Just sit tight, would you?"

I was too preoccupied to discuss herpetology at that point.

"I just wish I could see," he whined.

"Why don't you light a match?"

"Is that a good idea? There might be sewer gas in here."

I sniffed the air.

"I don't smell any methane," I said.

"Methane is odorless, boss."

"Someone tell that to my digestive tract. I thought you carried a pocket flashlight?"

"The batteries are dead."

"Then I guess we wait in the dark."

I wasn't very comfortable down in that sewer either, but there was still a heap of hubbub above us, and no way was I going to pop my head up into that meat grinder at ground level.

Carmine suddenly got excited.

"Hey boss, I see a light at the end of the tunnel!"

"It's nice that you're optimistic, but this is no time for corny metaphors."

"No, really! Come down and take a look!"

I climbed down the ladder, although I wasn't really in the mood to indulge Carmine's fervid imagination.

He probably just saw a mirage that got lost and was trying to make its way back to the Sahara desert.

When I stepped off the bottom rung of the ladder, my feet splashed into a few inches of water. We were obviously standing in a horizontal tunnel.

"This must be a storm drain," I said. "We'd be asphyxiated by the stench by now if it were part of the sewer system. Now where the heck is this..."

"Over there!" Carmine whispered.

I saw it, maybe twenty or thirty yards away. It was a canary yellow light (don't ask me for the Pantone™ number, because I'm not so good with colors). It flickered in the dark, its hue flashing whiter every few seconds, then settling back to yellow. I had to admit it was an unexpected sight.

"What could it be?" asked Carmine.

"I don't know," I replied. "Why don't we go find out?"

"Oh, no. Not me! You go ahead."

"Suit yourself. If you'd rather stay here in complete darkness with something crawling up your leg..."

I could hear Carmine's lips trembling with fricative fear.

"I suppose I'd better come along in case you need backup," he said.

"Come on, then, let's head for the light. It's good practice in case one of us has a near-death experience some day."

We followed the tunnel by running our fingers against the concrete walls, the light serving as our beacon. As we got closer, the tunnel got brighter. We could make out the features of the passageway as our pupils adjusted and our imaginations stopped filling in the unseen blanks with spooky details. I could hear faint clanking and crackling noises ahead, interspersed with a sound like someone attached a circular saw to a jackhammer and was trying to use both at the same time.

Finally, the tunnel we were in came to a T-intersection with another tunnel, and straight ahead of us was the source of the light: a crumbled-out hole in the concrete, about the height of my waist and the size of a tennis ball.

"It's down at your level," I whispered to Carmine. "Take a peek and tell me if you see anything."

The tunnel got darker as Carmine put his brain-basket up against the hole.

"Wow, boss," he whispered. "You're not gonna believe this!"

"Easy prediction, kiddo. I never believe anything."

"No, really! I mean it!"

"So what is it? Martians? Sasquatch? Chupacabra? The Yeti? Some kind of cannibalistic humanoid underground dweller?"

"Elves!" he said breathlessly.

Talk about anticlimactic. *Elves?* I thought. Sure, it was kooky, but so what?

I pulled Carmine away from the hole, bent down, and had a peek for myself.

On the other side of the wall was a big cavernous room that was obviously part of the storm drain system, a place where several tunnels came together. It was an impressive work of modern-day civil engineering.

Oh yeah: and it was full of elves.

But these weren't the usual garden-variety elves you read about in Christmas stories; that would have been an odd find in this kind of place, but not nearly as disturbing. Instead of the lively, rosy-cheeked manikins with the pointy hats, long beards and high voices we're all used to, there was something about these elves that was queerer than Cole Porter's face on a thirteen-dollar bill.

For one thing, they moved like cured beef: all jerky-like. Their beards were stiff and shiny, as though made of Bakelite instead of hair, and their glassy eyes showed no emotion. Their movement was mechanical, and they went about their tasks more like wind-up toys than living, breathing creatures.

Their tasks weren't the usual cutesy elfish activities, either. I had no idea what they were up to, but there was a full-scale construction project going on: the elves were hoisting and welding steel I-beams together, cutting lengths of rebar with power cutters, and grinding and shaping big pieces of metal. Showers of sparks were going up everywhere.

At one side of the room was the opening of a tunnel they were obviously digging out and reinforcing. It was one hell of a dangerous ruckus, and there wasn't a hardhat or safety vest in sight.

All the arcing and sparking explained the flickering of the light that we saw from the tunnel. Good thing for us the elves were making so much noise that none of them noticed us spying on them.

"What do you suppose they're up to?" asked Carmine from behind me.

"Anyone's guess, kid. It looks like they're tunneling towards the building. Maybe Santa's sick of going down chimneys?"

"Don't know why he'd prefer this," he said with a shiver. "It's so cold and clammy down here. I hope I'm not catching a...a...a...A-CHOOOOOOOO!"

The elves stopped what they were doing in an instant and turned their heads in synch straight towards my peephole. The din went completely quiet, but Carmine's sneeze continued to echo against the walls.

Now I don't consider myself a coward by any measure, but something about the clockwork movement of these elves gave me a galloping case of the creeps. A trembling spasm of dread sprinted from my tailbone all the way to the top of my head and back down again.

With perfect coordination, the elves dropped what they were doing and ran off in a single direction to the left, shouting "Intruder! Intruder! Intruder!" in high-pitched metallic voices.

I could only assume they were headed for an access point that would lead directly to our tunnel. I didn't want to wait and find out what they intended to do if they caught us, so I stood up, grabbed Carmine by the arm, and took off down the tunnel, back towards the ladder and the manhole.

I ran as fast as I could while dragging Carmine's miniscule frame behind me, my feet splashing in the shallow stream of water.

There was a rumbling sound behind us.

"I hope that riot is over, kid," I panted, "because like it or not, we're going topside."

"Fine by me, Cisco!" he replied. "But do you mind if I use my own legs?"

Actually, I did mind, but I was too out of breath to answer. Carmine's dachshund limbs weren't exactly suited for the hundred-yard dash, although I was no greyhound either.

With my eyes now adjusted to the darkness, I could see a little bit of dim light filtering through the holes in the manhole cover above us, which helped me locate the rung ladder.

As we climbed like methamphetamine monkeys up the ladder and out of there, the rumbling that I assumed was elf footsteps suddenly got a lot louder. It sounded like it was coming from a crowd of thousands, way more than I'd seen in that cavern.

I pushed up the manhole cover, crawled out onto the pavement, and helped Carmine climb out, just in time to see an avalanche of red, white and blue striped India rubber balls rush past us in the tunnel below.

Whew, that was close. Just one of those things can cause a bad bruise, let alone thousands hitting you all at once. I put the manhole cover back in its place, hoping those creepy elves would assume we'd been done in by the whiff of their rubbery grapeshot.

Then I remembered there was supposed to be a riot going on. But when I looked around me, I realized it was all over: no snowmen, no cops, no protest picket signs or placards, just a big mess of empty tear gas canisters, loose cobblestones, and spent batons. The lobby of Plotzky's condo building was empty, with just a few uniformed officers guarding the entrance. Obviously, the crowd had been dispersed.

Carmine exhaled with relief.

"That was close, boss," he said. "Maybe we should have just tried to take cover in the car."

"There was no time for fancy thinking. Besides, have a look."

My car was covered in dents. I suppose it might have been safe enough for us to hole up inside it, but in that kind of situation, you can't be sure: rioters love tipping cars the same way frat boys love tipping cows. We climbed in. At least the engine was still a bit warm, so it only took about nine tries to get it fired up. I cruised the bruised beast out of the visitor parking lot and onto the street.

"Where to now?" asked my sidekick.

"You heard Murray: they soaked up the puddle and sent it to forensics. That means the coroner's lab. Which is nice, 'cause I can always use a gander at her gams."

"Aw, I hate going to the coroner's," Carmine replied. "I can't put my finger on it, but there's something unsettling about that place."

"Maybe because it's full of corpses?"

"That's it!"

"Going there is part of the job," I said, "so figure out what you hate more: the coroner's lab or the unemployment line."

"Fine. Can I at least play the radio?"

"Only if by that, you mean you're going to sit very still and pretend you're a radio."

Chapter 6: The Coroner's

The coroner's lab wasn't far. It was in a plain, clinical building with polished floors that reflected like mirrors, so you could see all the gum and other gunk that was stuck to the soles of your shoes. The building housed the morgue, which made it a popular field trip destination with the kindergarten kids. There was also a five-pin bowling alley and mini-golf course in the basement, where they hosted birthday parties and bar mitzvahs.

Carmine and I walked through the corridors of the main floor, heading towards the coroner's wing. As usual, my sidekick started kvetching as soon as we arrived.

"This place gives me the creeps. Don't they have a morgue in the basement?"

"Not anymore."

"Really?"

"It got too full. Now they keep the bodies on the floors above us."

"Yikes!"

Carmine crossed himself.

"My hands are like ice," he moaned. "It's almost as cold as Plotzky's in here."

"They've got to keep it cold," I replied. "Otherwise, the stiffs will spoil."

"Well, I don't like it."

"You shouldn't be afraid of dead people, boyo," I said. "It's the live ones that are trouble. And this coroner is a live one, alright."

I licked my fingers and spit-shined my eyebrows, then did a quick check on my reflection in a nearby window. The coroner, a rather delectable specimen of the fairer sex, had only recently been hired as a replacement for the previous one—poor old Thomas "Tops" Nodsworth, who'd had an accident in the lab with some embalming fluid and became her first client (may he rest in peace).

"Have you met her before?" asked Carmine.

"Haven't had the pleasure yet, but I've seen her around. I've been looking for an excuse to shake her hand."

"I don't know if I wanna shake her hand. What kinda woman dissects corpses for a living?"

"The kind you don't want to cross. If she offers you her hand, you'd better not refuse it if you know what's good for you. But if she offers anything else, I'm calling dibs."

We reached a door marked, "Coroner's Lab."

"This is it," I said as I turned the knob.

"I'll bet it reeks in there," said Carmine.

I swung the door open.

"Will you stop complaining? It's not so bad..."

Then it hit me.

"Sufferin' sassafras! What is that stench?"

A nasty pong smacked us full-force in the nostrils. It smelled like someone figured out how to get buttermilk from a sow and made Limburger out of it.

Carmine coughed as his eyes started to water.

"P.U.," he hooted, "with a T.R.I.D.!"

I covered my mouth and nose with a handkerchief and looked around.

The laboratory was full of workbenches, sinks, and Bunsen burners, and loads of medical and scientific equipment straight out of Dr. Frankenstein's pantry. There was a desk in one corner, and a life-size skeleton hanging next to it that likely wasn't just a leftover Halloween decoration.

We couldn't figure out where the smell was coming from.

Then with a terse clacking of high-heeled footsteps, the coroner herself rushed in from another room.

Cue the wolf whistle: she was a lithesome brunette with a tight ponytail, horn-rimmed glasses, a lab coat, pencil skirt, and a pair of nylons covering the shapeliest legs this side of a Clydesdale ranch. I'd admired her architecture from afar while conducting other business in this building, and couldn't help thinking it was a shame that I didn't get very many murder cases.

"Sorry, gentlemen," she said. "I shouldn't have left that eggnog out of the fridge for so long."

She grabbed a small drinking glass from one of the workbenches. Inside it were multicolored layers of viscous fungal slop that sloshed around as she lifted it, the sight of which made my stomach do backward handsprings on top of my liver.

"Telling me, doc," I exclaimed. "What a honk!"

Eggnog! I didn't think it was even possible for the stuff to get more disgusting than it already was.

The coroner emptied the glass into one of the sinks, tossed it into a garbage chute, and gave us the kind of mischievous smirk that only a dame who handles human organs on a regular basis can deliver.

"Well, there it goes," she said breezily. "Won't bother you again unless it grows legs and crawls back out."

She nudged Carmine.

"Then it would be 'leg nog.' Get it?"

He shuddered.

"If you don't mind, ma'am, I've already got the heebie-jeebies bad enough without the puns."

"Have it your way, junior," she replied, a bit miffed.

"It still smells in here," said Carmine. "Maybe I should just light a match."

He took a box of matches from his pocket and struck one before she could answer.

"Don't!" she shouted.

"Okay, okay," he replied, and tossed the lit match into the sink.

"Not the sink!"

A burst of flames shot up from the drain. The three of us ducked.

"Don't do that again," she said as the smoke cleared, "or you might end up as my next customer."

"Wow," said Carmine. "What kinda rum did you put in there?"

"The house brand," answered the coroner. "It's a little bit overproof, but great for calming the nerves."

She lifted an empty test tube from a rack, held it under a nearby tap at the end of a copper coil, and filled the tube with clear liquid.

"Cheers."

She knocked back the shot of mortuary moonshine in one gulp. I figured I'd better get to the point of our visit before my sidekick did any more damage.

"Look here, Miss...uh..."

I realized I didn't even know her name.

"It's Doctor, not Miss, if you don't mind," she said testily. "Fabienne DeMontré, M.D."

So she had French blood! My temperature rose by a couple of degrees as a few extra hormone glands kicked into gear. I couldn't help it: society was so homogenous back then that French gals were considered exotic. France was still the world's number-one exporter of va-va-va-voom, along with wine, cheese, phallic Gallic bread, and *je ne sais quoi*.

She held out her hand, so I shook it carefully. I might have goofed by calling her "miss," but in my defense, I didn't see any ring on her finger.

"So how can I help you?" she asked. "I've got clients waiting in the fridge."

I gave my badge the ol' flip-and-flop.

"We're here on the Plotzky case, doc," I said. "Just wondered if we could get a peek at his autopsy report."

"The snowman from last night?" she asked. "I didn't know it was so urgent."

"It's a matter of life and death," I replied.

"Can't help you much with the 'life' part," she said, "but give me a few minutes, and I'll tell you what I found out."

Her heels clicked as the left the room. She shut the door behind her with a loud bang, which snapped me out of the trance her shapely hips had put me in.

"She must be a pretty good doctor," I muttered to my sidekick. "The sight of her cured my sore eyes."

Carmine was having none of it.

"Brrr," he said as he hugged himself to keep warm. "This place is so creepy."

"What are you, some kind of wimp?"

"Are you kiddin'? I'm the blueprint for wimp!"

Couldn't argue there.

We had some time to kill. Normally, if I have to wait for a doctor, there are at least some outdated issues of *National Geographic* to skim through, but the lab didn't even have a prescription pad to doodle on.

Bored, I checked out some of the coroner's fancy equipment. There were Erlenmeyer flasks, graduated cylinders, condensation coils, centrifuges, and autoclaves—words you'd be more likely to come across at a spelling bee than in my line of work. The science nerd kids would have had a field day if given the chance to have a field trip.

Speaking of nerds, Carmine took out my fingerprinting kit from his pocket and started dusting the place.

"What are you doing?" I asked him. "This ain't a crime scene."

"Just practicing, boss. I gotta do something to keep warm."

The fingerprinting kit was a Junior Detective model I got when I was just a tadpole. I'd outgrown it long ago, so I let Carmine hang on to it so he could do the dusting for me. That way, I could concentrate on important stuff, like haggling with cashiers over the price of expired bread.

He was right about it being cold, though. First we had to suffer in Plotzky's apartment, which was as chilly as a Russian funeral, and now the coroner's office, which seemed positively negative (in degrees Fahrenheit, that is).

I opened the valve on one of the Bunsen burners, lit it with a flint lighter from the workbench, and warmed my icy meat hooks over the flame.

"Come over here, Carmine," I said. "You can defrost your stubby sausages on this."

Carmine came over and cupped his mitts around the tiny blaze. Though our hands were now warming up, he still had cold feet, both literally and figuratively.

"Gee Wellington," he moaned, "why do we even have to be here? Don't we have enough information to make a bunch of assumptions and start fingering suspects?"

"What's the matter? You got an itchy fingering finger?"

"It's this dry weather making my eczema act up," he replied, taking out a little bottle of moisturizing cream and rubbing it on his digits. "So what do you say?"

"Nix and nay," I replied. "All we have to go on so far is speculation. Not to mention rumor, gossip, hearsay, conjecture, suspicion, hypothesis, intuition, and a good old-fashioned hunch."

"I can't help it if I have bad posture."

"Never mind that. We need to know how it was done. There's more than one way to melt a snowman."

"But what about the blowtorch theory?"

"At first I thought you were hot, but then I remembered my number-one rule of crime investigation: our first guess is always wrong."

"Oh, right."

Looking casually around the room, I spotted a galvanized tin bucket sitting on one of the workbenches, and remembered what Murray had said about them mopping up Plotzky's puddle.

I took a closer look. The bucket had a label stuck to it, showing a bunch of statistics. Handwritten in ballpoint pen above the stats, I could just barely make out: "The Snowman, Plotzky."

Jackpot! The bucket was full of water, obviously belonging to our famous liquid stiff.

I grabbed a syringe from the workbench and sucked water into it until it was full, then put a cap on it and stuck it in my pocket. You never know when a bit of evidence might come in handy, and I sure wasn't going to get another chance like that.

Carmine tried to look over my shoulder. (Actually, that was just a figure of speech: he was trying to look around my hip.)

"Boss, what are you doing?"

I turned around and clapped my hand over his mouth.

"Not now, buddy," I whispered. "O-nay estions-quay."

"Mmm-mmph?" he mumbled.

"Ut-shay up-ay."

"Mmm, mmp-umm!"

I let him go.

"I have no idea what you said, boss."

"Sheesh, don't they teach Pig Latin in night school?"

The sound of high-heeled footsteps signaled the return of the toothsome coroner, who came back with a stack of papers in a file folder.

Unfortunately, we'd left the Bunsen on. She immediately spotted the flame, shut off the valve, and glared at me.

"This is for roasting chestnuts, officer," she said. "Yours, if you touch it again. Here's the report."

She whacked me in the chest with it. The papers were full of charts, graphs, and mathematical equations, all in small, dense type. Staring at them was enough to give a minotaur a headache.

"Uh, could you just give us the condensed version, doc? It'd take a mental machete to hack our way through all this technical mumbo-jumbo."

With a roll of her eyes, she took the report back and read from it.

"Subject was a snowman, male, exact age undetermined. Exposed to severe hyperthermia, which led to complete liquefaction of the anatomical globules, a common cause of snowman death, known colloquially as 'Globule Warming.' This resulted in stage-four deglaciation."

"We know that already," I said. "But what did it?"

She smacked me in the chest with the report again.

"I'm getting to that part! We suspect it was caused by a chemical weapon."

"Chemical weapon?" Carmine and I blurted out in unison as we backed away from the bucket.

"Relax," she said. "It's nothing dangerous to us. We found a peculiar combination of precipitates in Plotzky's puddle."

"Sorry if this sounds like a stupid question, doc," I said, "but who participates in what combination again?"

She briefly looked up at the ceiling.

"There are no stupid questions, officer," she muttered. "Only stupid people."

She scanned through the report again.

"Let's see...iron particles, charcoal, salt, and a dash of pepper. The mixture causes an exothermic reaction that releases heat when dissolved in water. It's what you find in heat packs and heating pads."

"So he musta been murdered, huh doc?" asked Carmine.

"Oh, I wouldn't bet the Bunsen on it," she said. "It could have been suicide."

Carmine scoffed.

"Plotzky, a suicide? That's crazy."

"I've seen some oddball suicides, shorty," she replied. "Just last week we had a man who hanged himself."

"Lots of people hang themselves, doc," I said.

She crossed her arms, clearly losing patience with us.

"I didn't say 'hanged.' I said 'hung.' As in on the wall, like a painting, with several large nails."

"Ugh," exclaimed Carmine, "I'm gonna be sick!"

He doubled over and started to retch.

I couldn't stand to see him like that, so I turned away (besides, it's impolite to stare while someone's giving their lunch the old heave-ho). But I did give him some words of advice.

"For Pete's sake, Carmine, at least try to aim for the sink! My aunt gave me that fingerprinting kit!"

I stood between him and the coroner so she wouldn't have to watch, and tried to distract her with small talk.

"So, Doctor DeMontré, how does a lady like you get into this line of work?"

"By ignoring male chauvinist creeps," she said with a huff.

"I didn't mean any offense," I offered. "It's just that I've always been fascinated by medical science."

"If you're thinking of changing careers, you'll have to finish high school first."

Whoa. She shot me down like a chickadee under anti-aircraft fire.

"Now if you officers don't mind," she continued, "I have a few dead bodies I need to attend to before they go all gooey...or get used as props in some low-grade zombie movie."

"Okay, thanks, doc," I said, with a sinking feeling that I wouldn't be getting a second chance to make a worst impression. "Let's take the A train, Carmine."

I turned around to see my sidekick wiping his face with a handkerchief.

"Phew, that's better," he said. "Good thing there was a bucket right there."

"What bucket?" asked the coroner with alarm. She rushed over to where Carmine had been tossing his cookies. Sure enough, the evidence in the bucket was, um, slightly compromised. By vomit.

"You meshuggenah midget!" she cried. "That had the snowman's remains in it!"

"But...but...I...it's just that..."

Carmine looked to me for defense.

"Excuse my partner, doc," I said. "He's got a stomach made of feathers."

"Both of you, get out!" she shouted. "And try not to throw up into anything else while you're at it!"

She hustled us out the door and slammed it shut on our tailbones. A second later, we heard her holler again, but this time at someone else.

"Hey! You with the movie camera! Get away from there!"

Her footsteps broke into a run.

"I already told you! NO FILMING ON THE PREMISES!"

We stood stock still in the hallway for a moment. I turned to Carmine.

"You know what? I think she liked you."

"Really?" he asked. "How come?"

"She didn't tell you to shut up."

We headed back towards the exit. I tried to give some thought to the implications of what we'd just learned, but Carmine couldn't walk without flapping his peanut trap, the same way a pigeon can't walk without bobbing its head.

"Now don't that just take the biscuit?" he rambled. "Heat packs! I mean, what will they think of next? I never woulda guessed in a million years. A million and a half, maybe, but..."

"Weird way to go, alright," I interrupted.

I patted the pocket into which I'd snuck the syringe containing Plotzky's liquid remains.

"That coroner is too cautious to jump to conclusions," I said, "but I'd bet my last centavo that this was bonhomicide, cut and dried. Committed in cold blood."

"Are you saying it was a reptile that done it?"

"Let's not get too far ahead of ourselves. What I'm saying is this heat pack business is subtle. It tells me the killer put thought into it, planned it all out beforehand. Plotzky wasn't just melted in the heat of the moment: I'm talking premeditation, and I don't mean sitting cross-legged and going 'om'."

"Of course not. I'm sure it's that thing that you said, boss."

We continued down the antiseptic hallway.

"Now that we know how it was done," I mused, "it would help if we could figure out a motive."

"How do we do that?"

"We have to ask, *cui bono*?"

"The Sicilian guy with the organ-grinding monkey who sells tangerines filled with white powder outside the stock exchange?"

"No, I mean..."

"The brother of the short guy with the moustache and the greasy hair who sings on TV with the tall Armenian chick with the go-go boots and the thick eyebrows with the tight dress and the vim-vooms on her nay-nays with the ya-yas sticking out?"

"What the backflipping bacon-burgers is wrong with you?"

It sounded like my sidekick needed a reboot, so I gave him one.

"Ow!"

As I put my boot away, I tried to explain.

"*Cui bono*. It's kosher Latin, not the pig dialect. It means, 'who profits?' Who stands to gain the most by killing the most successful snowman of all time?"

We walked along in silence, pondering away at the puzzle.

An attractive woman in scrubs approached us in the hallway, wheeling a covered corpse on a gurney with a toe-tag dangling from the little piggy that wasn't gonna go "wee-wee-wee" all the way home anymore.

Carmine did a double-take as she walked past.

"Cisco," he whispered as he tugged at my sleeve, "that gal just winked at me!"

I gave him a corrective smack in back of the head.

"Don't get delusional. She probably just had something in her eye."

"No, really!"

A few minutes later, another attractive woman in scrubs appeared, also pushing a stiff on a gurney. The body she was pushing suddenly sat up and pulled back the sheet, almost causing the two of us to leap out of our boxer shorts. On the gurney was yet another good-looking dame, her skin crisscrossed with stitches like the Bride of Frankenstein.

"What's the deal?" I asked, steeling my nerve. "You almost gave us matching heart attacks."

"There's a post-Halloween party going on downstairs," said the gal on the gurney.

"Isn't it a little late for Halloween? Christmas is tomorrow."

"It's never too late for a 'post' party, dum dum. You boys want to join us? Free bowling until midnight."

"Sorry ladies, but duty calls," I said.

"Suit yourselves."

"I'd love to, but we don't have any costumes to suit ourselves with."

Carmine turned his head to gawk at them as they passed us by. I was too preoccupied thinking about the case to do any gawking.

"Cisco! Cisco!" he said as he tugged at my sleeve. "This time that dead gal winked at me!"

"She wasn't dead, Carmine. Believe me, I know the difference."

"But I thought the morgue was only for stiffs."

"Just drop it, sport. Let's get back on track and figure out our plan."

He settled down like day-old seltzer.

"So we know what Plotzky died of," I said. "What's next?"

"We go to every store in town and check up on sales of heat packs?"

"Hey, maybe night school is paying off."

"I wasn't being serious, boss!" he exclaimed. "There's hundreds of stores in this burg. And who'd still be selling heat packs this late on Christmas Eve?"

We arrived at the lobby near the front entrance of the building, where there was a pay phone mounted on the wall. I lifted the phone's receiver from the cradle and picked up an old directory from the shelf below it.

"Carmine, old friend, to find that out, we use the oldest book in the book: the Yellow Pages."

We heard a musical stinger. I leaned over and noticed the shabby brass band from the police station, now gathered in the lobby.

"Hey!" I shouted at them. "I'm trying to use the phone over here!"

I opened the directory to let my fingers do the walking. Bits of shredded paper fell out like flakes of yellow snow (which isn't really the kind of image I wanted to conjure up in your head just now, so I apologize). The center of the book had been hollowed out, and the thing was occupied: inside it was a family of mice sitting down to a Christmas dinner with all the trimmings.

The Papa Mouse was dressed in a pinstriped vest and an adorable little ascot, and was carving a garlic-parmesan crouton into slices and serving them out on cute little plates.

"Hey, you big palooka!" he squeaked in his angry little mouse voice, "We're trying to sit down to a family meal in here!"

"Oh, sorry," I said. "I just need a couple of pages."

"Someone always wants to make a call just as we're sitting down to eat," he grumbled as the Mama Mouse, who was dressed in a gingham gown, shook her head and sighed.

I hurriedly tore out the pages I needed and apologized.

"Sorry to bother you," I said. "Enjoy your meal, and Merry Christmas."

"Beat it, ya big lunk!" squeaked the Papa Mouse.

As I closed the phone book, he waved. Or maybe he was showing me his ring finger's big brother; it was hard to tell from his tiny paws.

I put the directory back on the shelf, and we hauled our cans out of the morgue, while behind us, the brass band played "God Rest Ye, Merry Gentlemen." Normally that might have been appropriate, but I doubt there was a single gentleman corpse in the entire place.

Chapter 7: The Sporting Goods Store

We climbed into my car and sat down to do a bit of research. I flicked through the pages I'd swiped off the family of mice.

As Carmine's attempt at sarcasm implied, there was no way we could check every single store in the city; besides, all the ones that offered credit had banned me ages before. The trick was to thin out the list by a process of methodical elimination.

In those days, heat packs weren't as common as they are now. They were a specialty item, mainly used by athletes for sore joints and muscles, so I only tore out the directory pages that listed the sporting goods stores.

I scanned the lists of business names on the yellow sheets. Some of them specialized in a single sport, like Gaga-For-Golf or Javier's Jouse of Jai Alai. Those ones were ruled out. Others specialized in low-impact activities you could do while drunk, such as fishing or bowling. Also out. Then there were the stores that sold collectible merchandise for fans, like autographed Lou Gehrig socks or those stupid foam hands that say "We're #1!" Those ones were out as well. That left just a handful of stores to check out, which was good because the car was running low on gas.

I started the engine and we set off. The snow kept on falling, to the delight of lucky children whose parents didn't force them to shovel it.

As we motored along, we saw roving gangs of agitated snowmen on the sidewalks, looking like they were out to hunt down a helping of trouble. Some were knocking over newspaper boxes and trash cans, taking out their frustration on whatever they could find that wouldn't fight back.

Carmine rubbed the foggy window with his sleeve to get a better view.

"Boy, those snowmen sure look steamed," he said.

"Can't really blame them," I replied. "They must be burning to serve up a nice cold dish of revenge for that riot. Let's try not to attract their attention."

We passed by the first few stores on my list, but they were already closed up for the day. Then we came to an old mom-and-pop shop, "Sketchley's Sporting Goods." Its window display was plastered with huge "SALE" signs (maybe the sign shop had a sale on them?). To our surprise, the lights were on and there was an "OPEN" sign dangling from the door.

As we got out of the car, I realized that I recognized the place: I used to drop in there on occasion when I was caught short of bullets. Normally I bought my rounds in bulk from the discount ammo warehouse in a place across town from me, since they were cheap, offered free parking, and I could always scarf down some complimentary bagel crisps from the bakery next door. But the warehouse was a bit out of the way, and there are times when convenience trumps thrift (although it always killed me to have to pay full retail price).

A bell rang as we opened the shop door; I assumed that meant that somewhere, an angel got its wings (for 50% off).

I bent down and whispered in Carmine's ear, giving him the rundown on our cover story.

"Remember: if anyone asks, we're just casual Christmas shoppers on a last-minute browsing spree. Try not to make eye contact with any sales clerks, and whatever you do, don't let them get you to try something on."

"Righty-o, boss," he said.

"Now let's find out where they keep the heat packs. Act natural."

We strolled through the aisles and inspected the shelves. Their inventory was scant, and the stuff they did have was sorely outdated; it was more like a sporting goods museum.

Carmine tiptoed up and whispered to me.

"I can't find them anywhere. You?"

"Nada. They need to hire a stock boy or fire the one they have."

There were a few paltry Christmas decorations on the walls, most of which looked like they'd been hanging since the previous year. For a second I thought maybe the place had been abandoned by its owners, but then I heard snoring noises coming from the back.

We followed the sound to the counter where the cash register sat. There was an old man standing behind it, his eyes closed, snoring away like a chainsaw suffering from engine knock. He was dressed in a grey tracksuit with matching head- and wrist-bands. Behind him on the wall was a big plate-glass mirror with a tall curtain beside it.

I wasn't sure if I should wake the old man or not. Wasn't it dangerous to rouse someone who's sleep-retailing? Or was that just a myth perpetuated by shoplifters? I tiptoed up to him, trying my best to be silent...

A deafening blast from behind me nearly punctured my eardrums. I turned to see Carmine holding an air horn that he'd picked up from a nearby display.

"Sorry!" he said, a sheepish look on his face.

I snatched the air horn from him and looked back at the old man, who to my surprise was still sawing logs, teetering back and forth as he snoozed on his feet.

"I just wanted to see how it worked," Carmine said.

"Apparently it doesn't," I replied as I snapped my fingers in front of the old man's face. "But I'll bet I know what will."

I jingled some change in my pocket. The old man reacted instantly, as though his wallet were on fire.

"Huh? Wha?"

He looked around, still in a daze. Maybe he wasn't sure where he was or what he was supposed to be doing, but in any case, he didn't seem to have all his pieces on the chessboard, if you know what I mean. Then he noticed us, rubbed his eyes, and cleared his throat.

"Oh, um, merry Christmas, gentlemen. Can I help you?"

"Hopefully," I replied. "You always open on Christmas Eve?"

"Of course. You never know when someone might need a dartboard or some last-minute roller skates for under the tree. Best day of the year to do business."

Carmine and I looked around, perplexed at the discrepancy between his words and reality. Other than us, the place was deserted.

"Best day?" said my sidekick. "Seems kinda dead to me."

"Shut up, Captain Killjoy," the old man snapped, the congeniality collapsing from his face like an avalanche. Then just like that, the flash of his friendly smile reappeared.

"So, gentlemen, what can I do for you?"

"Answer some questions for a start," I said as I flipped him my badge. (My flipping hand was getting a bit sore by that point.)

"Police?" he asked. "What's this all about?"

"Investigation. We're tracking sales of heat packs."

He drummed his fingers on the counter as if he were pleading the Fifth in Morse code.

"Oh, dear," he fretted. "I'd have to fetch our records for that. Not sure where they are right now. We've been doing a lot of reorganizing lately..."

"Find them, if you don't mind," I said. "I'd hate to have to charge you with obstetrics of justice."

"Oh, I don't want any trouble," he answered, "I just need to take a look in the back."

"We'll wait."

As he disappeared through the curtain behind the counter, it occurred to me that there might be an exit in the rear of the shop.

"I don't like this," I said to Carmine. "Go around the back of the store and make sure he doesn't try to make a break for it."

"Aw geez, Cisco, what's so suspicious about him? He's just an old shopkeeper."

"Exactly: they're the sneakiest, slipperiest snakes since the one that sold Eve a rotten apple."

"But he's..."

"Damn them all with their 'going out for business' sales and their discounts on stuff nobody wants...their coupons that always expire before you can use them...their endless flyers in your mailbox, even though you put up a sign on your door that says, 'No Flyers'..."

The Rant Raft had set sail and was carrying me adrift. Carmine shook my arm.

"Okay, boss, okay!" he said. "Don't start grinding your tonsils into powder over it."

He was about to head outside, but Sketchley came back through the curtain with a thick binder. He squatted down like an Olympic powerlifter and heaved the thing up onto the counter with a geriatric grunt.

"That's quite a workout," I remarked. "I'd watch my back if I were you."

His eyes went wide as he started looking furtively over his shoulder.

"Why? Are they following me again?"

"No, I mean your vertebrae," I clarified. "At your age, you shouldn't put too much strain on your spine."

"Nonsense," he huffed. "I jog five miles every morning and do two hundred crunches."

"I do crunches in the morning, too," interrupted Carmine. "On my Wheaty Flakes cereal."

"You already exercise your jaw too much," I told him.

"Best to avoid wheat," the old man said. "The gluten isn't good for one's digestion."

The shopkeeper assumed a bodybuilder's pose and flexed (at least that's what I had to assume, since I couldn't see a single muscle on his thin frame).

"I myself eat nothing but raw kelp, fermented yak milk, spelt bread and sesame seeds," he boasted. "Don't feel a day over sixty."

"How old are you?" asked Carmine.

"A day under sixty."

God help us: he was one of those "health food" nuts.

"Just show us the records," I said, "and spare us the nutritional advice."

Having to suffer fools gladly is part of my job, but time was a-wasting and I was getting impatient (also low on blood sugar).

The old man turned the binder around and shoved it towards me with just enough resentment to be noticeable.

"There's the figures for the last quarter," he said.

I foisted the binder on Carmine.

"Uh, you go ahead and read it, kid. The dog ate my glasses."

"But you don't have a do..."

HONK! I blasted the air horn in his face.

"I said *read*."

Carmine shook his head, opened the binder to the last few pages, and started checking over the figures.

"That's funny...they've been selling heat packs like hotcakes all through December," he said, "except yesterday and today."

"It's that up-to-date?" I asked.

Carmine pointed at the ledger.

"There's the 23rd and 24th marked down. They sold a referee whistle, an athletic cup, a set of crampons, a hockey puck, and a bag of trail mix, but no heat packs."

"If you weren't sure where these records were kept," I asked the shopkeeper, "then how is it that they're so current?"

"My daughter usually takes care of the books," he explained. "The old eyesight might be fading, but we still try to run a tight ship."

"Well, don't leave port, skipper," I replied. "We'll be asking you questions as soon as I can think of some good ones."

"Hey, Cisco," Carmine whispered as he nudged my elbow. "Don't he look a bit familiar?"

I took a closer look at the old geezer.

"Kind of. What's your handle, pal?"

"John Q. Sketchley," he answered as he pointed to the front of the store. "That's my name on the sign."

Carmine smacked his forehead, saving me the trouble.

"Now I recognize you!" he said. "Aren't you the tennis star who got busted for working with the mob?"

Sketchley cast his eyes down in shame.

"That wasn't my finest moment," he muttered.

"Busted, eh, Sketchley?" I asked. "What was the charge?"

"Racketeering."

"Figures. Usually I only got a memory for dame tennis players, but I remember seeing your mug shot in the papers. That arrest ruined your career, didn't it?"

"I'm legitimate now," Sketchley explained. "I just work here in my store, tending the counter, stringing the rackets, smearing Vaseline™ on the catcher's mitts..."

"Right."

"...boxing the sneakers, blowing up the beach balls..."

"Sure. Listen..."

"...and then there's all the sharpening: sharpening the skates, sharpening the lawn darts..."

"We get it."

"...sharpening the buck knives, sharpening the baseball bats..."

"Uh, you all right?"

Sketchley stuck a pencil into a sharpener mounted on the counter and started turning the handle, grinding the point to a stub, while shaking and foaming at the mouth (and maybe other places too). His eyes rolled back into his head.

"Day in, day out, I sharpen, sharpen, sharpen..."

"Judas on a jujube," Carmine exclaimed, "he's losin' it!"

It was clear that the bats in the old coot's belfry were flapping like hell to get out. Just as I was trying to decide whether to apply the Heimlich maneuver, hold his tongue down with a spoon, or perform an exorcism, we heard high-heeled footsteps coming from behind him.

The curtain was suddenly shoved aside by a radiant angel from paradise, who held it open while a pretty decent-looking broad walked through it. Though she appeared no older than mid-twenties, her hair was a striking shade of silver-grey. She had on a white dress with a floral pattern (at least, I think it was floral—it could have just as easily been vegetable, animal or mineral; textile design isn't exactly my forte).

She hurried straight to Sketchley and fussed over him like a nurse with her favorite invalid.

"C'mon, pop," she said, "time for your pill and your nap."

As she put an arm around the old man to lead him away, she eyed us with mistrust.

"What did you two jokers get him all worked up for?" she asked.

Carmine tried to explain.

"But all we did was ask him about...ouch!"

I stepped on his foot.

"I'll do the talking, Chatty Cathy."

The girl ignored us and turned her attentions back to Sketchley.

"This way, pop."

From "pop," I gathered that she was either heavily into onomatopoeia or she was Sketchley's daughter. There wasn't a whole lot of family resemblance, but maybe she got her looks from the maternal side.

She escorted the old man through the curtain and out of sight.

Carmine looked up at me.

"Bit of a looker, eh, boss?"

"Not bad," I mumbled. "I wonder what she'd look like in a tennis outfit."

"I wouldn't mind checking out her serve!"

Carmine made a wolf whistle that sounded more like it came from a hamster than a wolf.

"Cool it," I said. "This isn't a construction site."

"Fine," he said. "So what do we do now?"

"Let's just wait and see what develops."

The girl soon reemerged through the curtain and looked straight at me.

"So, if it isn't the famous Cisco Maloney," she said.

That caught me off guard.

"I see my reputation precedes me."

She sniffed.

"So does your cologne."

Carmine cracked up.

"Ha! She's got a tongue like a forked whip!"

"I see you taught your monkey to talk," she said, looking me straight in the eye.

I checked to see that her ring finger was unadorned, and turned the charm up to "Cary Grant."

"And I see you have the advantage of me, miss...?"

"Betty Sketchley," she said. "I had a feeling you'd show up here today, Mister Maloney."

"Oh really, now? Why's that?"

"You always end up short of bullets at the end of the month, and all the other stores are closed."

I confess, she had me nonplussed. Did I come here that often? Was I that predictable? I tried to get plussed again, and play it cool and casual.

"Nice guess, honey," I said. "I suppose you saw me coming in your crystal ball?"

"I saw you coming through the two-way mirror," she answered. "Normally, the first thing you do is head for the ammunition counter."

"Well, this time you're wrong about the reason," I said. "I'm here to..."

"Ogle the mannequins in the tennis outfits?" she interrupted. "That's the second thing you do."

"You seem to know me well enough," I said. "How come I've never seen you here before?"

"I'm usually in the back, looking out for shoplifters," she replied with a smile. "I wasn't watching you through the mirror just because you're so handsome, mister square-jaw-and-matching-head."

Ouch. Although this little honeybee's voice was sugar-sweet, her words carried an entire hive's worth of stings. Not to mention that her mixed signals had my radar in a frazzle. I felt like a catnip toy in the claws of a capricious Siamese cat.

She took out a file and started casually shaping her nails, barely even looking me in the eye.

"So if it isn't bullets, what do you want?" she asked. "Besides giving my poor father a coronary."

"We came to check your sales records."

That got her attention. Storm clouds of indignation gathered over her face as she noticed the binder on the counter and grabbed it.

"You don't have any right to look at those," she fumed.

"Too bad," I teased. "We already did."

"That's an outrage!"

"So's murder."

She put away the binder and laid her nail file to rest on the counter. I now had her undivided attention, but it wasn't the kind I'd have preferred. She arched a neatly plucked eyebrow at me, and then suddenly was all smiles again.

"Cut the baloney and start talking turkey, Cisco. What's your game?"

"You're aware that Plotzky the Snowman got the big melt last night?"

"It was on the radio."

"He was killed by heat packs," I said, "and you sell 'em. Lots of 'em. Right up until yesterday."

She shrugged a pair of shapely shoulders; I couldn't help but notice what smooth and tanned skin she had, like an amphibian with a timeshare in Florida.

"It's been a cold December," she said. "Our stock ran short. Tell me," she added, "why do you care about a melted snowman, anyways?"

"A certain thousand-dollar reward made my heart bleed."

Her laughter was both dismissive and attractive at the same time.

"And I thought there were no idealists left."

She was silent for a moment: either waiting for me to leave or thinking up a good putdown.

"I actually might have some information for you," she finally said. "But first I want to know if you're planning on sharing that reward."

Carmine butted in.

"He's already sharing it, thank you very much!"

I leaned over the counter a tad.

"Here's your reward, Betty," I said quietly. "Help me solve this case, and it'll take the heat off your old man."

"But he's innocent," she replied.

"The cops won't assume that. They'll be tracking heat pack sales, just like me. They're bound to go through your father's records. Maybe bring him in for questioning. Or even arrest him to show Joe Public that they're making headway on the case."

"Preposterous."

"Is it? The heat is on, Miss Sketchley. There's already been a riot. Out in the streets, Plotzky's kinsmen are going snow-ballistic. Believe me, I know the city's finest like the back of my cupboard. Johnny Law will gladly pin the blame on a patsy if it will prevent a race war."

She tossed her head back and stuck out her chin at just the right angle to get the shadows accentuating her fine cheekbones.

"They couldn't pin the tail on a pack-ass," she said haughtily. "My father's innocent until proven guilty."

I felt I was hitting a nerve, so I pressed on.

"Your dad's got a rap sheet, don't he?"

"That was ages ago. He served his time."

"Doesn't matter: a prior record never looks good."

"But he's a sick old man!"

"Even worse. People have been known to make false confessions under interrogation. Given your papa's condition, it wouldn't take too much time under the hot lights to make him crack like a soft-boiled egg..."

"How dare you threaten my father!"

With lightning speed, she slapped me right in the face.

Even as she connected, I couldn't help but admire the muscle tone in her arm. Ordinarily, a smack that hard would do more harm than good, but after getting whacked out of place by the trollop at the precinct, Betty's blow actually popped my loose disc back where it belonged.

"Ah," I said as I rubbed my neck with relief. "That actually feels much better."

She swung at my mug with the other arm, but this time I was ready: I caught her by the wrist and clamped on tight as a bear trap. I hate to get physical with a dame, but sometimes it's essential for self-defense.

For a second, I thought it was going to be like trying to hold an angry cat down in a bathtub; the wild look in her eyes suggested she was desperate enough to chew her own arm off to escape. But she suddenly composed herself, and started fussing and using her free hand to smooth down her dress, the way most women do after they catch themselves resorting to unladylike violence.

"Okay, Cisco, you win," she said, lowering her voice to a murmur. "I know someone who's been buying up quantities of heat packs recently."

As guilt, curiosity and arousal competed for bandwidth in my brain, I let go of her arm. What can I say? I was a bit of a sucker for the lively ones, and it doesn't hurt if they're easy on the eyes.

"Alright, señorita," I said, "spill the frijoles."

She rubbed her wrist.

"I won't say his name, but I'll give you a hint: he's got long ears, hops around a lot, and he's in the chocolate business."

Carmine's flabber was gasted.

"I don't believe it!" he said. "You mean the Easter Bun..."

She cut him off.

"You didn't hear it from me! Listen, Cisco: my father needs care, and I'm all he's got. If something were to happen to me, he wouldn't last a day."

Sensing that I was being fed a shipload of bunk, I threw her my trademarked Hard Stare™.

"Are you actually trying to tell me you're afraid of retaliation from a silly old rabbit?"

"I can't afford to take any chances," she said. "Now look, you got what you came here for, so why don't you leave? And take your monkey with you."

Carmine and I looked at each other.

"What do you say, boss?" he asked.

"I never cross a dame, buddy," I answered. "My little black book is thin enough already. Why don't you go wait for me by the door?"

"Whatever you say."

He shuffled his feet as he made for the exit, polishing the floor as he went. I heard the sound of a sad trombone in the distance and felt a bit bad for shooing him off, but I wanted a word with Betty in private...all out of professional motives, of course.

I doffed my hat in the dame's direction.

"Thanks for the tip, Miss Sketchley. We'll keep it between you, me, and the monkey over there."

"You swear?"

"Can't. This story's barely hanging on to its PG rating as it is. Oh, and I almost forgot; I think I'll need that pack of bullets after all."

Without so much as a downward glance, she lifted a box of bullets from under the counter, smacked it down in front of me, and cracked a wry grin.

"Forty-five, right?"

"You know my size?"

"I figured you used a big gun to make up for deficiencies elsewhere."

"Such charm. If you keep it up, I'm going to start expecting it."

"I expect payment. That'll be $2.95."

I fumbled around in my pocket, fished out a trio of dirty singles, and handed them over. She smoothed them out, stuck them in the register one by one, and then rung up the sale with a loud "ka-ching," making smoldering eyes at me the whole time.

I felt like a cobra being teased by a mongoose as I picked up the box of bullets: ACME brand, my favorite.

"I don't suppose you have any idea where I might find our lucky-footed friend?" I asked.

"Try this address."

She tore the receipt off the cash register and scribbled on the back of it with a pencil, then gave me the slip, together with my change.

As our hands briefly touched, I could feel the back of my neck getting red. Damn those involuntary bodily functions...even the voluntary ones were hard enough to control.

Our eyes met, and introduced each other.

From out of nowhere, I heard romantic string music swelling up like an allergic kid who ate a peanut.

I knew I should say something, but needed a second to untie my tongue.

"I...uh...thanks."

Smooth, that's me.

"You're welcome anytime," she cooed.

Now listen: I'm not some newborn greenhorn when it comes to reading women, but the way she switched from hard-assed harpy to flirty coquette had me scratching my head harder than a hydra with dandruff.

I was all out of things to say, so I finally turned and headed for the door.

"Let's go, Carmine."

I didn't see him anywhere, but guessed that my sidekick had gotten lost among the mannequins in the front window. A sign above them read: "SALE ON LADIES SPORTSWEAR." Sure enough, they were modeling the latest in women's athletic clothes, and this season was just like the last: strongly stitched architectural corsets designed to hold everything in while the wearer gave it everything she had.

I finally spotted Carmine. Like a teenage boy practicing for a heavy date, he had his arms around one of the mannequins and was struggling to undo its heavily barricaded brassière.

Oh, brother, I thought. *Not again.*

The kid was worse than a tomcat in a sardine shop. I walked over and gave him a swift kick in the cushions.

"I said let's go, Carmine!"

"Ow! I'm comin'!" he yelped.

He stumbled and knocked over the mannequin he was holding, which fell against another mannequin, which fell against another mannequin, which toppled over and knocked against a bowling ball on a shelf, which rolled off and landed on one end of a skateboard, which flipped up and did a somersault, then landed on an inclined weightlifting bench, then rolled down and bumped into a medicine ball, which tumbled off and bounced off a mini-trampoline, then sailed through the air and swished through a basketball net, then crashed into a cluster of bowling pins, which scattered all over the floor.

Rube Goldberg would have given it a four out of ten.

I grabbed Carmine and got ready to beat a hasty retreat, but Betty called out after me.

"Cisco, wait!"

The romantic string music started up again.

"What is it?" I asked.

"You dropped your receipt."

The string music screeched to a halt.

"Oh."

You know how they say when you leave something somewhere, it's because you want to go back? I guess it's true.

I went back for the slip of paper, but she ran out from behind the counter and beat me to it. She picked it up and tucked it in my pocket. We were face-to-face.

"There," she said. "Now it's safe."

"I guess I'll be seeing you around," I stammered.

"Sure," she answered demurely as she walked back to the counter. "Come back when your monkey is house-trained."

"Sorry about your store, miss!" Carmine blurted out as I hauled him out of there.

The bell on the door jingled as we stepped out onto the sidewalk.

"It's lucky she didn't bill us for the damage," I said to my sidekick. "You've got to stop playing the proverbial bull in the porcelain boutique."

"I can't help it if gravity always follows me around."

We almost crashed into a busking string quartet that had set up shop outside the store.

That explained where the romantic string music was coming from. And here I was thinking my life had become worthy of its own soundtrack.

The quartet gave us dirty looks as it struck up a requiem. We got the hint and hurried back to the car, almost tripping over a sad old dented trombone lying on the curb.

Chapter 8: The Message

As we got to the car, I heard an aggressive ringing behind me. What now?

I turned around and saw Santa. Not the real Santa, of course, but a guy dressed up in a Santa suit, holding a brass bell in one hand and a fishbowl in the other, which bore the red and white shield of the Salvation Army.

The ersatz Claus waved his bell at us. It clanged hard enough to shake my hypothalamus loose.

He stuck out the bowl.

"Give to the Salvation Army?" he asked.

The way he said it, it sounded more like a dare than a question.

"Sorry, buddy," I lied. "I'm on my way to work."

"Fine," he said with two generous scoops of scorn. "Just remember that some children don't get a Christmas."

And with that he turned away, ignoring me completely.

If there's one thing I can't stand (and don't worry, there's plenty more than one thing I can't stand), it's pushy charities that try to lay on the guilt trip. Not wanting to let him think he got the last word, I tapped him on the shoulder.

"Hey, pal," I asked. "Why do you guys call yourselves an 'army' anyways? Is it because you 'rifle' through people's pockets?"

"I know a reason," added Carmine. "The only 'tanks' they have are septic!"

I wished my sidekick would run his lines by me before trying them out on a live audience.

"I don't know what's cheaper," sneered the Salvation Army Santa as he turned around. "You or your shots."

I took a closer look at the man behind the beard. Names escape me, but I never forget a face I want to punch.

"Say, I've seen you downtown before. Weren't you raising money last summer to save the trees? Or maybe it was the grass?"

I suppose he'd mustered up all his indignation with that last comeback, because he started walking away too fast for me to catch up. I guess he didn't relish the thought of further conversation.

At last, Carmine and I headed back to my car. We got in and did up our seat belts (the car was built before the belt laws, so mine were homemade jobs made of braided rubber bands).

"Get the map and find the quickest route to this address," I said as I handed him the receipt Betty had given me.

Carmine opened the glove box. A powerful odor filled the car.

"Egads," I exclaimed, "what's that stink?"

"Not sure," Carmine said as he plugged his pug nose, took a telescopic pointer from his pocket, and poked around in the glove box with it.

I could tell from the guilty look on his face that he wasn't as forthcoming as he could have been.

"What did you leave in there?" I asked, giving him the stink eye.

"I think it might be a kumquat from last week," he said, cowering like a dog that got caught laying an egg on the carpet. "I was saving it."

He fished out a lumpy, fuzzy orange mass, about the size of a ping-pong ball, impaled at the end of his pointer.

"Crimony jickets!" I said. "I hope it's not having babies."

"It's just a rotten fruit, boss."

"Well, toss it out the window before it reproduces!"

"But that would be littering."

"So? I sure don't want it to have a litter in here."

"No, I mean it's against the law to throw garbage out of a car."

"And it's against my law to keep garbage *in* the car. Now chuck it!"

He rolled down the window and flung out the composted 'quat. I wondered what else might be lurking in the glove box that wasn't gloves.

I also wondered why it was taking my sidekick so long to do his job.

"What are you waiting for?" I asked him. "Get the map out!"

He peered reluctantly inside the tiny space.

"I don't wanna put my hand in there," he said.

"You want to put your hand on the reward money, don't you?"

He winced as he reached in, took out my city map, and shut the glove box as quickly as he could.

The map was a bit ragged, having been used as a coaster, a tablecloth, a picnic blanket, a pup tent, and a parachute (long story), but he managed to find the location.

"Here it is, and it's not far," he said. "Make two rights and then a wrong."

"You got it."

I followed his directions. We ended up on a wide four-lane boulevard with a median strip in the middle. Traffic was moving well for a change.

And then I heard the wail of a police siren behind me.

"Aw nuts, the fuzz," I said.

Although I didn't think I was going too fast, I admit I hadn't been checking the speedometer, but that's only because it had fallen through a rusted hole in the dashboard ages before. I usually judged my speed kind of the same way sailors do, by throwing a brick tied to a length of rope out of the car and timing how long it took for the rope to go taut.

I really didn't need the holdup, but I pulled over anyways, knowing darn well that the rusty old bag of bolts I was driving had no chance of outrunning a police cruiser. I'd have to use a mix of wits and congeniality to talk my way out of it, since my badge sure wasn't going to get me uncanned from this pickle. All I could do was hope and pray that the cop pulling us over had a little bit of seasonal goodwill in him...or that he didn't know me, either personally or by reputation.

Looking in my rearview mirror, I saw a massive lump in uniform get out of the police car and walk purposefully towards us. I recognized the lump as Wencil Hampfizscht, who'd been freshly recruited from the Amish country just before I quit the force.

Raised on a farm and big as a barn, Wencil had muscles whose only job was to help hold up his bigger muscles. His shadow darkened the car as he rapped on my window with a thick, callused knuckle that knew no pain and took no prisoners.

With trepidation, I rolled the window down and tried out a cheery greeting.

"Merry Christmas, Wencil! Long time no see."

"Season's greetings, Cisco," he replied in a voice that sounded as though it was coming from the bottom of the Marianas Trench.

He stuck his face through the open window so we were nose-to-nose. Though his mouth was closed, I could tell what he'd eaten for lunch that day from the breath coming out of his nostrils (Black Forest ham on pumpernickel with a dollop of grainy mustard and a gherkin on top).

"Got a message for you from Chief Murray," he said.

"Really?" I asked. "What is it?"

"The Chief says he's got to hand it to you..."

WHAMMO! He smacked my face with his open palm.

"You sure do know how to stick to a case..."

SMASH! He busted my side-view mirror with his nightstick.

I cringed, not only from the puns and the pain, but also in dread of where the next blow would land.

"But he's not too ebullient with reference to your impertinent disregard for the line of demarcation between the authority of a civilian and that of a police officer," Wencil concluded.

"Uh...come again?"

"Murray says to quit using the badge and back off the Plotzky case," he said. "Exclamation point!"

ZOCKO! He threw me a right hook across the chops that knocked all my fillings out. Forget stars; I was seeing entire galaxies spinning around my head. I rubbed my sore jaw and opened and closed my mouth a couple of times to make sure the hinges weren't loose.

"Jeez, whatever happened to 'serve and protect'?" I asked, woozy from the wallop.

"That was you being served," Wencil replied. "And the lesson ought to protect you from getting any more. By the way, I believe this is yours."

He tossed something small, orange and fuzzy into the car through my window.

"Next time I catch you littering," he continued, "I'll make sure you get thirty days' community service picking up garbage from the roadside with your teeth...if you have any left."

As the putrid smell filled the car, Wencil walked back towards his cruiser. He climbed in and pulled away, cutting off oncoming traffic.

"See, boss?" chirped Carmine. "I told you it was littering!"

"Ah, put a sock in it!" I shot back. "There's plenty of things worse than littering. This god-forsaken fruit, for instance."

We choked on the horrible smell, our eyes watering and our tooth enamel flaking off. As soon as Wencil's car was out of sight, I bent down, picked up the offending kumquat and tossed it as far away as I could, then rolled up the window.

"Check the glove box for some aspirin," I said to Carmine. "Suddenly, I have a headache that's reaching all the way down to my ankles."

He poked around in the glove box again.

"Sorry, Cisco. Looks like we're all out."

"Forget it, then," I replied. "I need something stronger anyways if I'm going to make it through this day with my head in one piece."

I might have been smarting, but I wasn't smart enough to give up on the case, so don't think we were going to be dissuaded that easily. Despite Chief Murray's hand-delivered warning, I had no choice but to press on. My face could roll with the punches, but my wallet was ready to throw in the towel: two good reasons for us to keep at it and leave no turn un-stoned.

"Uh, boss?"

There was a tremor in Carmine's voice; I'd say about a 3.6 on the Richter scale.

"What is it now?"

"There's a bunch of snowmen coming our way."

I looked outside and spotted a matlock of snowmen marching towards the car. ("Matlock" was the commonly accepted collective noun for a group of snowmen, like "murder of crows" or "shrewdness of apes." Don't ask me why; I wasn't asked to pitch in when they invented the English language.).

The one in the front of the group had a dent on his forehead and was holding something in his hand.

"Hey, wiseguy!" he shouted at me. "Did you throw this?"

Damn that blasted kumquat.

I slammed my foot on the gas pedal. The car's tires screeched as it lurched forward, every gasket groaning from the effort. I cut off several cars as I swerved onto the lane, but driver etiquette had to take a back seat this time. Horns honked behind us as the snowmen gathered on the road, shaking their fists and blocking the traffic.

Through the rearview mirror, I watched as angry drivers got out of their cars to yell at the snowmen for standing in their way. An all-out brawl broke out, and I wasn't sticking around to declare the winner.

"Let's just get to the Easter Bunny's place in one piece," I said to Carmine. "And from now on, no more funny-named fruits in the car. New rule."

"I'll add it to the rulebook, boss," he replied with a sigh.

Carmine took out a black notebook and jotted something down. Since I was always forgetting the arbitrary rules I made up on the spot, I'd bought him the notebook and made him keep a list. It seemed that the shorter my patience got, the longer that list became.

The car rolled along the snowy road as we closed the distance between us and the Easter Bunny's place. I didn't exactly have a plan for how to approach him once we got there, but plans are for people who like to make the gods laugh. Like a jazz musician, I preferred to improvise...and like most jazz musicians, I suffered from the delusion that I was good at it.

Chapter 9: The Warren

The Easter Bunny was well known in this town; a die-hard, dyed-in-the-wool bachelor, one part philanthropist, two parts philanderer. He was famous for his charity with children and his dexterity with women, to say nothing of his chocolate empire.

Not all the ladies loved him, though.

I'll explain: back in the days before the Temperance crowd went grog-wild trying to outlaw all substances that inspired pleasure, they were happy if we only dodged the draft (beer, that is). Totalitarian teetotalers focused their damnation on the silly-sauce; they didn't worry about stimulants like opium, cocaine, khat, betel nut, or cocoa, because none of those were the reason their husbands came home late from the bars (come to think of it, booze wasn't always the reason either, but let's not shove the hard truth up their well-meaning, upturned noses).

To the Anglo-Saxon xenophobes of the Temperance movement, cocoa was viewed as just another unpleasant exotic substance, presumably used by immigrants for voodoo rituals and homemade aphrodisiacs. They had very little interest in restricting it.

That all changed when the Easter Bunny came up with the idea to add milk and sugar to the stuff and sell it in solid bars wrapped in foil. As a shrewd promotion strategy, he started giving it away in egg form at Easter, right when many Christian kids were coming down off forty days of Lenten deprivation and dying for an indulgence that they could later purchase an indulgence for (man, that Catholicism sure is a funny faith).

A chocolate craze erupted, which caught the Temperance ladies with their bloomers down. Sensing a new threat to juvenile morality, they kicked their knickers into overdrive and did their damnedest to ban the stuff. Petitions were signed, factories were picketed, chocolatiers were boycotted, and finally, the Anti-Cocoa Amendment was signed into law by presidential veto (I don't really know much about how the Executive Branch works, but you get the idea).

Quite predictably, this drove the Easter Bunny and his enterprise underground, where it flourished. Naturally the government overreacted, launching a full-scale Campaign Against Cocoa at home and sending Marines overseas to eradicate cocoa production in plantations as far away as Guam, Guatemala, Guinea Bissau, Guyana, and the Guays (Para and Uru). (In those days, our men were invading other countries alphabetically; we were at the letter *G*.) But despite the best efforts of our doughboys abroad and a gaggle of busy-bodied old biddies stateside, the Easter Bunny continued to make a fortune off his illicit cocoa cartel, always keeping himself just one hop ahead of the law.

Then out of the blue, the President backed down and reversed his decision, though nobody was sure why. Rumor had it the Easter Bunny made a large donation to his campaign chest; another rumor said he caught the Commander-in-Chief in a compromising position with a special lady who wasn't the First Lady (and wasn't the *last* lady, either). According to that particular line of scuttlebutt, the conniving rabbit obtained photographic evidence of the sordid affair and blackmailed the heck out of our head of state, forcing him to take a compromising position with respect to the legality of chocolate.

Whatever the motive, the Anti-Cocoa Amendment was overturned overnight, making the rabbit a legitimate business-bunny and a "made" member of the Chamber of Commerce. From then on, he was hailed as an entrepreneurial success story, accepted into all the social clubs, and got his picture in all the gossip columns, usually while standing on a red carpet with some painted starlet on his arm. He was suddenly the most eligible bachelor in town, with plenty of speculation as to who might claim his heart, but it seemed that no woman would ever manage to get him marching down the aisle and saying "I do."

I pulled up to the apartment building at the address Betty had given me. It was upscale, no doubt, though not as ritzy as Plotzky's place.

We were offered valet parking service, which I refused: mostly because I couldn't afford it, but also because I'd be embarrassed to let a stranger see the filthy interior of my car. What can I say? Nature abhors a vacuum, and I abhor a vacuum cleaner.

I decided it would better suit my budget to park on one of the side streets behind the building, but when I drove around, I found a small lot for employees, deliveries, and service personnel. Perfect. I tucked the car neatly into an empty spot, and we walked back around to the front entrance.

Once inside, we encountered an imposing concierge who sat at a massive security desk. Although it looked like he was buried in his newspaper, I could tell by the sideways glance he gave us that he knew darn well we didn't belong there.

Figuring my best defense was a good offense, I rushed towards him as if it were a matter of life or death.

"Oh, you've got to do something," I said, panting like a panicky puppy. "There's a bum wiping down people's windshields in the parking garage. And his cloth is filthy!"

The concierge immediately abandoned his post and raced outside. Meanwhile, Carmine and I bee-lined it for the elevators and went up.

That particular deception was a fun trick I'd learned when I was working as the house dick at a high-class ski resort in Alberta, Canada. I'd been hired by the owners to solve the Case of the Banff Whistler, a mysterious figure who would whistle from behind the trees and startle the skiers passing by, causing avalanches and confusing local cab drivers. As I got to know the hotel security staff, I learned that nothing got their dander up more than the idea of vagrant riff-raff tarnishing the premises with their disgustingly low bank balances. As a consequence, the easiest way to distract those snobby goons was to divert their attention to someone poorer and filthier than oneself. And if you couldn't find a real person who fit that description, an imaginary one would do (but seriously, you should also consider getting a job and taking a bath at least once in a blue moon).

Carmine hyperventilated the whole way up, clutching at a handrail for dear life.

"Seriously, you need to see a shrink about this elevator thing," I said. "It's just a big metal box dangling on a cable."

"I can't help it!" he whined. "All I can think about is how much empty space there is beneath our feet."

"Look at it this way: if we get stuck, at least I have a pack of cards to pass the time."

His knuckles whitened to match his face.

As soon as the elevator door opened, Carmine rushed out into the hallway and collapsed. Once his breathing got back to normal, I helped him up and we made our way down the hallway of the Easter Bunny's tony apartment building. It was slow going: the carpet must have been knee-deep.

Carmine counted the numbers on the doors.

"I still have a hard time believing it, Cisco," he said in a low voice. "Why would the Easter Bunny wanna kill Plotzky the Snowman?"

"Beats me, but it's the only lead we've got."

"His business is legit now. Even if he was on the wrong side of the law for a while there, he's not mean enough to have people killed."

"I know you're sympathetic, Carmine, but we're on a case. Keep your personal preferences personal."

"I'm trying, boss. It's just that I loved chocolate when I was a kid."

I gave him a look (not that one; the stern one).

"I was never addicted though," he added hastily. "I could quit anytime I wanted. I mean, I haven't had a bite of chocolate in months."

"You sure that's not just because you've been too broke to buy it?"

"Sure, I'm sure!"

He started scratching himself around the neck. Beads of sweat formed along his hairline.

"Look, boss, you wouldn't understand. You've never dealt with a chocolate habit."

"Don't jump to assumptions, kiddo. I've been there. Not Willy Wonka's, but someplace just as bad."

I had a sickening sensation as I felt myself slip into a flashback...

"It was back during the war. I forget which one, but we were fighting a cunning and relentless enemy, so it couldn't have been the Italians...maybe the Swiss? Anyways...four years in a POW camp and every week my mother sent me a care package. Don't ask me how she got the address. Each time she sent me the same thing: Dairy Milk bars. No crunchy peanuts, no creamy caramel, no soft nougat, nothing but that solid milk chocolate..."

"Sounds like heaven to me," interrupted Carmine.

"But it came at a price, and the price was a downward spiral into cocoa hell. By the end of the war, I was a full-blown addict, hooked like Charlie the Tuna. I was lucky to come home with any teeth left. We had no dental plan. My mother never forgave herself."

I snapped out of the flashback.

"Did she die of grief?" asked Carmine.

"No, appendicitis."

"Oh. So how did you kick the habit?"

"I was in and out of a couple of funny farms for a while, but there were bold new techniques being developed in the world of psychiatric treatment. Since I couldn't pay, they offered to work on me for free if I signed up for an experimental program: spooks from the Secret Service would slip LSD into my eyeballs when I wasn't looking."

"How'd they manage that?"

"They were really sneaky."

"Wow, boss, I had no idea you were once a chocoholic."

"There ain't a private dick in the world without a monkey on his back, Carmine, and I'm not about to buck the trend."

"So did the treatment work?"

"I was tripping my eyeballs off, but it didn't cure me. I finally managed to kick the habit and get back on my feet thanks to electroshock therapy and the G.I. bill that put me through the police academy."

"Oh."

I sensed that Carmine was already bored of my story; he went back to counting door numbers.

I took out my old service revolver and checked to see that it was loaded. Carmine gave me a sidelong glance.

"You're not gonna hurt him, are you?"

"If he's innocent, he'll get a chance to prove it in court."

I spun the barrel of the gun.

"Unless I'm forced to shoot him in self-defense, that is."

Carmine stopped at one of the apartment doors.

"Number 327," he said. "This is it."

"Then give it the old shave-and-a-haircut."

Carmine was about to knock on the door, but hesitated. He stared up at me like a dog that knew it was due for a trip to the vet.

"Uh, is one of us gonna play 'bad cop'?" he asked.

"To tell you the truth, I'm not really in the mood."

"Why not?"

"Because Betty Sketchley wrote her phone number on that receipt she slipped into my pocket."

"Aw, Cisco, since when did that kinda thing faze you?"

"Since it was my front pants pocket. And she did it like she was fishing a lipstick tube from out of her purse."

Carmine let out a low wolf whistle.

"So what does that mean, I hafta play bad cop?" he asked. "You know I'm no good at it."

"That's why you need the practice," I said. "For me, it's second nature. Now give the door a knock before we catch Legionnaire's Disease in here."

He tapped on the door with his pinkie knuckle and steeled himself for the role.

"Okay," he mumbled to himself. "I'm bad cop...I'm bad cop...a really bad, not-very-amiable cop..."

"Come on," I said, "get your arm into it! You're 'bad cop,' not Girl Scouts."

He knocked politely on the door with one of those be-bop rhythms the teenagers were crazy about. A bit louder this time, but not much.

"Are you kidding me?" I asked. "I've had Jehovah's Witnesses knock with more gusto than that, and they're afraid they'll go to hell if they breathe too heavily."

Finally, Carmine took a few steps back, counted to three, wound up, and launched himself with both fists flying at the door.

It swung open just as he was about to hit it.

"Whuuups!"

He tripped over the threshold and sailed into the apartment.

Holding the doorknob was the Easter Bunny himself, dressed in a red silk ascot and a matching silk robe. He stood off to one side as Carmine fell flat on his face inside the doorway with an appropriately dull thud, and stared down with bemusement at my fallen sidekick.

"I'm sure I said on the phone that I wanted Girl Scout outfits," he said in a smooth Ivy League accent, "But I also meant with girls wearing them."

"Sorry," I said, "we're not here on that kind of call."

"Then who the blazing heck are you?"

"Officer Maloney," I said with a flash of the badge, "and this here's my partner, Appelbaum. You mind if we come in, Mister Bunny?"

He took a step back and let go of the doorknob. His whiskers twitched.

"Can't see why not, other than the fact that it's Christmas Eve and this tiny cop is already passed out on my carpet."

He gestured for me to come in. Was it really going to be that easy?

I knelt down next to Carmine and waved my travel-sized bottle of smelling salts under his oversized honker. He revived. The Easter Bunny helped me get him to his feet.

"I thought you fellows weren't supposed to be drinking on duty," he said. "Still, I wouldn't mind a snifter of whatever your partner's been having."

He grunted a little from the effort; I got the feeling this playboy wasn't accustomed to any physical exertion that didn't involve a woman.

I took a quick peek at his pad, which was decorated like the typical swank digs of a swinging, bourgeois bachelor with money to burn on the latest in interior design: there was a teak telephone, rosewood rugs, abstract oil sculptures, and *trompe l'oeil* watercolors, all in bold and daring hues. Funky fiberglass lampshades threw mood lighting around the place with reckless abandon, while jazz musicians recklessly soloed for thirty-two bars each over "skittle-e-bop" versions of familiar Christmas carols, the sound coming from a top-tier audiophilic stereo cabinet.

The music stopped as the stylus came to the end of the record. The Easter Bunny casually walked over to the hi-fi set and gave the shellac platter a flip to the B side.

"I assume you officers have a warrant to enter my warren?"

Carmine launched right into his "bad cop" routine.

"Why?" he asked abruptly, making the rabbit's whiskers twitch again. "You hiding something? Well it's too late, buster, we're already inside! It's *habeas corpus* and *casus belli*, not to mention *a f-f-faye ac-com-plee!*"

The Easter Bunny cocked an eyebrow and smirked as he dropped the needle on the disc.

"I've got nothing to hide. At least, not for now. Easter's still a few months away."

A woman in a bunny uniform, complete with a satin one-piece, white rabbit ears, and a cotton tail, appeared through a nearby doorway. (I knew better than to ask what kind of sick, perverse fetish was going on here; I just call 'em like I see 'em...and I like 'em when I see 'em, too.) She handed the Easter Bunny a martini from a serving tray and trotted off in her high-heeled bunny slippers. Carmine's bad-cop routine stumbled a bit as we both stared agog at the tick-tock motion of her fluffy tail.

"Darn right you can't hide," he mumbled distractedly, "because we're seeking, uh, hiding and seeking...are you trying to say we're hiding something?"

The bunny picked out an olive from the glass and took a sip.

"I don't insinuate things," he said with a wink.

I nudged Carmine with the pointy end of my elbow.

"C'mon, buddy. Ad-bay op-cay!"

He shook his head to rattle that pea-brain of his, and gave the Easter Bunny a full-frontal frown with his substantial monobrow.

"You don't, huh? Well, we won't take 'no' for an answer! And we don't have a warrant and we don't have anything to hide! You know why?"

The Easter Bunny stifled a chortle.

"Do tell."

"'Cause we're not really cops! Ha-ha!"

I facepalmed so hard, a gypsy woman could tell my fortune by reading my forehead.

"Nice going, knucklehead. You blew it."

"Aw, sugar-honey-iced-tea! Sorry, Cisco."

The Easter Bunny handed his empty glass to yet another woman passing by in a bunny outfit and opened the top drawer of his hallway console.

"In that case..."

He pulled out a sawed-off shotgun from the drawer, cocked it with an impressive "ka-chack," and aimed it straight at us.

"Great MacGuffin!" yelped Carmine.

We stuck up our handwiches. In that hallway, at that close range, we were sitting ducks, liable to get our gooses cooked at any second. Or turned into stuffing, at least...

The Easter Bunny's knuckles whitened as he gripped his twelve-gauge.

"No fast moves, Maloney and Appelbaum. If those *are* your real names..."

"They're legit," I said.

"F-for realsies," added Carmine.

"So if you're not police, what's the point of your little game?"

"You heard that Plotzky got melted?"

"Plotzky the Snowman?"

He lowered the shotgun a tad.

"You didn't know?"

"I only got out of bed an hour ago. Start talking, and make it coherent."

"They found a puddle in his penthouse this morning," I explained. "Someone put out a big reward for anyone who figures out how it happened. We're just trying to chase up some leads."

He moved closer and shoved the gun barrel right in our faces, going from nose to nose. The oiled grey steel carried a faint whiff of aftershave lotion: the fancy, imported kind like you get from an airport duty-free.

"And you think I did it?" asked the bunny, with a lot more menace than I'd have expected from a fuzzy, cuddly rodent.

"Well... Not as such..."

Here's a law-enforcement tip: it's not a good time to let someone know they're being suspected of a crime if they happen to be aiming a gun at you.

The Easter Bunny cocked the shotgun again. I wasn't sure what all this cocking was supposed to achieve, but it was a lot more cocks than I was comfortable with. I especially didn't like so many cocks right in my face.

(Hey...what are you snickering for?)

The Easter Bunny eyed us from between both sights on the barrels of his crowd-disperser.

"Give me one reason, any reason at all, why I shouldn't blast you into mincemeat," he said.

Carmine and I winced.

"We might get lead poisoning?"

"Our blood would clash with the color scheme?"

And then he fired.

Relax! It wasn't what you think: there was a bang and some smoke, but two tiny chocolate Easter eggs popped out of the barrels, hitting us each in the middle of the forehead.

We shook our heads, stunned and surprised to be alive, albeit with choco-dots on our faces.

The rabbit giggled like a Japanese schoolgirl, put the shotgun back into the console drawer, and hopped on down the hall.

"Why don't you come into the kitchen and tell me about it?" he called out jovially over his shoulder. "I'm warming up some fresh zucchini bread."

It was obvious that he got a sick kick out of scaring us half to death. We hesitated at first, checking our pants to make sure we hadn't emptied our hearts of courage (I'm not too good with anatomy). Then we followed the bunny.

"Zucchini bread?" Carmine whispered. "I would've expected carrot cake."

"What am I?" the bunny hollered back, "A walking cliché?"

I guess those long antenna ears gave him some pretty decent hearing.

Chapter 10: The Kitchen

We stepped into the kitchen, a typically modern designer job for the well-to-do gentleman who mostly ate in restaurants: every pan hanging from the fancy wrought-iron rack above the island in the center was spotless and new.

"Sit, sit," said the rabbit, gesturing towards the tall, uncomfortable-looking chrome stools of his breakfast bar. He took a pair of oven mitts from a drawer beneath the stove. As he put them on, he hummed a bit of Wagner while his tail wagged a bit of...Humner, I guess?

We sat down; at least Carmine tried to, but he had to climb the horizontal rungs of his stool before he could even reach the seat.

Since the suave rabbit seemed to be in a cooperative mood, I decided to take the "bait and fish" approach: feed him little details about the case to see if he might let slip with some bigger ones and incriminate himself.

And then he fed us, literally. As I gave him a redacted rundown of what we knew so far (keeping a few pertinent details to myself), he bent over and heaved a loaf of zucchini bread out of the oven, steaming hot and screaming to be dunked into a cool pool of milk. My stomach had finished digesting those ham-on-ryes and was starting to nag me for more, but I wanted to keep my mind on the business at hand. So I looked around the room to find something to distract me from the tantalizing smell of the baked goods.

Walnut bookshelves surrounded the kitchen, (When I say "walnut," I don't mean the wood; I mean actual walnuts—pressed and glued together. They must have been from Sweden). They were stacked with paperbacks and a massive collection of gentlemen's-interest magazines with titles like *Titillation* and *Wink*.

"I'll be back in a jiffy, boys" the Easter Bunny said. "Got to refresh my drink."

He left the kitchen, bringing his martini glass with him.

"Carmine," I said, "have you seen all these shelves? The bunny sure is a bookworm."

He stood up and scanned the shelves.

"Not exactly the canons of Western literature, boss. It's mostly dime-store novels, pulpy paperbacks with preposterous plots about pulchritudinous paramours perturbing their parsimonious parents with their palpable peccadilloes."

"What?"

"There's also this thesaurus," he said, holding the book open at the *P*'s.

I pointed to the shelf on the wall behind him.

"What about those ones?"

He turned to take a look.

"All murder mysteries, boss. Check out some of these titles: there's *A Kill, The Kill, To Kill, Two Kills for the Price of One, The Killers, The Killing, The Killing Fields, The Killing Floor, The Killing Ceiling, The Kill Zone, Mr. Kildare's Killatorium, The Cabinet of Dr. Killagari, To Mock A Killingbird, Irish Towns From Kilkenny to Killarney, Killion Dollar Baby,* and *Faster, Pussycat! Kill! Kill? Yes, Kill! Didn't You Hear Me?*"

"That last one seems a bit unwieldy."

The Easter Bunny returned with a full glass in his mitt.

"I see you gentlemen are interested in my books," he said with a little too much pride.

I stroked his ego.

"This is quite a library you got here, EB."

"What can I say?" replied the rabbit. "I'm a voracious reader."

"Rapacious, even," said Carmine.

"I see you found my thesaurus, Mister Appelbaum."

He pulled a massive cook's knife from a drawer and grinned, showing two buck teeth that must have been the terror of Carrot Town. My guard shot up at the sight of the knife, but he turned back to the counter and started using it to cut up the zucchini bread.

I told my guard to stand at ease.

The rabbit served out the slices on colorful FiestaWare™ plates and handed us each a martini glass full of milk.

Carmine sat back down in a hurry when the food arrived.

"Mmmm, pickled onions!" he squealed as he fished one out of his glass and started crunching away, then tossed the toothpick and dove into his zucchini bread face-first. He stuffed his gullet like he hadn't had a meal in days, chasing it down with gulps of the onion-y moo juice.

"One slice at a time, Carmine," I told him.

"But I'm so esurient, boss."

"Put that damn thesaurus down."

I admit I was feeling quite hungry myself. I took a bite of the zucchini bread; it was moist, fresh, and delicious, but left an unexpected mint taste on the back palate as it went down. Apparently, Carmine didn't care, or else he didn't notice; he reminded me of a rat trying to gnaw its way through a tractor tire.

"Shucks, EB," I said, "you didn't have to lay out a spread like this just for us."

"Don't mention it," he replied as he stuck the knife in one of those newfangled automatic dishwashers and turned it on. Sheesh, these rich people and their modern conveniences...

"We noticed you're quite a fan of the murder books," I continued.

"I love crime stories," he replied. "Don't you?"

"Only if they line my pocket in the end."

He sat down at the table with us and nibbled at a piece of zucchini bread with his sizeable incisors.

"So what's your take on this whole Plotzky business?" he asked.

"We doubt it was an accident, and it sure wasn't a suicide."

"I'd put all my eggs on it," he nodded in agreement. "Plotzky wouldn't kill himself; it was against his religion."

"What religion?"

"Survival."

"Right. Only we have no clue why somebody would want him dead."

I watched him closely to get his reaction. His expression went blank.

"Obviously, he got too big for his britches and crossed the wrong person," he said.

Carmine paused the destruction of his dessert to interject.

"But Plotzky was popular. I used to love his song-and-dance act when I was little."

"You're little now," the bunny quipped.

Touché.

He leaned towards me, as if to confide something secret.

"I'm sure you're aware that kids didn't love Plotzky just for his charisma."

"What do you mean?"

"Are you that naive? He controlled the snowball trade, top to bottom."

This was a new one to me.

"Wait a minute, EB. 'Snowball trade'? 'Top to bottom'? It sounds like you're suggesting that not only are all those rag-tag snowmen peddling snowballs on the streets *organized*, but that Plotzky was their ringleader."

"Bingo."

"You're joking, right?"

"No joke, gumshoe. I should know: Plotzky and I came close to a turf war once."

It's not every day that someone manages to shock me (except for that time I was in the loony bin for PTSD after the war and that was part of the therapy).

"A turf war between a snowman and a rabbit?" I asked. "What could you two possibly fight a turf war over?"

"Kids don't have much disposable income," he explained, "so to keep from competing for their nickels and dimes, Plotzky and I had an unspoken agreement to keep things seasonal: he dominated in winter, and in the spring I'd kick off with my Easter promotion, then sell product until Halloween."

"Sounds fair enough," said Carmine, still thumbing the thesaurus. "I don't see what could possibly deteriorate an equitable arrangement like that."

"So you should shut up and let me finish," the bunny snapped. "It was working fine until a few years ago. Spring arrived, but for some reason, Plotzky decided he was going to push snowballs all year round. At first it was mostly a cold war, then tensions escalated. His snow-goons had to head north because of the warmer weather, so he hired former strikebreakers and other toughs for more muscle. They just about shut me down completely."

"So what did you do?" I asked.

"I could take a hint. I gave up selling to children."

"How have you been getting by?"

His harelip curled up into a sly grin.

"Turns out there's more profit to be had selling high-end product to the parents."

"You moved up-market?"

"Best thing I ever did. All along, I assumed adults only had a casual interest in chocolate, but if anything, they love it even more than the kids. It was the bunny- and egg-shapes that turned them off."

"So Plotzky did you a favor, I guess."

"In more ways than one. Most of the demand is from women, and that's a market I live to serve."

"I'll bet."

"But you still give chocolate away to kids at Easter," Carmine pointed out.

"Traditions die hard among us rabbits. But I finally realized that concentrating all my promotional efforts on just one day of the year was a ridiculous marketing strategy. Now I've got product lines for Christmas, Labor Day, President's Day, you name it. Not to mention Valentine's Day, when sales are even better than Easter."

"I could never keep track of Easter, anyways," said Carmine. "It keeps jumping around the calendar each year."

The Easter Bunny turned to me.

"You must be the brains of the partnership."

I wasn't going to let him butter me up (the butter dish on the table had done that to my sleeve already).

"That's right, EB," I answered. "And I've figured out a connection between chocolate and snow."

The rabbit knitted his brow.

"I don't quite follow you."

"They can both be melted by heat packs."

"Heat packs?"

I decided it was time to play my hand on the heavy side, so I drew my pistol on him. Not very subtle, maybe, but it got results.

He stuck his paws in the air, but didn't seem as surprised as I would have expected.

"We got a tip that you bought several dozen heat packs recently," I said. "Were they just to keep your lucky rabbit's foot warm?"

"What does that have to do with Plotzky?"

"It's a little too convenient, don't you think? You stock up on heat packs, Plotzky gets melted soon afterwards, and heat pack chemicals are found in his puddle. Oh, did I forget to mention that part? The prosecution loves an open-and-shut case."

"That's twenty years' hard time!" threatened Carmine, who suddenly slipped back into his "bad cop" persona. "Although they might knock it down to two for good behavior...but still!"

The Easter Bunny stifled a snicker as his countenance went calm again.

"You really need to work on that "bad cop" act, shorty," he said. "I bought the heat packs because I'm shipping out an order of fancy chocolate truffles for a New Year's Eve party."

"Why the fickle fire-truck would you need heat packs for that?" Carmine asked.

The bunny played it as blasé as could be.

"The forecast for New Year's Eve is freezing. Each truffle will be shipped with its own lace-embroidered heat pack, so that it remains at the optimum level of mouth-watering melty-ness."

Carmine drooled onto the floor a tiny bit.

"That sounds amazing."

"It's a very decadent party."

It sounded plausible, but now that everything was laid out on the table, I didn't want to cave in that easily. I kept the gun steady.

"So you haven't used those heat packs yet, EB? You can prove it?"

"They're still at my warehouse on the waterfront, all boxed up and..."

He stopped talking all of a sudden as his whiskers started to twitch. One of his ears swiveled around.

"Hang on a second..."

A giant snowball crashed through the kitchen window and landed on the table, scattering the slices of zucchini bread.

"Snowmen!" he shouted.

Keeping my gun trained on him, I jumped from my chair, rushed over to the window, and looked down at the street, where sure enough, about a dozen angry-looking snowmen had gathered. They were rolling up big snowballs and obviously weren't too shy to use them.

"Come on out, rabbit!" one of them hollered. "We got somethin' to ask ya!"

It was a funny thing about the snowmen: they all seemed to be male, with gruff, raspy voices. This one sounded like he'd been huffing gasoline fumes and gargling gravel.

As one of them wound up to lob another snowball, I yanked my head back like a turtle. I was just in time; the missile went "splat" against the wall beside me. I backed away from the kitchen window.

Carmine had ducked under the table, where he was stuffing his pockets with slices of zucchini bread.

The Easter Bunny was standing by his refrigerator, hiding behind the open door for protection. I crouched down next to him.

"They think I did it!" he said.

"Did you?"

"Of course not. I was in bed the whole time!"

"Any witnesses who can back you up on that?"

"Normally, there would have been at least two. But I was actually sleeping for once."

A half-dozen more snowballs flew in through the window and struck the opposite wall, punching holes in the plaster. It was obvious that each one had been loaded with a rock, the snowmen's calling card.

"I doubt they're going to believe you," I said.

"Listen, we can sneak out and hide at my warehouse," he replied. "I can show you the heat packs, then you can vouch for me! Deal?"

"No funny stuff?"

"Cross my heart and hope to end up in a stew!"

Another volley sailed through the window, making a mess I was glad I didn't have to clean up (I was a guest, after all).

To buy us some time, I ran to the window, stuck my gun out, and fired a couple of rounds in the snowmen's direction, then ducked back down next to the rabbit.

"Okay, EB, you're on. But how do we slip out of here?"

More snowballs came in through the window. There was a big one that had a lit fuse sticking out of it, which was hissing and sparking away.

"Oh, balls!" the Easter Bunny exclaimed. "This way!"

He led us down the hall to his bedroom. I didn't get much of a chance to look, but what I could see out of the corners of my eyes told me the Easter Bunny was fond of some rather unusual practices, and let's just leave it at that...lest this story get confiscated by the Postmaster General. He ran straight for a closet door and whipped it open. Inside, he pulled back a piece of loose carpet, revealing a trapdoor in the floor. He lifted it open.

"Come on, jump in!" he shouted. Then he leapt down the hole.

Carmine and I looked at each other, silently debating whether we should follow him or not.

"Women and children first, kiddo," I said.

"Oh no, I don't wanna go first!"

"You're smaller. Less likely to get stuck."

"But I've always had a phobia of falling down narrow holes."

"You've also told me you have phobias about sea urchins, strange shadows in your bedroom at night, squirrels with patchy fur that makes them look like they're going bald, and catching early-onset rigor mortis."

"What can I say? I'm complicated."

"Take it up with your shrink. Now jump in!"

There was a loud KABOOM from the kitchen as the snowbomb went blooey. Out in the hallway, bits of shrapnel and debris flew past the bedroom door, followed by flames and smoke.

Even if we might be headed into the fire, there was no point staying in the frying pan. I gave Carmine a shove down the trapdoor, holstered my gun, and jumped in after him.

It turned out to be a lot like a laundry chute, but lacked the funky smell of gym socks and mossy towels. We slid down like greased lightning in the dark, and the friction quickly started heating up my hindquarters. Maybe the Easter Bunny had enough fur on his tail to protect him, but my partner and I were in serious danger of losing a few layers of skin.

The steep slope of the chute started to curve and level off, and I saw a light ahead of us. We were thrown out into some kind of underground storage area, our momentum flinging us across the room. We landed in a pile of multicolored pastel cushions that looked like giant painted Easter eggs.

"Oof!" said Carmine.

"Ugh!" said I.

The Easter Bunny stood there, waiting for us impatiently.

"Come on! Come on! We can get out through the back door. You've got a car, right?"

"Sure. We just dress like people who take the bus."

"This way then, Beau Brummel."

We hurried after him through a series of concrete hallways that made the place look like a dictator's last-stand bunker. The Easter Bunny ran so fast, we had to hustle our hearts out just to keep him in sight.

Carmine panted as he ran alongside me.

"Man, he's quick."

"When a rabbit's afraid, kid, he bolts. He doesn't have any other instincts."

"Can we trust him?"

"I might sound soft as a mink brassière, little buddy, but I think he's playing straight with us. He could have snuck off and left us to tangle with the snowmen alone."

"I guess I goofed as bad cop, huh?"

"You fumbled it, alright. I'd better get my mind off Betty Sketchley, but soon."

"You know, Cisco," he wheezed, "sometimes you can only get your mind off a woman after you've gotten your hands *on* her. Know what I mean? Huh?"

He gave me a nudge.

"Like you'd know. You haven't touched a woman since you last shook hands with your mother."

"Can't we leave my mother out of this?"

"Just work on your bad cop routine."

I nudged him back. He bounced off the wall.

Then he stopped running and knelt on the floor, clutching his chest. I stopped, turned and walked back to him.

"Come on, kid. We need to hurry."

"I can't run any more," he gasped. "I think I'm going to have a thrombosis."

"A what?"

I saw a book in his hand.

"Hey, did you steal the Easter Bunny's thesaurus?"

I snatched the Roget's from his mitt and stuck it in my pocket, then picked him up and put him on my shoulders.

From up ahead, the Easter Bunny called back.

"Are you fellows coming, or what?"

"On our way, EB!" I answered, and ran along, carrying my sidekick.

When I finally caught up with him, the Easter Bunny was standing in front of a door marked "EXIT," peeping through a peephole. His tail flicked from side to side under his robe.

"Looks like the coast is clear," he said. "Now where's your car?"

"Let me have a look and get my bearings," I said as I put Carmine down. "You're sure this is the back of the building?"

He looked at me.

"Of course."

His tone made it clear he wasn't sure if I was skeptical or stupid.

Through the peephole, I could see a couple of dumpsters and old mattresses, as well as a few parked cars.

"I'm pretty sure my car's to the right. We'll just have to make a break for it. Follow me."

I cracked open the door and looked around to make sure the coast was clear. My car was parked about thirty yards away.

We ran towards it. I threw my keys back at Carmine, who managed to catch them.

"You drive!" I said.

He unlocked the doors and we all got in: Carmine in the driver's seat, the Easter Bunny in the passenger's, and me in the back. Normally I did all the driving, but I wanted to keep my eyes on the rodent.

Carmine started the engine while the Easter Bunny scoped out my corroded carriage.

"I'm surprised you don't have to get out and crank to start this thing."

"Don't you have a car?" I asked.

"It's an antique British roadster! I can't drive it in winter."

"Figures."

As Carmine pulled out of the parking spot, a gang of snowmen appeared around the corner of the building and spotted us.

"There they is!" one of them hollered.

I shouted at Carmine.

"Gun it, kid!"

He put his foot down as hard as he could, but couldn't quite reach all the way.

"EB, lend him your lucky rabbit's foot!"

"I'm on it," the rabbit replied as he stretched his left foot over and stomped on Carmine's right instep, squashing it down on the gas pedal.

The engine went "Grrr."

Carmine went "Owch! That smarts!"

A volley of snowballs went "Bud, ba-dump, CRACK, bumper-tea-bump" against the back of the car, doing further damage to the rear windshield.

"Faster!" I yelled as I ducked down low in the back seat, unsure of how much more pummeling the glass could take.

Once the old jalopy put a bit of distance between us and the hail-hurlers, I popped my head up like a periscope to check on the enemy's position. The snowmen tried to give chase, but they couldn't get much speed, seeing as how they didn't have any legs.

Perhaps it was the stress of the situation, but I had a mini-flashback, brought on by my experiences in the war (or maybe it was from the LSD experiments). In my vision, the snowmen transformed into pale white matryoshkas, those Russian wooden dolls that all fit inside each other like, well, like Russian wooden dolls. Was I coming down with the flu?

I heard Carmine's voice somewhere in the distance.

"Boss! Boss? Are you having a flashback again? 'Cause I could really use you up here!"

I snapped out of it and saw Carmine and the Easter Bunny wrestling over the steering wheel.

"Leggo!" yelled Carmine. "I had it first!"

"You drive like an old lady with gas cramps!" the Easter Bunny retorted. "Let me take over."

I took out my gun. Bullets were expensive, so I pointed it in the air and yelled "BANG!"

That got their attention. The struggle ceased as I stuck the gun barrel against the Easter Bunny's temple, just under the right ear.

"Let him have the wheel, EB; otherwise, he's never going to get past the learner's permit."

Carmine snorted in triumph as the rabbit released the steering wheel and settled back down in the passenger's seat.

"Is that thing really necessary?" he asked with a pout.

I put the heater away, feeling like a bit of a heel for threatening the guy who'd fed me in his own home just ten minutes earlier.

The Easter Bunny turned and smirked.

"I've had guns pointed at me before, you know."

"Sorry, EB. The pistola routine is just business. Nothing personal."

"That's okay. I'm sure it makes up for deficiencies elsewhere."

"Why do people always say that?"

Carmine and the Easter Bunny started howling with laughter.

"Alright, you two: knock it off."

Annoyed, I poked the Easter Bunny on his silk-robed shoulder.

"Just tell us how to get to your warehouse, you. And remember who helped pull your chestnuts out of the fire back there."

You'd think he'd have stopped laughing, if only just to be polite.

Chapter 11: The Warehouse

Thanks to the Easter Bunny's suggestion of a couple shortcuts, we made it to the waterfront faster than you could say "rotten egg."

Our footsteps echoed off the polished hardwood floors of his warehouse. Still in his bunny slippers, the rabbit's steps were completely silent, although he moved so fast, it was like his feet were greased.

The place was an enormous maze of wooden crates, all labeled with his trademark bunny logo.

"The heat packs are right over here," he said. "In the far corner."

I have to admit, by that point I was out of breath from chasing after this rambunctious rodent. I was also surprised at the scale of his operation, and the fact that the warehouse was completely deserted.

"Some digs you got here, EB," I wheezed. "You don't hire no one to watch the place for you?"

"No need, Mister Maloney."

Carmine huffed and puffed as he lagged behind us.

"You ain't even got a guard dog?" he asked.

"A dog? I'm a rabbit, you dope! A dog would sooner bite *my* leg than any burglar's."

Carmine tried to change the subject. He read some of the labels on the crates.

"Jumpin' Jersey Milk! Have you seen these, boss? There's Swiss brown, Belgian white, even the raw beans, right from the pod! I've never seen so much chocolate in my whole life."

"Take it easy," I said.

He started drooling like a puppy with a gland condition.

"But look at it all! It's like I died and went to heaven...without having to die first."

"Sheesh, you fall to bits faster than a house of cards in a hailstorm."

The bunny's voice echoed from somewhere ahead of us.

"Help yourself to a sample, Mister Appelbaum. It's the least I can do for helping me escape the snowmob."

"Don't do it, Carmine."

"But Cisco!"

"I said knock it off!"

I gave him a smack in the face. I didn't like having to whack some sense into him, but I wasn't going to miss the opportunity, either.

Carmine rubbed his cheek and shook his head.

"Thanks, boss. That's actually a nice change from the kicking."

We finally caught up with the Easter Bunny, who was standing next to a stack of smaller crates and holding a crowbar.

"You keep him on a short leash," he said to me.

"I don't tolerate weakness, EB; that goes for highballs and sidekicks."

He nodded his agreement, bent over one of the crates, and pried it open.

"Here they are. You can see for yourselves."

He stood up and leaned back against a post, then took a cigarette from a monogrammed, gold-plated case, put it in an abalone cigarette holder, and lit it.

I peered into the crate. Sure enough, it was full of heat packs. They were still sealed, each one individually wrapped.

"How many are in there?"

"Five dozen, all accounted for."

I counted the top layer and calculated the total using some of the more advanced math I'd retained from elementary school.

"Looks about right, from what I can see."

The Easter Bunny started blowing giant, egg-shaped smoke rings. The rings suspended in the air in front of him as he drew Easter egg patterns in the smoke with strokes of his furry finger.

"How long did you say you've had these?" I asked.

"A couple of days."

"Have you got a receipt?"

"It went to my accountant. I'm not running some little Peter-Cottontail cottage industry, you know."

"I'm sure the story checks out," I said. "Say, EB, can you spare a cancer stick?"

"Go right ahead."

He handed me the open cigarette case. I reached in and took one, taking note of the trembling of his hands.

Carmine butted in.

"But Cisco, you don't...ow! Not again!"

That's right: I kicked him. Carmine didn't realize I was using an old cop trick to find out if a suspect was nervous.

"Your hands are shaking, EB. What are you so fidgety for?"

He finished his smoke and stubbed it out on the post he'd been leaning on.

"I don't like violence. Especially when it's directed at me."

"So what's up, doc? If you're innocent, those snowmen will back off once they figure it out."

"It's not the snowmen I'm worried about. Whoever took out Plotzky obviously means business. He isn't going to rest on his laurels."

"You think you're next?"

"It's a possibility."

"Don't flatter yourself, EB. All this square-footage might impress a simpleton like Carmine here, but aren't you just a successful chocolatier? Not exactly public enemy number one."

He lit another tumor-tube while Carmine snooped around some of the other crates.

"I control every ounce of chocolate coming into Wurstburg, Mister Maloney. As you can see, it's no small potatoes. If the killer's ambition is to take over the snowball trade, he's surely noticed how much profit there is in my line of business. The next logical step would be to come after me."

It sounded to me like the Easter Bunny was suffering from paranoia of the ego.

"I guess humility is the one thing you don't indulge in," I said. "So what are you going to do, leave town?"

"Better to be a rabbit on the lam than a dead duck."

"What did I tell you, Carmine? When a rabbit's afraid, he bolts."

I looked around. No sign of my sidekick.

"Carmine?"

There was a loud bang.

"Get down!" I shouted as I hit the deck.

The Easter Bunny stared at me like I'd just checked into Hotel Cuckoo Clock.

"Why are you lying on the floor?"

I suppose the answer had something to do with that POW camp.

Carmine popped his head out from behind some crates. His face was covered in chocolate, his mouth was full, and he was chewing on something; my guess was that it wasn't Brussels sprouts.

"My bad!" he said. "I stebbed on a barty balloon."

I shouldn't have felt ashamed if I suffered the occasional bout of shell-shock, but it wounded my pride to have to get up off the Easter Bunny's floor and dust myself off just because of a popped balloon.

"You can't be too cautious," I mumbled by way of explanation.

The rabbit chuckled and blew another egg-shaped smoke ring.

"We're perfectly safe here, Mister Maloney. Now, I expect you gents are satisfied that I'm innocent?"

"We're cool, EB. Sorry for the intrusion, but frankly, we had no other suspects."

"Better to be eliminated as a suspect than eliminated, full-stop. Now if you boys don't mind, I've got travel arrangements to make."

He turned and waved for us to follow him.

"Where are you off to?" I asked.

"I was thinking I'd take a trip to the English countryside. Maybe do a little fox hunting."

"That's a cruel sport," Carmine said as he licked his fingers.

"You ever see what a fox does to a rabbit?" the Easter Bunny hit back. "I wouldn't mind scoring a few points for my side."

We followed him back towards the warehouse exit. Carmine's face was a mess of mocha.

"Wipe your mug, for the love of Peter, Paul and Mounds."

"Sorry, boss, I couldn't help myself."

"Looks like you helped yourself plenty."

"It was worth it!"

I sighed, more concerned about the dead end in the case than my sidekick looking like the world's shortest blackface minstrel.

"This does us no good, kid," I sighed. "We got no leads."

The Easter Bunny overheard me.

"You could try talking to Saint Nick," he said. "He's usually quite well informed."

"On Christmas Eve? I thought he'd be giving out his presents to the kids tonight."

"Ha, 'presents'...more like payoff."

"I don't follow."

"You've got a lot to learn, Helen Keller. Try looking for him at Cupid's. It's in the alley behind the House of Hearts gift shop on Fourteenth Street. Red door. Ask them to validate your parking."

"Isn't Cupid that Valentine's Day baby with the matchmaking service?" asked Carmine.

"He's not much of a baby anymore. And it's the kind of 'matchmaking' where you pay by the half hour."

"What would Santa be doing at a place like that?"

"The old perv's got a thing for Eskimo massage attendants."

"Shouldn't you say Inuit massage attendants?"

"Seriously? Shut up."

I clapped a hand over Carmine's blab-trap before he dug himself in deeper.

"Thanks for the tip, EB," I said. "We'll check it out. By the way, what did you mean about 'payoff' when you mentioned..."

I was cut off by a "shwoop" sound.

The Easter Bunny gave us a funny look.

"Guh!" he grunted, then collapsed on the floor.

We knelt down beside him.

"EB! Are you all right? What happened?"

"I...I think I've been shot," he wheezed.

"Are you sure?"

"I don't know...it's my first time. What's it supposed to feel like?"

I looked around, trying to figure out where the shot might have come from. Then I heard a crate fall over, followed by rapid footsteps.

"Stay with him," I said to Carmine as I ran for the exit.

I was just in time to see the warehouse door slam shut. I opened it and stepped out into the inky night.

I heard the footsteps running away. They sounded like they were heading down an alley to my left, so I sprinted in that direction. Sure enough, I came to a dead end: there was nothing but a solid brick wall blocking my way. (I almost "hit the wall" myself; usually the only part of me that did any running this time of year was my nose.)

In the middle of the empty alleyway, I spotted something shiny lying on the ground. It was a leather strap, about eight inches long, with a set of jingle bells stitched into it. I picked it up.

When I got back to the warehouse, I found Carmine crouched beside the Easter Bunny, who was lying unconscious on his back. He was holding the bunny's wrist.

"His pulse is fading," he said. "Should I try mouth to-mouth?"

"I don't know, but clean your face first, for crying out loud."

Carmine wiped the chocolate off his face with a handkerchief.

"Did you see who did it?" he asked. "Was it a snowman?"

"He got away. But whoever it was dropped this."

I crouched down next to the Easter Bunny and gave the strap a shake next to his ear.

"EB, can you hear me? Does that sound ring a bell?"

He didn't appear to be breathing.

"We should call a real doctor," I said to Carmine. "This is beyond your Boy Scout training."

"But I earned the Band-Aid badge!"

Carmine checked the Easter Bunny's pulse again. He tapped the furry wrist a couple times, and then put his ear to it.

"Sweet hereafter, I think he's dead! But what coulda killed him?"

"I'm not the one with the Band-Aid badge," I said as I grabbed the Easter Bunny by the shoulder and rolled him over, "but I think it could have been this."

There was a feathered crossbow bolt sticking out of his back.

Carmine turned paler than the ash on a Transylvanian cigar at the sight of the pool of jugular-juice spreading out on the floor under the stricken rodent.

"Ick, blood! Uh, I gotta go!"

He ran off and retched behind a stack of crates.

"Don't be so squeamish, kid! Blood is nothing but rusty water."

It didn't take a Florence Nightingale to see that the Easter Bunny had kicked the proverbial bucket. I took out my handkerchief, put it around the bolt, and slowly pulled it out from between the rabbit's ribs. It was a sleek, mean-looking missile with a needle-sharp point and red and black fletching. Whoever had fired it was no dilettante in the archery department.

Carmine reappeared, wiping his mouth with the cleaner side of his hanky.

"Phew, so much for all the chocolate I ate," he said. "On the other hand, that was the most delicious vomit I've ever tasted."

I tried to suppress a wave of nausea as I wrapped the bolt in my handkerchief and tucked it in my pocket.

"First Plotzky, and now the Easter Bunny...and it isn't even rabbit season."

We heard a musical stinger, and looked over to see the shabby brass band huddled together near the warehouse entrance.

"How did they get in here?" Carmine asked.

"Damn it, I must have left the door open."

The band played an upbeat version of Chopin's "Funeral March." For some reason, that seemed even more depressing than usual.

Chapter 12: The Cabaret

With the body count now doubled, I knew we were getting hot: two famous figures crossed off the list of the living, and it wasn't even time to open the presents yet.

Pulling the crossbow bolt out of the Easter Bunny's back probably hadn't been my smartest move, but I desperately needed any evidence I could get, and the bolt and jingle bell strap were my only clues. The fulfillment of the rabbit's paranoid prophecy that he might be the next target—right in front of my eyes, no less—convinced me that whoever had killed Plotzky was also responsible for the leporicide, and was diversifying his murder portfolio (I would have bet dollars to donuts on it, but my bookie was diabetic). My gut feeling told me that if I found the mystery marksman, I'd also find a snowman killer...it also told me that the ham in my sandwiches was a few weeks past the due date.

I confess to an additional motivation: taking the bolt would leave a piece of the puzzle missing when the police finally discovered the bunny's skewered body, throwing a monkey wrench in their investigation. Although I had no hard feelings towards my former buddies in blue, it would be a disaster for me if they cracked the case first, which would screw me royally out of what was starting to become a very hard-earned reward, indeed.

With nothing left to do but follow the rabbit's advice, we hot-footed it to Cupid's, desperately seeking

Santa Claus. On our way there in the car, Carmine treated me to his opinion about my unethical pilfering.

"I think we should bring that bolt to the police."

"Use your knuckle, noodle head," I replied. "This could be the only ace up our sleeve."

"But isn't it against the law to tamper with a crime scene?"

"Listen, kid, the cops still get paid at the end of the month whether they solve a crime or not. But if we don't get that reward money, our office will be a refrigerator box on the Lower-Lower-Lower East Side. We're keeping the bolt."

It always annoyed me when Carmine played understudy to my conscience.

Cupid's Cabaret was located in Bricktown: the old industrial part of Wurstburg dating back to the Steam Age. Until recently, it was a place where the *derrière-garde* bohemians would rent out warehouse space to work on their "action paintings" and throw wild parties, slumming it among the hustlers, drug dealers, and speakeasies. But Bricktown had gotten gentrified like everywhere else, and the artists, dope dealers and addicts had moved to cheaper pastures.

Bricktown had become a trendy haunt for the pony set, with its quiet wine bars and jazz piano nights, and pretentious restaurants with no menus and no service. Everything in the neighborhood had been scrubbed clean except the alleyways, which were still covered in high-quality graffiti left by the old residents. Apparently the neighborhood business association felt it gave the place the kind of gritty charm that attracted phonies with money to burn.

There was no place to park except a fancy indoor garage that treated customers to a first-class fleecing. We soon found ourselves in a dark alley behind some warehouses that were probably gin mills back in the

Prohibition days. Sure enough, we came across a weathered but solid-looking red door that matched the bunny's description. Its only feature was a sliding peephole panel at eye level.

There was burlesque music coming from inside.

"This is it," I said as I rapped on the door with my favorite knocking knuckles.

"How do you know?" asked Carmine. "There's no sign."

"That's the idea, nitwit. This is the kind of business that doesn't like to advertise."

Carmine stepped up closer to look at the door and stumbled over a bag of road salt—the enemy of leather wingtips everywhere.

"Didn't the Easter Bunny say it was a red door? This looks more like a burgundy."

"Shut up or I'll strangle you with your own uvula."

I knocked again, a bit more insistent this time.

"I just don't think it's a good idea to go in there, boss."

"Aw, sprout a combo, will ya? It's like you've got Obsessive Cowardice Disorder."

I knocked a third time. The sliding panel on the door opened and the burlesque music got a little louder. A massive, unfriendly face appeared, filling up the rectangular opening.

"What's the password?" asked the face in a guttural, simian voice.

"Password?" parroted Carmine.

"Aw, dang it," I muttered. "What did the rabbit say? Something about barking?"

Carmine scratched himself.

"My dog has fleas?"

"Nice try," said the face.

The peephole slid shut. Carmine shrugged.

"Oh well, looks like we'll never know what's in there," he said as he tried to scurry away. I grabbed his coattail and yanked him back.

"A Maloney doesn't give up so easily."

"Well, an Appelbaum sure does. I'm lucky I was even conceived."

"Just plant your paws and stick around."

I knocked again. The peephole slid back open.

"Password?" asked the face.

"Now just give me a minute to think," I said. "It's been a while."

I realized I was buying time on thin credit.

Putting my hands in my pockets, I felt the slip from the parking garage.

"Hey, do you think you guys could at least validate my parking?"

The peephole slid shut again, but then the door opened. In front of us was a giant hulk of a man, dressed completely in black, with the widest face I'd ever seen.

"Come in," he said.

I waved the parking slip in front of his enormous visage.

"Actually, I meant it. Those garage rates are extortionate."

"Only for paying customers," he grunted as he ushered us in and shut the door.

We found ourselves on a small landing at the top of a flight of stairs. The doorman led us down the steps and pulled back a red velvet curtain blocking a doorway. The bump-and-grind music got louder, now mixed in with the sounds of a big crowd.

"Remember the rules," he said. "Be neat, be discreet, and don't ask for receipts."

He gave us a shove through the curtain.

We stumbled into the plush main hall of Cupid's establishment. The décor was uncompromising in its hues: red walls, scarlet leather sofas with pink and white heart-shaped cushions, rosewood booths with crimson velvet curtains separating them, and tables stained in dark cherry.

There was a bar off to one side, all glass shelves stocked with top-dollar liqueurs and a giant mirror behind it. Tending it was a staff of ladies so sophisticated they only needed to wear the cuffs and collars of their blouses, eschewing the rest.

Waitresses in skimpy white angel costumes stood out in contrast to the dark color scheme as they flitted back and forth from the bar to the tables, hustling drinks to the patrons.

Clearly, this was a moneyed crowd, compared to what you'd normally find in establishments of low virtue. There were three-piece banker's suits everywhere, expensive gold watch fobs dangling from vest pockets that bulged over well-fed bellies, and fat fingers wrapped around lowball glasses of aged Scotch whiskey that predated Hadrian's wall. Every other mouth had a cigar stuck in it, and the heavy aroma of Havana's finest hung in the air like Batista after the commies strung him up (or maybe I'm thinking of Mussolini?).

"Wow," Carmine gushed. "Just look at this place."

"First time in a bordello, kid?"

"First time in a heart-shaped room, boss. What would Santa be doing in a joint like this?"

"Probably research. He has to find out who's been naughty, right?"

"But it's Christmas Eve. Shouldn't he be getting ready to deliver all those presents?"

"Beats me, bucko. Let's just hope he's around."

I felt a bit self-conscious in that place, but no one even noticed us; the crowd had its prurient interest keenly focused on what was going on in the center of the room.

There was a small circular stage. Beside it, in a sunken orchestra pit, was a familiar sight: the shabby brass band from earlier, playing the burlesque bump we'd been hearing ever since we'd arrived in the alley. Jumpin' jiminy, these guys must have been the hardest working brass band in "blow" business. I was starting to wonder how they always seemed to be either following me around, or one step ahead of me.

But the crowd wasn't there for the band. On the stage was a well-developed dancer in mid-peel, about to reveal the particulars of her chesticulars, much to the delectation of the hormonal audience. The hoary old hound-dogs clapped, cheered and catcalled with remarkable class at the sight of her pastied puppies, and roared with approval when she did the stock whirligig routine. I never found that move to be all that attractive, myself; *if anything, it reminded me of the twin props of a double-engined Douglass-Winthrop C-29 "Spaniel" taxiing on the runway for a takeoff, bringing home all the troops too badly wounded to keep fighting in the war, and leaving me behind...*(Whoops, almost had another war flashback there.)

Carmine and I didn't want to just stand there like a pair of cigar-store Indians, so we headed towards a group of sofas in a lounge area that had been set aside from the main hall. In amongst the settees and recliners were low coffee tables with stacks of men's magazines on them. You know the kind: pinup cutie on the cover, and articles inside on a wide range of subjects such as reproductive biology, conjugal visitations, close encounters of the third-base kind, philandering, makin' whoopee, and good old-fashioned you-know-what. A handful of customers sat and skimmed through the magazines, presumably waiting their turn for service. I didn't see the point of leaving these kinds of mags around, seeing as how the place already had more 'horn' than a Witwatersrand watering hole.

I figured we'd sit down for a spell and case the joint, searching for any signs of Santa.

Between the waiting area and the bar was a chest-high reception desk, heart-shaped like the room, and built to completely enclose its occupant. Standing inside the desk, wearing a silver lamé tuxedo, white shirt, and red bow tie, was a gentleman with silver hair combed up in a preposterous pompa-do. I'd never seen him in person before, but my powers of deduction told me he had to be the proprietor, none other than Cupid himself. Despite the grey mane, he looked like he was only middle-aged, though he certainly wasn't so cherubic anymore.

I turned to Carmine.

"Follow me and remember to stay quiet, kid. You're way out of your element here."

We got up and headed straight for the silver tuxedo. The crowd went wild—not for me, obviously, but for the dancing miss who was busy reenacting the helicopter chase scene from the Garden of Eden story for their entertainment.

As we approached Cupid, the phone at his reception desk rang. It was one of those ridiculous "princess" phones that looked more like a tabletop chandelier. He answered it.

"Hello, Cupid's!"

I thought I detected a slight lisp. Despite my order to zip it, Carmine started to babble.

"Is that who I think it is?"

"Just keep your mouth shut and your eyes and ears open."

We approached the desk, which stood in front of an ornately carved red door that must have led to the areas where customers could grope other kinds of areas.

Cupid was arguing on the phone with whoever was at the other end; it sounded like a dissatisfied customer.

"Look, there's no need to get sore," he said. "I mean, if you got a sore, you should call a doctor. What makes you so sure you got it from here?"

There was a brief pause.

"Maybe you got it from your wife. Or maybe your mistress. Or your girlfriend. Or the maid. Or the toilet. I'm not suggesting you've been getting chummy with the plumbing, I just meant that... Fine then, go ahead and sue me if you want: every judge in town drinks here for free. Good day, sir."

He hung up the phone on the rococo receiver and noticed us for the first time.

"Welcome to Cupid's," he said as he gave us a good scrutinizing. "You aren't private members, are you?"

"Nope," I replied. "Just a couple of private dicks."

"This isn't a pun parlor, pal. You here for a bit of relaxation, or what?"

"That sounds innocent enough," said Carmine.

"So do you, homunculus," said Cupid. "First time here?"

We nodded.

"In that case, I suggest starting you off with something light: Swedish massage? Turkish bath? Oriental rubdown?"

"Shouldn't you call it an 'Asian' rubdown?" asked Carmine.

(Ugh, him and his sensitivities. I'm only sensitive to the wormwood in absinthe, which makes me break out in hives, hallucinations, and early-onset dementia.)

"It's best to be specific," bristled Cupid as he took out a world map and smacked it with a pointer stick.

"Asia goes from way west in Turkey to far east in Japan; from down in Ceylon all the way up to Siberia. And frankly," he added as he poked Carmine in the chest with the pointer, "you don't look like you'd survive a Siberian rubdown. Of course, we can always arrange it if you sign the appropriate waivers."

"No thanks," said Carmine, backing off a bit. "I get your drift."

Cupid rolled up the map and put it away, chuckling. I tried making small talk.

"So you're Cupid, huh?" I asked. "I thought you'd be younger."

"Boy, you sure know how to flatter a guy."

"Sorry, it's just that..."

"I'm only yanking your chain, Bowser," he said with a wink. "Most people know me from my baby pictures. What, can't a baby grow up without causing a scandal?"

He took out a pocket mirror and dabbed his chin with a powder puff.

"Nothing implied," I said. "So how's business going?"

"Not bad for the off season."

"Off-season? The place looks jam-packed."

"Not really. I prefer when we have at least double the fire-code capacity. But for most gents, this is the one night of the year they have to spend with their families, so it's a bit slow. Now would you like to choose from our expens—I mean, extensive catalogue? Something for every taste and persuasion..."

He picked up a glossy color catalogue from the desk and handed it to me. It was covered in red hearts and genuine silver leaf, a good indication that Cupid's business was doing very well indeed. I admired the four-color separation and 200-lb. card stock, but didn't take it from him.

"To be honest, Mister Cupid, we're after information, not gratification. We're hoping to find someone here."

He gave me a pinched look.

"Sorry, I can't confirm or deny the presence of anyone in my establishment. We have rather strict rules protecting the privacy of our clients."

He leaned in close and lowered his voice.

"Most of them are paying for the alibi, not the lay-by. Get my drift?"

He winked unnecessarily.

"We catch the current," I said.

It was then that I realized I was receiving an urgent call from Nature on the red phone.

"Say, Mister Cupid, mind if I use the restroom?"

"Sorry, restrooms are for patrons only."

"How about validating my parking, then?"

"Pa-trons on-ly!" he said in a singsong voice (high tenor).

"All right then, fine. I'll buy something. Gimme that catalogue."

"All yours."

He handed it over and turned his attention back to the club, probably making sure nobody was having a good time without being billed for it. I passed the catalogue to Carmine, who started to read, his eyes bulging at the pictures inside it, which made the Kama Sutra look like an in-flight emergency instruction card.

"How's the Singapore Sling?" he asked.

"Bouncy," offered Cupid.

"How 'bout the Bangkok Backrub?"

"Steamy."

"Orgasm On The Beach?"

"You're reading from the cocktail menu, sir."

"Right. It's hard to tell."

Carmine skimmed over a couple more pages.

"This is all kinda pricey, Cisco."

"No kidding," I said. "And since we're not working for a client, I can't charge it on expenses."

Carmine paused at one page.

"What's this 'St. Valentine's Day Massacre' all about?"

Cupid beamed with pride.

"That's the house specialty. In one package, you get the complete "made" service: we start with a full-body, deep-tissue beating with a bag of oranges; then bathe the feet in soothing, exfoliating cement; follow that up with a soaking from head to toe in mineralized seawater; and top it all off with the Kiss of Death."

"What's the 'Kiss of Death'?"

"You die at the end. I guess it's not really much of a metaphor."

Carmine nodded and kept reading.

"How about this one: 'North Pole Noserub'?"

Cupid suddenly got all cagey; he turned his head back to look at the door behind him.

"I'm afraid the attendant who provides that particular service is booked for the rest of the evening."

"Oh yeah?" I asked. "She wouldn't happen to be rubbing noses with Santa Claus, would she?"

That put some starch in his upper lip. His tone took a sour turn.

"As I said, I'm not at liberty to tell."

He snatched the catalogue out of Carmine's mitts.

"I'm a busy man, gentlemen, so if you're not buying anything and have forgotten the way to the exit, I can always have our security staff jog your memory."

"No need to pull a heavy," I said. "We'll find our way out."

It looked like I was going to have to find relief in the alley, but as we turned around to leave, the door behind

Cupid cracked open. A voice boomed out; it was a *basso profondo* as deep as the Grand Canyon.

"Hey Cupid, got any more tissues?"

Cupid's spine shot up straight.

"Yes, sir. Right away, sir."

He grabbed a silver tissue box from his desk and hurried to the door. Standing there was an older, portly gentleman, his bald head jammed between the door and the jamb. He was wearing rimless spectacles, sported a full white beard, and was naked save for a white towel around his waist and a pair of flip-flops with pom-poms on them shaped like two giant snowflakes. I thought I could see a few faded prison tattoos, but it was hard to tell in the dim light. They might have been liver spots.

Cupid handed him the box of tissues. He took one and honked into it with his rosy, bulbous schnozz.

For the first time that day, it seemed like Lady Luck was cutting me some slack: there was no shortage of lecherous old men in this town, but I knew we were standing within ten yards of the only one they called Saint Nick.

I leaned in close to Carmine.

"Well, well, well: if it isn't the oldest 'trick' in the book," I murmured. "Get it? 'Trick'?"

"North Pole Noserub!" Carmine exclaimed. "That's why he's always got the red nose. I just figured it was windburn from riding in an open sleigh."

Santa noticed us gawking at him.

"Stare much?" he growled. He turned to Cupid and jerked his thumb at us. "Who are these jokers?"

Cupid rushed back towards his desk.

"I'm so sorry, Mister Claus. I was just kicking them out."

It looked like this was going to be my only chance.

"Santa, I'm Cisco Maloney, private eye, and this is my associate, Carmine. We'd just like a minute of your time to ask you about..."

"They won't bother you much longer, Mister Claus," Cupid cut in.

He started ringing a bell on his desk. I slammed my hand down over it, muffling the bell, and finished my appeal to Santa.

"...to ask you about Plotzky the Snowman."

"Security!" Cupid shouted at the top of his lungs, trying to be heard over the sound of the brass band and the crowd going ga-ga over the lady on stage, whose tasseled pasties had come unglued.

The enormous doorman rushed in through the front curtain. He saw Cupid pointing at us and ran across the floor, dodging between the rowdy customers. With a mighty swing of his fist he decked Carmine, who tumbled head over heels and crashed onto a couch, sending several patrons scattering for cover.

I bravely leapt over Cupid's desk and ducked behind it. The doorman moved in menacingly as Cupid tried to shove me away.

"Get out of here, you smelly brute!" he said with all the petulance he could muster. "This is a scent-free workplace!"

(Guess I *had* put on too much cologne that morning.)

I dodged from side to side as the doorman took a couple of swings at me with his hulking fists. He narrowly missed Cupid's head.

"Whoa!" shouted Cupid. "You're supposed to get *him*, not me!"

As I danced around his lefts and rights, I made a mental note that my New Year's resolution would be to get more exercise, and maybe take some lessons in self-defense. I sure didn't want what poor Carmine got; he was still lying unconscious on the couch.

Then from behind me, Santa spoke up.

"Plotzky the Snowman, you say? Cupid, take five will you? Go string your bow or something."

"Yes, sir, Mister Claus."

Cupid snapped his fingers.

"Mungo! Back off, beefcakes. Let's go hit the steam."

He stepped out of the reception desk, took Mungo by the arm, and led him towards the red door. They strolled past Santa and disappeared into the mysterious back rooms of Cupid's Cabaret.

I'd never had to go so badly, but there was no way I was leaving now.

Chapter 13: The Fat Man

I helped Carmine get back on his feet.

"You alright, kid?"

Carmine rubbed his bruised cheekbone and waved away the tweeting birds and twinkling stars orbiting his head.

"I'm not really sure," he said, "but I think I'm actually starting to like it."

The poor guy was in shock, but don't worry, he had a lot of spring left and could easily bounce back.

Santa chuckled and waved us towards the red door. He adjusted his towel.

"You fellows better come on in here. I don't need this much exposure."

He held the door open as we hurried in.

Inside was a long hallway with dim red lights. In the darker space, I noticed Santa's eyes were glowing slightly.

Or was it the secondhand cigar smoke playing tricks on my mind? Either way, I couldn't give it much thought; it felt like my bladder was going to burst.

"Any chance I could use the little boys' room, Santa? My back teeth are going down for the third time."

"Go ahead. Second door to the right."

My feet chafed the broadloom as I ran over and flung open a door. Inside was nothing but mops and buckets.

"That's the cleaning closet," said Claus.

I opened the right door this time, and was so grateful to see the words "American Standard" stenciled on the white porcelain that I saluted. Not that I want to go into too much detail, but let's just say I managed to write not only my full name on the back of the urinal, but my address and social security number to boot.

I stepped out of the W.C. and back into the hallway.

"Thanks for hearing us out, Nick," I said. "You don't mind if I call you Nick, do you?"

"All my friends call me Nick."

"Great."

"But you're not my friends. You've got five minutes."

I spat out the Coles Notes version of our story.

"We're on the trail of Plotzky's killer, Mister Claus. We were hoping you could help us out. I don't suppose you could give us any leads?"

Santa walked over to a sofa in the hallway and sat down.

"If that were the case, I wouldn't have put up a thousand-dollar reward."

"That was you? How come?"

"Nobody in this town kills someone like Plotzky. Nobody."

"Oh. Were you...very close?"

"Nobody kills Plotzky unless they clear it with me first," he continued. "I'd be an idiot to just let it slide. Do I look like an idiot to you?"

His stare bored a hole right through us.

"No siree, sir."

"Damn straight. Who do you think keeps the streets clean around here? Can't have rogue elements going around whacking whoever they want."

"So you have no idea who could have done it?"

Santa shifted his substantial weight on the sofa. The springs groaned.

"Normally I'd put a few elves on the case, but this is peak season. I thought a reward would help speed things along."

"What have you got planned for the killer when you find him?"

The corner of his mouth curled up in a cruel smile.

"Dangle him from my sleigh and ask him a few questions."

I had a vision of Santa riding his sleigh, speeding along through the cold night air, a taut length of strong rope tied behind him. The other end of the rope was tied around the ankles of a man dressed in black, with a red gift bag over his head. The man dangled upside-down, swaying in the wind, his screams muffled by the bag.

Santa cracked his whip, urging his reindeer on.

"Ho, ho, ho! Now who's been a naughty boy?"

The vision disappeared and I snapped back to reality, shaking my noggin. It wasn't a flashback; was it a flash-forward?

Carmine was staring at me like a dog that had just been shown a math textbook. I looked Santa in the eye.

"We heard Plotzky was the ringleader of the snowball racket."

"That's old news, Johnny-Come-Lately. He was on my naughty list, but so long as he kept his snow out of my beard, I let him run his little song-and-dance."

"I always wanted to be on his show!" said Carmine.

I smacked him and turned back to Santa.

"Mister Claus, we don't know who did it yet, but we know Plotzky was killed by heat packs someone put in his mitts and boots. Now get this: we followed the trail to the Easter Bunny, but he checked out clean. Problem is, he also checked out for good when someone put a crossbow bolt between his ribs."

"The Hopper's dead? You saw it happen?"

I showed him the bloody bolt.

"In his warehouse, about a half-hour ago."

"Did you see who did it?"

"Nope. It was a clean job, real professional. That rabbit was afraid he might be next, and he was right. The last thing he said was to check with you for any tips. He told us where to find you."

"I see."

Claus took out a Meerschaum pipe from god-knows-where under his towel.

"Don't mind if I smoke."

"Go ahead."

Santa struck a match.

"I wasn't asking you; I was telling you. The pipe helps me think."

He held the match to the bowl and took several puffs, blowing thick smoke that definitely didn't smell like tobacco.

"Also gives me the munchies something fierce," he added.

Carmine whispered to me.

"Now we know what keeps him fat and jolly."

"Shut up," I said.

Santa blew two vortices of smoke out his nostrils that intertwined with each other in a crazy interference pattern. He muttered aloud, but more to himself than to us.

"So that's two dead without my nod. I've got a gut feeling it was one and the same killer."

"That's what I said earlier!" Carmine exclaimed. "Only with different words."

"And I said to zip it, half-pint! Sorry about him, Mister Claus."

Santa didn't seem as bothered by Carmine as I was; it was obvious that something else was on his mind.

"You know, the police came to my condo earlier today to ask a bunch of questions," he said.

"Really? What happened?"

"I sicced my lawyers on 'em like a pack of pitbulls on a poodle."

"I didn't know lawyers worked on Christmas Eve," said Carmine.

"They do when they work for me. A good attorney is the best protection a man can have."

"A lawyer wouldn't have been much good to Plotzky or the Bunny," I said.

Santa frowned. He tucked his pipe back under his towel, stood up, and smacked his palms together.

"Good point. Speaking of working on Christmas Eve, I'd better get back to that nose rub. The elves should be done weighing up the packages soon, and I can't be late for the evening's drop."

"We capiche."

"But I'm doubling the reward now."

"Really?"

"I want to get this wrapped up before the year is out."

"Wow, Cisco," said Carmine. "Two thousand!"

"And we can use the money," I replied. "If I miss a payment on that electric eggbeater I bought, I'm screwed."

"Why did you buy an eggbeater if you hate eggs?"

"Because I hate eggs. Why else?"

"Must have been a hell of a salesman."

Santa headed down the hallway towards a bunch of numbered doors. He grabbed one by the doorknob and turned back to us.

"Um, I'm just going to go ahead and let you two work that out for yourselves. In the meantime, here's a little advance to keep you going."

He took an object out from under his towel and tossed it to us. Carmine caught it.

It was a tiny box, wrapped up like a Christmas present with a bow tied around it.

"Don't wait 'til Christmas," I said. "Open it!"

He tore it open and found a rolled up bill inside.

"Wow," Carmine exclaimed. "A C-note!"

I looked up at Santa.

"Warm up your checkbook, Mister Claus, 'cause we're gonna catch that killer one way or the other."

"You get him soon and you might find the rest in your stocking tomorrow morning."

"Thank you, sir. And Merry Christmas."

"Whatever."

He opened the door, walked in, and slammed it shut behind him. We heard his voice booming from inside the room.

"Ho, ho, ho! All three of you get over here! And bring the nose drops! And some cheese and crackers!"

We stood in the hallway for a minute, speechless.

"Probably best that we mosey along, Carmine," I said. "I like a story with a happy ending, but this is a little too close for comfort."

As we headed for the door leading back to the main hall of the cabaret, Cupid and Mungo returned from the steam bath, their hair soaking wet. Carmine shuddered at the sight of the doorman who'd decked him, but Mungo ignored us as the unlikely pair passed by.

As Cupid followed his muscle-bound meat mountain, he shot us a dirty look.

"Are you finished harassing my best customers now?" he hissed, his voice filled with pique.

"We were just leaving," I said.

We entered the main hall. Cupid had gone back to his place at the desk.

The burlesque show was having an intermission, and the audience was howling for more entertainment.

Cupid picked up a microphone and made an announcement over the club's loudspeaker system.

"Gentlemen, Cupid's is pleased to announce an exclusive engagement, all the way from San-Ho-Zay. Get ready to put your hands together (but don't expect to get them unstuck) for Heddy Hollinger and her Harvest Moon!"

A new dancer came on as the band started playing "Turkey in the Straw." She was balancing a cornucopia of fruit on her head, and was clad entirely in fresh produce. At this time of year, it must have been an expensive act.

The crowd went ape for her bananas. Maybe they were vitamin deficient.

As Mungo held open the curtain for us at the exit, Carmine cringed and tucked his head under his collar like a turtle. Mungo only barely grunted his acknowledgement as we headed up the stairs.

Once we were safely out of range, Carmine popped his head up again and tugged my sleeve.

"Say, Cisco, when we get the rest of Santa's money, is it going to be an eighty-twenty split like always? I think I deserve more if I have to take abuse from other people besides you."

"Don't bother me with figures, Carmine. We got some serious drinking to do."

"You mean thinking?"

"I mean *both*."

Chapter 14: The Alley

We left Cupid's club and stepped out into the cold alleyway. As soon as the red door shut behind us, we bumped smack into a snowman.

"Sorry," I said. "I didn't see you standing there."

"That's okay," he growled with a crooked smile. "We tend to blend in."

A second snowman popped out from the shadows.

"And if one of us melts," he added, "things start to get very clear. Transparent, even."

Before you could say "the sheik's seventh son spent seventy cents on soldered solenoids," we were surrounded by a half-dozen of them.

The second snowman, who I assumed to be the leader of the group on account of him wearing the loudest scarf, stepped up to me and gave me a poke in the chest with his stick finger.

"Have a nice time at Cupid's, Maloney?"

That upset my apple cart; how did he know my name?

"Sure," I stammered. "I mean, I didn't have *that* kind of nice time...it was purely business-related."

"We couldn't afford nothin'!" squealed Carmine.

The snowman leader came a step closer. He pulled a corncob pipe out of his mouth.

"So if it wasn't pleasure business, then maybe it was *murder* business, huh?"

"That's something I was hoping to talk to you guys about," I said. "I'm looking for Plotzky's killer, just like you."

"You don't say? And how's the investigation going?"

"Not too great. I feel like I'm just getting started."

"And yet, look at the friends you've made so far," he snarled. "First you play 'good egg' with the Easter Bunny, and now you're bellying up to the Fat Man."

The others added their two cents' worth.

"Taking a walk on the wide side, are we?"

"They're in cahoots!"

"He's hand-in-glove with the White and Red!"

"Clobber the collaborator!"

"Sickles out, boys!"

The snowmen pulled out foot-long icicles, which they brandished in their little stick hands like daggers. The frozen spikes had needle-sharp points that gleamed in the yellowy sodium glow of the alley's street lamps.

They closed in. Carmine and I backed against the wall and put our hands up. Reaching for my gun would be risky; there wasn't much else I could do except try to talk my way out of the situation.

"Look here now, fellas...no reason to jump to conclusions. We had nothing against Plotzky, and I'm pretty sure the bunny and Saint Nick weren't involved."

The leader got right in my face. His breath smelled like wintermint.

"So you're vouching for your buddies, huh?"

"I only met them today for the first time. The Easter Bunny had a decent alibi, and there's no point going after him anyways, because he's dead."

"Not yet, he isn't!"

The snowmen cackled in their horrible, frigid voices.

"He was killed tonight," I said. "We saw it happen! Have a look..."

I reached into my pocket for the bolt and got the pokey parts of half a dozen icicles in my face.

"No funny stuff, gumshoe," growled the leader.

"I was just going to show you what killed him."

I carefully took out my hanky and unwrapped it for them to see the bloody bolt. The leader looked at it with a snort.

"Bah, that's no proof. For all we know, you were using that oversized toothpick to dislodge a booger and gave yourself a nosebleed."

"I swear on my mother's grave expression that she makes whenever I swear," I said. "I heard Plotzky and the Bunny had their differences, but he didn't seem like the type who'd try to murder a business rival."

"They had an argument over a girl," said the leader. "The rodent was jealous 'cause she picked Plotzky over him."

"He seemed like the type who'd do it over that!" said Carmine.

I smacked him.

"That's probably just circumstantial," I said to the snowmen. "As for Claus, he's offering a reward to whoever finds the killer. Why do that if it was him?"

They laughed again, although this time, it was starting to sound a bit forced. The leader stabbed his icicle in the ground to make his point.

"You know how Claus gets his dough, don't you?"

"Smart investing?" ventured Carmine.

"Shut up, knee-high," he snapped. "It's the kids. When they send him letters, he gets them to slip in a couple of their parents' blank checks. With all the bills at this time of year, they don't notice Claus dipping into their bank accounts."

"It's a Christmas ka-ching!" said another snowman.

"His presents are payola!"

"Not quite the jolly old Saint Nick you've read about!"

"Claus is as crooked as they come!"

"Now if you know what's good for your health," said the leader, "you'd better start telling us what we wanna know."

"I already told you everything," I said.

(Okay, more like I *pleaded*.)

As they closed in, it got pretty clear that we needed an escape plan. Too bad I wasn't much good at planning things in advance...as mentioned previously, I wasn't all that great at improvising, either. But I *did* notice an open sack of road salt lying against the brick wall behind us, right next to Cupid's door.

I looked at Carmine. He must have read my mind, because he started shaking his head and waving his hands with his "oh no!" signal. I turned back to face the matlock.

"I can tell you this, fellas: I've never assaulted a snowman before..."

I bent down, grabbed Carmine by the ankles, and swung him around in a circle.

"Eeeeek!" he screamed.

The snowmen backed off. I reached down and grabbed the salt bag with my other hand.

"...but it's never too late to start!"

I swung the bag in an arc, spraying them with the contents. The snowmen screamed blue murder as their snowy hides were melted by the chunks of coarse salt. Turns out their language was even coarser; they squirmed around on the asphalt like slugs, cursing and swearing up a storm.

I put Carmine down.

"Let's leg it, kid!"

Needless to say, we dashed out of the alley as fast as we could.

Now it might have just been my imagination playing tricks on me thanks to the rush of adrenaline, but I thought I heard a whirring sound behind us, like the insides of a windup toy. But when I looked over my shoulder to check, all I saw was an alley full of really angry snowmen.

"We'll get you for this, Maloney!"

We ran back to my expensively parked car.

Chapter 15: The Lakeside

It had been the busiest Christmas Eve of my life, and it wasn't even dinnertime yet. All that action had made me incredibly thirsty; I needed a glass of hundred-proof perspective so I could soothe the ol' cerebellum, and the Lakeside Bar & Grill was just the place to get it.

Drinking probably wasn't the best idea at a time like this, but desperate times call for desperate measures, and I was desperate for a few measures of my favorite single malt. So we drove over to the Lakeside, my regular watering hole.

We sat at the bar on our usual stools—the ones that afforded a clear view of both the front door and the bar counter. From there we could watch who was coming and going, and more importantly, what was going into our glasses.

My sidekick and I could both sense that we were getting warmer; we just needed a tender shove in the right direction. All the way there, Carmine wouldn't stop blabbing about what he was going to do with his share of the reward money, so I figured I should stop up his yap with a few shots.

"Shisco, yer my besht buddy, ya know that? You can kick me anytime ya wanna."

Too bad the drinks produced the opposite effect. Oh well, I was a few sheets to the wind myself.

"Shishco! Are ya lishening to me?"

The Lakeside was a typical downscale dive whose customers were trying their best to leave their troubles behind them. It was doing some unusually good business that evening, and I couldn't figure out why.

I surveyed the room, looking from face to face.

There was the usual crew: Bobby No-Slacks, Vinnie the Tool 'n' Die Guy and his granola-munching brother, Benny the Tie-Dye Guy, Jake the Knife, Eugene the Spoon, Honey Stirrups, Lush-Lips Frankie, Mojo Scrofula, and Itchfinger Brown. (Mind you, I didn't personally know these people; those were the nicknames Carmine and I had given them. Customers at the Lakeside weren't very sociable).

There was also a slew of irregulars whose faces I didn't recognize. For a minute I was worried that my dear old dive was starting to get trendy, but then I realized why the place was so full: that gol' dang shabby brass band was setting up on a makeshift stage in the corner.

The crowd gathered around as the band struck up a slow, maudlin version of "Merry Christmas To You." Boy, was it depressing...a perfect fit.

"Hey Shishco, lookit! They're playing mushic!"

I counted the empty glasses on the counter in front of us, trying to figure out how much we'd drunk. The Lakeside had the cheapest booze in town: a business strategy guaranteed to pack 'em in with bottom-feeders. It was no place to bring a date, but at least they let me run a tab. Heck, at least they still let me through the door. It was like perpetual happy hour, minus the happiness.

"Shishco, who're you talking to?"

Damn, was I narrating out loud again?

"Just my imaginary friends, Carmine."

"Oh. I had a imashinary friend once...but we had a falling out, and from then on, he acted like I didn't even exisht."

He knocked back his drink.

"Sorry to hear it, buddy."

Behind the bar, Max the barman was wiping a glass with a towel, stopping on occasion to swat flies with it, then going back to wiping the glass. I used to wonder how flies and cockroaches stuck it out in the winter and my new theory was that they all took shelter at the Lakeside. So long as they dodged Max's towel, they had a good chance of surviving 'til spring.

Max poked the towel in his ear with his index finger and gave it a twist, as though there was a loose screw in there. He sniffed at the waxy extraction, then wiped the bar down and collected some of our dirty glasses. I watched to see if he was going to use the same towel to wipe them clean.

Yep, he sure did.

Carmine hiccupped. The air around us turned green for a second and smelled like hydrogen sulphide. I picked up a cocktail list and waved the cloud away.

"Ugh! What have you been eating?"

"I had a few overshized mintsh from that jar over there."

"Those are pickled eggs, kid."

"No wonder they were sho shoft."

His eyes fell on a shallow bowl of water with a lemon floating in it on the bar counter. Carmine picked it up and took a sip.

"That's to clean your hands with, you know," said Max.

"Ick!" Carmine said as he spat out the water. "I *thought* it tashted shtrong!"

"People around here do some really nasty things with their hands," said Max.

Carmine put the bowl down. Max refilled it.

"'Nother round, Cisco?"

"Sure, Max. At these prices, I can't afford to stay sober."

Max turned back towards the shelf of bottles and measured a couple more snorts of fool fuel. He was a stand-up guy, and the only bartender I could trust not to pour me short. The Lakeside's other barman was the proprietor, a balding old bastard with a colossal comb-over who was easily the most miserable small-business owner I'd ever met. He put too much ice in the drinks, then poured half measures, then moaned that you didn't tip him enough. I once phoned the Better Business Bureau to complain about him, but their line had been disconnected after they gave the telephone company a bad rating.

"Here ya go, Cisco," said Max as he put two glasses down in front of us. "On the house."

Max was grateful to me 'cause I once looked after his pet anaconda while he was doing time in the clink for stealing bras off of clotheslines. As far as I was concerned, he must have been framed: Max was more of a hosiery-and-garters man.

"Shishco! You gonna introdouche your imashinary friend, or what?"

Carmine was slurring up a storm (you might want to break out the Oxford Dictionary of Modern Slurs to translate). I sipped at my malt and reminded myself to stop narrating out loud.

"I tell you, Carmine, something bugs me about this case."

"What'sh 'at?"

"I can't figure out why Santa Claus would put up two grand just to find Plotzky's killer. It doesn't make a hot lick of sense."

"He wants to keep the streetsh clean, he shaid. I had a dog onshe; I know what he meansh."

"That story's fuller of holes than a hole filled with holes is full of holes."

"Sho why didn't you call him on it?"

"Because I didn't want to end up even more full of holes.

"Oh."

"It's as if Claus is afraid of something... But what? Just 'cause someone kills Plotzky and the Easter Bunny doesn't mean they're the world's baddest badass. So why would Santa be shaking in his big black boots?"

"Maybe hish feet are cold."

"He runs a big operation. Can't he spare a single elf? Why would he have to contract out?"

"The elf union musht be angry."

"Maybe the reward is just a ploy to draw the blame away from himself and firm up his alibi. What if Claus is guilty, and he's sending everyone on a wild goose chase?"

"No chasher for me. I've had enough."

"You know what? I smell a big, fat, jolly rat."

I took another sip of my scotch. The whiskey burned with a peaty tingle as it went down my throat, but the questions burned even more.

Suddenly, Carmine got all animated.

"Hey Shishco, check out the broad who just walked in!"

"You're seeing things. The only woman to set foot in this place is the cleaning lady, and that's once a year, tops."

"No, really! Boy, she's shtacked like the Empire Shtate; makesh ya wish ya wush King Kong! Raowr, raowr, raowr, with a side order of va-va-vavoom!"

"Calm down, you rummy Romeo."

I turned around and looked. Lo and behold, my peepers peeped a peepful of a woman wearing a fur shawl and not a whole lot much else.

"Hey, wait a minute," I said. "She's the Jezebel who walloped me this morning at the precinct."

Carmine blinked.

"Wow, Shishco, she'sh coming thish way!"

The call girl approached the bar, spotted me, and slinked over with a smirk of recognition on her face.

"You're Maloney, right?" she purred.

"I'm right most of the time."

She frowned with one eyebrow.

"We met at the police station this morning, remember?"

"I do, and so does my bruised cheek. No hard feelings about what I said?"

She shrugged.

"My skin's thick enough."

"Thick and plenty visible!" Carmine hooted. "Wowee-wow-*whoopsh!*"

He toppled off his barstool. The call girl watched with amusement as I helped him back up.

"How'd you get bailed out so soon?" I asked her.

"Let's just say the way to a judge's heart is through his zipper."

"A-hem!"

I didn't really need to clear my throat, but it felt like every ear in the place was listening to us.

"So," I said in a low voice, "do you require my services?"

"No, but I'll bet you could use mine."

She poked me in the chest with her stiletto finger. I hoped it was clean, because it had been more than seven years since my last tetanus shot.

Carmine guffawed and slapped the bar counter as he teetered on the stool.

"Heh, she mushta had her tongue sharpened!"

"That's nothing," replied the call girl. "For the real abuse, I charge an arm and a leg."

"I suppose they get what they pay for?" I asked.

"Sometimes more."

She winked, sat down on the stool next to mine, and scissored her bare gams like a Radio City Rockette as she crossed them. The dress she wore under the fur shawl was cut with barely enough cloth to mummy-wrap a kielbasa.

Carmine pointed at her pelt.

"That looksh familiar. Ish it rabbit?"

"The real thing. Just picked it up."

"Man, thoshe furriersh work fasht," he slurred.

"So what do you want?" I asked her.

She leaned in close and breathed in my ear.

"I hear you're on the Plotzky case."

"Me and the rest of creation. What about it?"

"Plotzky was a good client of mine. I paid him a visit last night, in fact."

"Is that so?"

"I saw something funny as I was leaving his apartment," she continued.

"Funny 'strange,' or funny 'ha-ha'?"

She gave me a look of disdain.

"Funny like the circus clown who knocked up your mother, gumshoe. You want to hear the rest, or what?"

"Sorry. Go on."

She planted her fists onto her shapely hips, giving the impression of a peeved hourglass.

"Just for that, it's going to cost you."

I knew this old routine well, and shrugged as I reached for my wallet.

"Here we go...are you charging by the minute, or by the word?"

"Breathe easy, Buckminster," she said. "Just order me a stinger for a start."

I turned to the barkeep.

"Hey, Max! Stinger for the lady!"

Max mixed the drink, poured it into a highball glass, and shoved it over to the call girl. She picked up the glass and inspected it; inside was a live scorpion.

"Say, they *do* make 'em strong here."

Without so much as a flinch, she fished the scorpion out like it was a swizzle stick and flung it away.

Somebody shrieked.

The call girl sipped the drink with approval as a customer ran by screaming, the scorpion gripping his earlobe in its pincer.

"We also take things very literally," said Max.

I crossed his palm with a dollar tip and faced off with the tippling teaser.

"Okay sister, gimme the lowdown on the skinny."

"I left Plotzky's apartment around two o'clock," she said. "A few blocks away, I realized I forgot my cigarettes. When I got back to the lobby, another girl was going into the building, ahead of me. She buzzed Plotzky's apartment and he let her in."

"Was she one of your—how shall we say—associates?"

"Maybe, but her getup wasn't exactly standard-issue."

"How so?"

"She wore a man's overcoat and was carrying a tweed suitcase."

"What else?"

"She had her hair tied back in a tight ponytail and was wearing sunglasses. She looked like some kinda spy. Know what I mean?"

"That's odd."

"If Plotzky liked playing dress-up games, he never told me. I mean, another girl so soon after...I didn't know he was so hot-blooded! It bruised my ego a bit."

"It's understandable."

"So I didn't go back for the cigarettes," she continued. "Professional courtesy, you understand. One doesn't intrude."

"Of course."

"It didn't seem that suspicious at the time, but then I heard in the joint that Plotzky'd been melted, so I started to think maybe something wasn't right."

"What made you come to me?"

"When I overheard the cops talking about Plotzky in the station, they mentioned you a lot."

"Really?"

For a minute I thought maybe my former colleagues weren't such a bad bunch of guys after all.

"Sure," she said. "They were having a laugh at the idea of you chasing Plotzky's killer all over town."

"Oh, brother. How did you know you'd find me here?"

"They said you'd probably be here, drinking away your sorrows after coming up empty-handed."

"Okay, that's enough of that, thanks," I said. "Tell me more about what the mystery girl looked like."

"She was about twenty-five, thirty at the max if she uses a good quality skin cream. Platinum-blonde hair and really bright white tennis shoes. After Labor Day, I might add."

I dropped my glass. It crashed on the floor.

A group of Orthodox Jews at a nearby table yelled "Mazel Tov!"

At another table, a group of Orthodox Greeks smashed their plates and yelled "Opa!"

Next to them, a group of orthopedic surgeons sat quietly. There was nothing unorthodox about them.

"Say, Maloney, what bit ya?" asked the call girl. "You know her or something?"

"I...I think I've got her phone number in my pocket."

The brass band played a musical stinger. Max hollered at them.

"Stick to the Christmas tunes, fellas! And play something a bit more up-tempo!"

A skinny teenager at the drum kit launched into a frantic solo.

"Man oh man, that kidsh a whiz on the trapsh!" said Carmine, clapping off-tempo. "Go, little drummer boy, go! *Whoopsh*!"

He fell off his barstool again.

"Carmine!" I shouted over the din. "Remember the little sneaker prints we found on Plotzky's carpet?"

"Yeah, bossh!" he said from down on the dirty floor.

"I'll bet you dimes to ducats they were tennis shoes. Very small ladies' tennis shoes!"

I turned to Max as I hauled my sidekick up.

"Max, get the lady another drink and put it on my tab, will ya? Come on, Carmine. We've got a sudden appointment."

"Sure thing, bossh!"

I dragged him away as Max puts another stinger on the bar in front of the call girl. She flung the arachnid away. Somebody shrieked.

"Cheers, boys!" she toasted as we left. "Feel free to ask me things anytime!"

She downed the drink as the brass band honked away to the tune of pa-ra-pa-pum-pum.

Chapter 16: The Parade

The call girl's tip set my mind racing faster than a greased warthog down a waterslide. I was starting to think maybe I'd gone all loop-screwy; Betty Sketchley, a murderer? It ran counter to all my instincts as a detective, which is why, come to think of it, I should have suspected it all along.

We headed for the sporting goods store. My car moved silently through the city, mostly because I was coasting down every hill to save gas.

I was experiencing a bit of double vision, so I covered up one eye with my hand: problem solved. Good thing it was okay back in those days to drink and drive.

Carmine passed the time by drunkenly plucking out the melody of "Jingle Bells" on his rubber-band seatbelt.

"You really fink Betty Shketchley done it, Cisco?"

"I hate to think of her as a suspect, Carmine. But then again, it gives me an excuse to go peeping through her window."

He looked outside at the city passing us by.

"Either I'm sheeing double, or people put out twiche as many Chrishmash lightsh thish year."

"We'd better sober up."

"Maybe we should get shome coffee?"

"Coffee doesn't sober you up; that's just a myth. We'll need to give each other a hard slap in the face. You go first."

I stuck my cheek out at him. Carmine wound up and slapped it; compared to the facial abuse I'd been taking that day, it was like getting a flick of a feather boa off Liberace.

"Did it work?" he asked.

"Not quite. Put some more pepper into it."

He wound up and slapped me again, a bit harder this time. The constellation for my astrological sign did an orbit around my head.

"That's better. Now I'll do you."

Carmine closed his eyes and stuck out his cheek. I gave it a hard slap that sent him spinning like a top in his seat. He steadied himself and put his hand to his face, then shook his head, rattling his tongue against his tonsils.

"You feeling clearer-headed?" I asked.

"Yeah, but this cheek is sure gonna hurt in the morning."

"Don't worry. Once we get that reward, you'll be able to buy a steak for it."

The traffic started to slow down. I sat up straight to get a better view and see what was turning the road into a parking lot, but couldn't see much, other than a cop standing on the sidewalk. I rolled down my window and got his attention.

"What's going on, officer?"

"Illegal Christmas parade," he replied. "They made a goulash out of the next few blocks."

"Who's 'they'?"

"Mostly Trinitarians, but we've also got some Albigensians, a few Abecedarians, and the Flat Earth folks. It's pretty schismatic over there. Things are getting tense."

"Isn't Jesus the reason for the season?" asked Carmine. "Can't they all agree on that?"

The cop laughed.

"You expect any of it to make sense?"

Not on that day, I didn't.

"So is it a parade, a protest, or a punch-up?" I asked.

"Beats me," said the cop with a shrug. "Wouldn't be surprised if the whole mess turned into a religious rumble. We're trying to send them down the side streets."

"Okay, thanks," I said, and rolled up the window.

We moved along at a snail's pace, bumper-to-bumper. I noticed the right lane was empty, so I switched over to it. Big mistake: it was a dedicated turn lane, and the traffic on the left was too thick for me to move back over. I put on my turn signal, but nobody was letting me in. Damn the road hogs in this town! Then I realized my turn signal light probably had a busted bulb, so I rolled the window down and stuck out my hand to signal a left. All I got was a couple of high-fives on the side.

We were forced to follow the lane and turn right down a street that the police had used to divert the parade. Sure enough, we ended up behind a flotilla of Christmas floats.

Cops were lined up on either side of the road, herding the participants along in an orderly fashion. The last place I wanted to end up in was a parade, but I didn't want to have to turn around and go back to the main drag, where traffic had become a major pain in the hind cushions. Sometimes if you can't beat 'em, you gotta join 'em.

I was signaled to stop by a cluster of cops.

"Hey officers, are we too late to join in?"

They turned and looked at me, then at my car.

"Is this your parade vehicle, sir?" one of them asked.

(Sheez, all this "vehicle" nonsense... How come cops can never just say "car"?)

"Yeah," I answered. "Sorry we're a bit late. If we could just sneak on through..."

"It doesn't look like a Christmas float. Where's the decorations?"

"See the ribbon?"

I pointed to the tattered remains of a red ribbon tied to the coat hanger that served as my radio antenna. I must have gotten it for supporting some charitable cause or other. (I can't remember which—it could have been cancer, or heart disease, or maybe engine knock. I was more likely to deal with charities from the receiving end rather than the giving end.)

The cop stared at me for a second, shook his head, and waved his hand.

"All right, it's your funeral." He turned to his buddies. "Let 'em through!"

The cops stepped aside to clear the way as I drove smack-dab into the middle of the motley-est crew of Christmas cranks I'd ever seen.

The float to my right was driven by a group that seemed hell-bent on keeping the "Christ" in Christmas (I mean phonetically; they wanted it to rhyme with "iced" instead of "wrist"). I couldn't recognize their particular denomination, but their Puritan uniforms made me hungry for oatmeal.

The float to my left was occupied by moon worshipers who demanded a return to traditional solstice values, denouncing the commercialization of Saturnalia (or something like that...it was hard to read their placards and drive at the same time).

I was a bit nervous, as it was clear to me that many of the paraders were packing heat, their right hands stuck in the breast pockets of their overcoats, ready to unholster and fire at the slightest provocation. It wasn't so much a parade as a Mexican standoff on wheels, but at least it was moving along.

"Kooky crowd, eh kid?"

I looked over at Carmine; he was fast asleep.

I spotted the float belonging to the Hare Krishnas. What were *they* doing here? Singing and dancing and chanting, that's what. The shaven-headed devotees were standing barefoot on their flowery, garlanded flatbed, wearing nothing but saffron robes. I had to give 'em their due; it was a brave choice of clothing in this kind of weather.

I figured theirs would be the safest float to follow, if only because they lacked the two-thousand year history of killing each other over differing interpretations of some stuff Jesus said about being nice to people. So I squeezed my car in behind them and stayed as close as I could while we rolled along at a parade-speed crawl. Their float left a trail of their signature whiff behind it, a heady mix of sandalwood incense, asafetida, and curried vegetables. I covered my nose with my hanky, but it was no match for the power of reincarnated okra.

My car was suddenly bombarded by a volley of slushy snowballs hitting us on the passenger side, waking Carmine from whatever strange dreams he was having.

"Remember the à la mode!" he sputtered. "Batten down the hat checks!"

He blinked a couple times as the mushy missiles dented the car; obviously, each one was loaded with a rock.

"Holy free holies, Cisco! What's with the snowballistics?"

"What do you think? Looks like they found us."

Sure enough, we'd been spotted by a roving gang of snowmen at the side of the road. Word must have gotten out among them of our altercation with the gang in the alley behind Cupid's, and that was bad: I'd never heard of anyone being targeted by the wrath of this ballsy bunch, but couldn't imagine that it would be easy to mollify their refrigerated rage.

We had to get out of there, fast. I stepped on the gas and bumped up against the Krishnas' float, shoving them forwards. I doubt Krishna would have approved of the language his followers used as they stumbled around on the flatbed.

That push helped get us out of range of the snowmen, but before you could shout "free vegetarian buffet," the Krishnas suddenly abandoned ship and scattered in all directions. Obviously, they must have seen something coming that I couldn't. Then sure enough, BLAMMO! Their float exploded.

Dead ahead of us was a T intersection where the rest of the parade had been forced to turn right. Through the cloud of smoke, I could see what looked like a big black circle surrounded by a metallic ring on the opposite sidewalk. As we got closer, I realized what it was: the snowmen had set up some kind of cannon that was aimed straight at us, and I was looking down the barrel. They were loading it with a giant snowball. Who knows, maybe it was a lower body part from one of their fallen brethren? But more likely, it was a bigger version of the snowbomb they'd chucked into the Easter Bunny's kitchen. Man, when these fellas started a snowball fight, it was no child's play.

The Karavan of Krishna Konsciousness™ had been reincarnated into little scraps of chicken wire and paper-maché, possibly as karmic payback for that unfortunate acronym. It was no longer suitable cover. There wasn't time to do a U-turn or a three-pointer; we would have been like sitting ducks at the ol' carnival shooting gallery. Instead, I went into kamikaze mode, gunning the engine full speed ahead while swerving the car from side to side in a serpentine motion to make us a more difficult target.

"Whoa, Cisco," moaned Carmine, "I'm gonna be carsick!"

"It's liable to become fatal if we don't dodge that blizzard-bomb!" I shouted as I played Waltzing Matilda with the steering wheel.

The snowmen lowered the cannon straight at us. I turned the wheel for a hard right, but the car started to spin out and kept skidding straight ahead, as I'd been too broke to invest in a set of winter tires that season. (Or any year, for that matter. Now might be a good time to mention my sponsor, Nubbly Brand SureGrip Tire Swing Co. Ltd. Inc. All Rights Reserved.)

It was looking bad.

The professional advice dispensers always tell you that if your car spins out of control, you should do something completely counter-intuitive, like turn in the same direction you're swerving, or let go of the wheel and play dead, or start a kangaroo breeding program. (I don't know why cars don't just do what you want them to, but who am I to question the laws of physics?) Although I'd passed my driver's test with flying colors (that is, by throwing rainbow ribbons to distract the examiner so I could change the scores on his tally sheet), I was unable to remember any concrete advice that might be useful. So I waved my arms over my head and started singing "Down By The Old Mill Stream." Confused, Carmine joined in, but he stepped all over the contralto part; the kid sure did put the "harm" in harmony.

At that point, the snowmen fired.

We must have hit a spot on the road that wasn't black ice, because the tires suddenly gripped the asphalt as we entered the intersection, and the car started to turn the corner. The giant snowball grazed our left side, caught the back bumper and tore it loose, then landed on the pavement and exploded behind us, rattling the chassis and shaking one of my fillings out.

It was a close one, but there wasn't time to heave any sighs of relief: the snowmen were dead ahead and the road was coming to an end at the T intersection. I yanked the steering wheel to the right and the car swerved ninety degrees. Carmine started a prayer to Saint Christopher but the tires squealed like pigs getting turned into bacon, drowning out his pleas.

Fortunately, we were out of there before the snowmen had time to turn their cannon our way. In my rearview mirror, I could see them shouting curses and shaking their tiny stick fists in impotent rage. But I couldn't gloat back in anger for long: the parade-goers ahead of us had scattered in mass panic after the explosions, leaving a fleet of derelict floats on the road. I tried to dodge them as best I could, but still ended up playing smash-up-derby with a few. Good thing they were all built just as flimsily as the Krishnas' float.

We were lucky to get away in one piece. I wondered how much longer our luck would hold out.

Carmine checked his seat belt, breathing heavily.

"I hate to say it, Cisco, but that carnival job is looking much more attractive all of a sudden."

"You don't quit now just because of a bump in the road," I said.

"Bump? More like a bombardment!"

"Come on, kid, where's your nerve? Danger is something we put in our morning coffee, remember?"

"I don't remember you ever saying that."

"What, can't a guy improvise?"

We drove on in what would have been silence, if not for the clattering of my back bumper, hanging by a thread (literally: last time it fell off, I used thread to tie it back on).

It was almost dinnertime, but food was even farther from my mind than from my stomach. I had a very important rendezvous to make ASAP, with or without an RSVP.

Chapter 17: The Dame

I slowed down the car and stopped about a half-block from Sketchley's Sporting Goods.

Parking the old heap made me nervous: the snowmen knew what it looked like, and I didn't want to come back later to find an explosive device left underneath it as a present. Those fellows were clearly in the mood to bomb first and ask questions later.

"Wait here in the car," I said to Carmine.

"But I wanna come too!"

"No way. You've got to stay and keep an eye out in case any snowmen show up."

"S-s-s-snowmen?"

He trembled like a leaf.

"Also, make sure the girl doesn't try to make a getaway."

"G-g-g-girl?"

He trembled like a leaf glued to an epileptic chicken.

"Oh, just watch that I don't get another ticket."

"T-t-t-ticket?"

His teeth bit the Morse code for "SOS" on his fingernails.

"Pull yourself together, you poltroon! If you see a meter maid, just drive around the block and come back."

"But what if she gives me a dirty look or something?"

Sheesh. Sidekicks...am I right?

As I stepped out of the car, Carmine stuck his head out the window like an abandoned puppy. I chucked him my keys. He caught them in his mouth.

"You sure you won't need some backup?" he pleaded. "I could go in there and give her my best 'bad cop' yet."

"No way, ho-zay. This is going to take the finest finesse I can scrape up. I can't afford to have you botch it."

"Aw, nuts," he grumbled as he sat back inside the car. "I never get to do any peeping."

"When you run your own detective business, then you can spy through the girls' windows."

Without another word, he sat back in his seat and pouted.

I should have appreciated Carmine's willingness to plunge headfirst into what might have been a dangerous mission, but there are some jobs that the boss has to do alone: namely, anything that might turn up an eyeful of delectable demoiselle.

I headed towards the store. All the windows were dark. Next to it was a narrow alleyway a couple of feet wide, just big enough for the raccoons to use as a thoroughfare on their way to the Pot 'o' Garbage at the end of the Refuse Rainbow. So I tiptoed along the side of the building to see if I could get a better view around back.

In the alley behind the store were a few garbage cans and some flattened boxes for larger items like bicycles and canoes and—bingo—a fire escape that led up to the apartments on the upper floors.

I looked up and saw a light on, so I climbed up the fire escape to investigate. Turns out, it was the window to Betty's bedroom: there she was, strutting back and forth in her nightgown, stuffing clothes into a suitcase that was lying on the bed. As an added bonus, it looked like she was going through her lingerie drawer.

I felt the blood rushing up my neck as I stood on my toes to get a better view (for professional reasons, you understand). Now before you get all judgmental on me, remember we're not called "private eyes" for nothing. Watching people is about ninety per cent of this gig, and although a little accidental voyeurism was one of the inevitable perks of the job, I happened to consider it to be perfectly ethical: after all, I was primarily doing it for money.

But back to the scene: I watched transfixed as Betty deftly folded her lacy gossamer unmentionables like some kind of pervy Japanese origami. Although she was packing her suitcase with great care, she also seemed pressed for time.

Once the suitcase was full, she took a lacy pink and white evening gown from her closet and packed it on top, followed by a tiara and a sparkly wand. It was plain as plain this bird was flying the coop, but who knew what she was packing those funny feathers for?

She closed the lid, leaned over, and pushed her hands down on the suitcase. I estimated her weight at somewhere between one-twenty to one-thirty (nicely distributed in all the right places), and she did her best to use all of it while trying to get that case closed.

It looked like I was finally about to close a case of my own.

I snuck into the building by my usual method. (Sorry folks, but I can't reveal my trade secrets for gaining entrance into people's apartments, or else everyone would start doing it and no television set would be safe again.)

Once inside, I found my way to Betty's bedroom door, flung it open, and made my patented dramatic entrance.

"Going somewhere?" I asked in my most authoritative voice.

"Cisco!" she exclaimed as she heaved on the suitcase. "How did you get in here?"

"I used the cat flap."

"I don't have a cat flap."

"You do now."

She wiped the perspiration from her brow. To my surprise, she didn't seem all that upset to see me.

"Fine then, you're here," she said. "What do you want?"

"I got a hot lead in the Plotzky case," I answered. "Thought you might like to hear about it."

"I'm a little bit busy at the moment."

I took a few steps towards her.

"Need a hand with that?"

"It's a suitcase, Mister Chivalry. I might be just a woman, but it involves clothes, so I can handle it."

I had to admit, her sarcasm really got my sap rising.

She flattened her palms on the suitcase and bounced up and down a couple of times, but the latches wouldn't catch, so the lid popped back open when she let go of it. I snuck up and ran my pinky finger inside the suitcase.

"Don't touch that!" she shouted. Then she regained her composure. "I told you, I can handle it."

"Touchy, aren't we?"

She struggled to close the suitcase again and finally managed to get the latches shut. Then she reached for an ornate golden box from a nearby dresser and put it on the bed next to the case.

Watching her like a hawk, I gave my pinky a lick.

"Leaving the country?" I asked.

"Why would you think that?"

"I just figured if you wanted to skip out on a murder rap, you'd have to run real far."

She closed her eyes and rubbed her temples, as though trying to squeeze a headache out from her skull like a massive pimple.

"I realize you're trying to imply something," she said, "but I'm too tired for guessing games. Whatever it is, why don't you just spit it out?"

I tasted the tip of my pinky again and spat out onto the floor.

"Sister," I said, "in this case 'it' just happens to be the bitter, alkaline taste of heat-pack chemical residue."

She looked me square in the eye and sniffed derisively.

"No wonder you're talking loopy talk: you smell like a hobo's campfire cocktail."

"And you smell like..."

I sniffed back. The place had a familiar aroma.

"Is that zucchini bread?"

She took a long white coat from her closet and started putting on her scarf and gloves.

"I did my Christmas baking this morning, but it's all gone. You're too late."

"Don't speak too soon, Betty," I snapped. "There's more heat in your suitcase than in your oven."

She laughed, but I could tell she was getting anxious.

"You're drunk," she said. "It's kind of endearing, but you really should go home and sleep it off."

"You brought it to Plotzky's last night, didn't you?"

"Now why would I bring an oven to Plotzky's place?"

"Leave the playing dumb routine for my sidekick, sweetie. You can't hold a dim candle to him."

She put her coat on.

"Love to hear your theories, Sherlock, but I have a train to catch..."

She reached for the suitcase, but I grabbed it first, holding it tightly by the handle and pushing down hard so it wouldn't budge. She tried to pull it away with those thin, supple arms of hers.

"Stop it!" she grunted. "Let go of that!"

"Not 'til you come clean."

We fought a brief tug-of-war over the suitcase, yanking it back and forth between us. With a heave, I freed it from her grip, but accidentally knocked the gold box off the bed and onto the floor. The lid on the box popped open, and out spilled the biggest collection of children's teeth I'd ever seen. (Actually, it was the *only* collection of children's teeth I'd ever seen, and I sure hoped it would be the last...talk about creepy.)

I stared at the pile of teeth on the carpet.

"Now look what you did!" she wailed.

She fell to her knees and started to scoop up the teeth and put them back in the box.

"Boy," I said, "you sure do have some weird hobbies."

"They're my baby teeth from when I was a kid, you brute!"

I folded my arms into my most skeptical pose.

"You're telling me all of those are yours, Betty? Or should I say 'Tooth Fairy'?"

There was a musical stinger from outside. I flung open the bedroom window and looked out to see the shabby brass band standing in the alley, looking up at me expectantly, like a posse of puppies staring at a bitch's nipples (don't look at me like that; it's the appropriate word).

"Hey! Stop following me around!" I shouted down at them. "If you want a tip, you're barking up the wrong bush!"

I slammed the window shut. Betty was just about done putting the teeth back into the box.

"Of all the tall tales I've ever heard," she muttered. Tooth Fairy? That's ridiculous. Where do you get these crazy ideas?"

"I'll draw you a map," I said as I started pacing the room. "You're the Tooth Fairy. You and the Easter Bunny were in cahoots: he rotted the kids' teeth with his chocolate and you got to harvest whatever fell out. You must have made quite a team, a regular Bunny and Clyde...only it doesn't really work with you as Clyde."

"But..."

"I'm not finished quipping yet. Plotzky was competition with his snowballs; all the kids wanted to 'get stoned.' So you applied a targeted heat-pack attack to force him out of business the hard way. It was supposed to be smooth sailing for you and the bunny: once the deed was done, the dish would run away with the goon. But you were spotted outside Plotzky's building late last night, and you forgot to clean out the heat-pack residue from your suitcase."

"But..."

I was on a roll, and not about to let myself get sidetracked. I took a breath of air to recharge the ol' bellows, and nipped her off at the "but."

"When I came snooping around, you fed me a tip about your Cottontail Casanova to try and draw suspicion away from yourself. The chocolate truffle alibi was all planned out in advance, so you were certain the bunny would be able to hop off the hook with his sweet talk. But that didn't protect him from the crossbow bolt that sent him to the big Easter egg hunt in the sky."

I paused for effect. Betty looked at me, confused.

"Crossbow bolt?"

"You heard right. And although I *am* glad to see you, Miss Sketchley, this is actually a bolt in my pocket. I pulled it from between the rabbit's ribs just about an hour ago."

I took out the stained handkerchief, unwrapped it, and showed her the bloody bolt.

"Have a look. That stuff ain't ketchup."

Her lips trembled.

"No!"

She collapsed on the bed in tears, moaning into a pillow.

"No! It can't be true! Not my Hoppy!"

"Sorry to break the news, kid, but the Easter Bunny's a goner."

I sat down on the corner of the bed while she bawled all over the pillowcase, leaving a Rorschach test of runny mascara on the white linen. I was never much good at offering consolation back when I'd been a cop, and sure didn't get any better at it as a private eye.

"So it looks like I was right about you and the Easter Bunny at least," I said. "What about Plotzky?"

She sat up and wiped her eyes with a lace doily (which wasn't very absorbed in its job).

"It's true," she sniffled. "I killed Plotzky."

I heard another musical stinger from outside. Man, those brass band guys had perfect timing.

"Okay, honey, tell me from the beginning."

She turned her head away in shame and started to sing like a canary.

"I snuck into Plotzky's apartment last night and emptied the heat packs into his mitts and boots."

"I mean the very beginning. What made you do it?"

"Do you want the long version or the short version?"

The hemline of her nightgown was hovering just north of the legal limit. I wasn't in a hurry to run away from a nice pair of legs when my vantage point made for the perfect ogling angle.

"Take your time," I said.

"Hoppy and I were in love," she explained, "but father didn't approve. We were planning to elope and move somewhere far away. I suggested Easter Island, but he said it would be too obvious. Then we considered Guam, but we didn't like the way it sounded off the tongue. We considered Fiji, then the Seychelles, and had an argument over the Falklands versus the Malvinas. Can you believe he thought they were the same islands?"

Holy sweet heck, was she gabby. I looked at my watch and half-expected the brass band to cue the "wrap it up" music.

"...so we finally settled on the Maldives, even though I had a sinking feeling about them."

"What were you going to do when you got there?"

"We planned to have lots of children: he was a rabbit, after all. And I was sick of having to pay kids for teeth."

"So what stopped you from going?"

"Hoppy wanted to do one last truffle deal and get a nice nest egg saved up before he quit the business. But Santa got wind of his plan. Claus took a piece of his action and didn't want to lose the goose that laid the chocolate eggs."

"Are you saying the Bunny was paying Claus off? What for?"

"Protection. The fat man is worse than the tax man; every time money changes hands in this town, he nicks a cut. Why do you think he's called 'Saint Nick'?"

"I just figured he was Greek."

She gave me a look that told me I had a lot to learn.

"So let's get back to Plotzky," I said.

Her expression hardened.

"Santa always thought the snowman was a cold thorn in his pudgy side because Plotzky refused to kiss

Kringle's ring. He told us if we got rid of Plotzky for him, he'd let us go."

"And help himself to the snowball trade and the rabbit's chocolate business, I suppose?"

"Naturally."

"So you iced the snowman."

She looked at me, her eyes red and swollen.

"It was horrible, Cisco! Horrible! He was screaming, his arms and legs were melting...it took so long! I didn't want to stay and watch, but I had to make sure it was done. It was the worst thing I've ever seen."

She turned on the waterworks again and dabbed her tears with the doily.

"How come *you* had to do it?" I asked. "Did the Easter Bunny not want to get his paws dirty?"

"Plotzky knew him; Hoppy never would have gotten close enough."

"And I guess the Bunny would have been too obvious a suspect. You knew that when you gave me his address, right?"

"I knew Hoppy could convince you he was innocent, but I also didn't trust Santa to keep his word."

"I don't quite follow."

She cast a downward glance.

"I gave you his address because I was hoping you might be able to protect him."

"Sorry to let you down, sweetheart, but if I'm expected to dive in front of crossbow bolts, I charge double my usual fees."

She clutched at me as though for dear life; it felt like she had my liver in a headlock.

"Santa double-crossed us, Cisco! He killed Hoppy to wipe out the trail! Like Little Jack Horner, he's trying to corner the market and get his fat fingers in all the plum pies!"

"Easy Betty, don't squeeze so hard."

She relaxed her grip on my internal organs.

"I know why Claus put out the reward," she continued, a little melodramatically. "He wants to put himself above suspicion! We never should have taken his offer, but what else were we going to do? Whatever were we going to do?"

She tore at the doily and wrung her hands like an arthritic Lady Macbeth.

"Okay, just take it easy," I said. "Let me think."

She fainted in my arms with a moan. I held her up, which wasn't too hard, thanks to her ergonomic figure. She was warm and soft, and smelled like talcum powder, with a dash of mint. Man, the scene was straight out of one of those awful radio dramas Carmine likes to listen to, except with full color picture and stereo surround sound.

So that was it: Santa wanted to be the boss of all bosses...the *capo della tutti capi*...the *tutti* of all the *frutti*. It was hard to believe Betty was the Tooth Fairy, but I always did fall for the crazy ones. For a minute there, I didn't care about Plotzky, or the Easter Bunny, or even Santa Claus...

Then Carmine burst into the room.

"Cisco, there's a meter maid out there, but so far she's just doing some light dusting and mopping..."

He noticed us and did a double-take.

"Holy hot tamales! I wondered what was taking you so long."

"It's okay, Carmine," I said. "The girl is innocent."

Yeah, you read that right: I lied to my sidekick through my teeth.

"But what about what the call girl said?" he asked.

"I ain't buying it. I'll bet that two-bit floozy got her bail paid off by dirty old Saint Nick in exchange for putting the finger on poor Betty, here."

At the sound of her name, Betty started to revive.

"So... Uh... I don't get it," Carmine said. "Are you saying Santa Claus done it?"

"That's right, and we've got to take him down and rope him in. Go get the car started."

"But boss..."

"If there's time for questions, there's also time for kicking," I threatened.

"Okay, I hear ya, already! Whatever you say."

Carmine backed out of the room as Betty came to.

"Sorry about your door, Miss," he said.

"That's alright," she replied woozily.

We were alone again. Betty held me close and whispered in my ear.

"Thanks, Cisco."

I felt the goosebumps popping up on my forearms as her lips brushed against the hairs growing from my earholes, which made me glad that I never bothered to trim them.

"I don't care what you did to Plotzky," I said. "Just get out of town and don't leave a trace."

"Come with me!" she murmured.

I looked deep into her pale blues and could have easily gotten lost in there, but harsh reality nagged at me.

"I'd love to, baby, but if I don't deal with Santa, he'll find you. And you'll get worse than coal in your stocking if he does."

I stood up. She followed suit.

"Cisco, before you go..."

"What is it? Did I drop something again?"

She grabbed me by the collarbones, yanked me front and center, and kissed me hard enough to bruise both lips.

Boy, did that ever bring the fireworks. My life flashed before my eyes (everything after puberty, that is). The hairs on the back of my neck did a standing ovation. Romantic string music swelled up in the background like a party balloon with the mumps.

I realized the music was coming from outside and swiveled my eyeballs to get a gander out the window.

The string quartet was clustered together in the alley behind the building, sawing away at their viols for dear life. Standing nearby was the shabby brass band, arms folded and not too impressed with the intrusion upon their turf.

Before I even got a chance to savor the moment, Betty decoupled from the lip-link. Although I was sore in the mouth, I wouldn't have minded keeping it up a bit longer (told you I was a sucker for the crazy ones.)

"I'd better get going," she said. "We're already attracting attention."

"Will you let me know where to find you?"

"I'll leave a note under your pillow," she replied. "Farewell, but not goodbye, Cisco Maloney! 'Parting is such sweet sorrow, so I shall say goodnight till it be morrow.' Because if I don't split now, I'm never going to get a decent seat on the train."

She let go of me and tied up her overcoat. Then she shut the suitcase, grabbed it and the box of teeth, and rushed out of the room without closing the door.

I was left standing in a puddle of hormones squeezed out of me by my schoolboy crush. It wasn't cold, it wasn't a first pressing, and it sure wasn't virgin, but it was real, alright. I don't normally get all gaga over a kiss, but Betty locked lips like she was giving mouth-to-mouth to a mastodon. She probably could have revived a frozen one, too.

It was the hardest I'd ever fallen for a dame.

My romantic daze was snapped by faint whirring and clicking noises from outside, followed by rapid footsteps on the fire escape. I rushed to the window and threw it open again, looking out just in time to see a short elf-shaped figure disappear into the darkness of the alley.

I shut the window and stroked the hairs on my chinny-chin-chin. It looked like old Claus could spare some elfpower that night after all...and there was definitely more to the puzzle than met the eye...

Chapter 18: The Chase

As I climbed back down Betty's fire escape, I wondered why one of Santa's elves was spying on her apartment. Then something in my brain went "click," and I remembered the elf engineers in the sewer; it couldn't have been a coincidence that they were tunneling so close to Plotzky's apartment. Were they looking to dig a way in? Was Saint Nick working on a backup plan in case Betty and the bunny got cold feet, or else failed in their mission to dispatch Plotzky the Snowman?

I had no real reason to doubt that Betty was giving me the straight goods (and I needed much incentive to believe her after experiencing the "goods" close up). But was she was just a pretty pawn in Kringle's crooked game? Or was there more going on beneath the surface? To be honest, I didn't care if she killed Plotzky and got away with it. The thought of that beautiful girl rotting in prison on account of a corrupt snowball pusher and that corpulent bully in the red suit made my blood boil (then again, so did the thought of seeing her in a tennis outfit). To me, her only crime was stealing my heart.

Corny, right? That's how smitten I'd become.

I snuck back around the front of the building and saw Carmine arguing with a stout meter maid. The front end of my car was hitched up to a tow truck, inside which the driver sat patiently, waiting for the two of them to hash it out.

"What seems to be the problem, ma'am?" I asked the meter maid.

"Who are you?"

"The owner of this car."

"Oh, then you can pay the twenty-dollar fine," she said as she scribbled in her ticket book. "You're parked in a Snow Removal lane. See the sign?"

Frankly, I hadn't. I swear it wasn't there when I first parked.

"Twenty dollars?" I said, trying to sound outraged. I gestured at Carmine. "Okay, him and I share the car."

"Cisco!"

I got a good look at the meter maid, or at least, as good a look as a look at her could get. She was built like a linebacker, with yard-wide shoulders and a slight hunch, and her hair was all tucked up under her navy cap, except for the strands on her neck that avoided the general roundup. She had a bulbous nose, a cleft palate, and a warty growth of some kind that would have been situated between her eyebrows if she'd had two of them. I'm not one to judge a person's worth based on their looks, but it's fair to say she'd been dealt a low hand in the beauty department.

"If this is a snow removal lane," I asked her, "how come they never remove the snow?"

"The city's backlogged 'til June."

Typical.

She paused from writing the ticket, stuck out her tongue and licked the tip of her pencil, which reminded me that I needed to pick up some bologna on the way home.

"Listen," I said, "we were just leaving. You can tell Tommy Tow Truck over there that we won't be needing him."

"I still have to serve you the ticket."

"Fine. Did you get the license plate number?"

"I was just about to..."

"Let's beat it, Carmine!"

We jumped into the car. Carmine started it up.

"Throw it in reverse!" I shouted.

He shifted gears and slammed on the gas. The car lurched backwards with a screech of bald tires on asphalt; sometimes the old girl remembered how to dance.

We narrowly missed the meter maid. The tow truck cable hooked to the front bumper started to unspool, but it wasn't a problem for long: as it pulled taut, it tore the bumper from the chassis. We were off the hook.

Carmine spun the steering wheel and skidded the car into a 180-degree spin, shifted gears, and took us out of there (I admit it was impressive driving, if you're into that kind of thing). I looked back to see the meter maid stamping her feet and shouting at the tow-truck driver, and then throwing her ticket book on the pavement and kicking it for good measure.

It was a minor victory, but at that point I'd take anything I could get.

"Nice work, kiddo. You really earned your burned rubber wings back there."

Carmine's face turned red as he shifted up.

"Thanks, boss. Does that mean we can go get some ice cream?"

"Hell, no. We've got business to attend to."

"You mean go after Santa? On Christmas Eve he could be anywhere in the world. The farther, the better."

"I just said that to impress the girl. Take us to the police station and we'll let the boys in blue handle it. Santa's too big a fish for us weekend anglers."

Carmine breathed a sigh of relief.

"I like that you're coming around to my wimpy way of thinking."

"Well, bravery is admirable and all, but sometimes it's also Nature's way of kicking you out of the gene pool."

We were silent for a few minutes. Then Carmine tuned the radio to a country music program. At least I assumed it was country music, but the country might as well have been Wail-and-Moanistan. I couldn't tell if the singer was pining for a forsaken lover or bemoaning the loss of his missing wallet and keys. It was all plucky banjos, high-strung fiddles, and sliding lapsteel guitars, over which a nasal tenor hillbilly hiccupped a ballad. Something about losing his wife in an arm-wrestling match, or maybe losing his arm in a wife-wrestling match...it was hard to discern the Appalachian dialect.

"Would you mind turning that off? You know how I feel about country music."

"But it's Saddleass Sam's Lonesome Cowboy Hour. He's playing my favorite group: Sandy Kitchenheimer and the Three-Minute Eggs."

"Ugh, it sounds like an earthquake hit a pawnshop."

I flicked the radio off and thought again about buying a harmonica. Mention of pawnshops got me thinking maybe I could pick one up second-hand...then I realized I'd be sharing lip-space with someone so desperate that they had to pawn off a two-dollar harmonica...and then I remembered that I was a guy who couldn't afford a two-dollar harmonica, so maybe I shouldn't be so snobby...

I could tell Carmine was deep in thought too. Finally, he asked me the question that was on his mind.

"Uh, Cisco, if Santa *did* kill Plotzky, how does it make sense for him to give us a reward for catching him?"

"It doesn't, and he won't. The reward is just a smokescreen to put himself above suspicion. Claus has no intention of paying it out."

"You mean all day long we've been wasting our time?"

"Let's just say you might want to get in touch with the carnival and see if they have any openings."

"Aw, nuts and bolts."

"What was your job there, anyways?"

"I was a calliopist."

"What the heck is that? Some kind of foot doctor?"

"I was the guy who plays the calliope."

"Once more, with feeling: what the Sam Hill is a calliope?"

"It's the steam-driven pipe organ they play carnival music on. You know, like 'March of the Gladiators'."

"Come again?"

"The tune they play when the clowns come out."

"Oh, that one. Say, I didn't know you played music."

"I learned when I was growing up. Started on melodica, then advanced to accordion, then got demoted to concertina, but eventually worked my way up to grade ten calliopist."

"Bit of a limited instrument, isn't it? It's not like you're ever gonna play Carnegie Hall on one of those."

"It has its own solemn dignity, boss."

I didn't argue the point. The only thing I knew how to play was solitaire, and nobody ever wanted to join in.

We sat in silence as we headed for the police station. Neither of us wanted to acknowledge it, but going to the cop shop was an ego-smacking admission of defeat. My old colleagues on the force would have a good laugh at our fruitless efforts, mocking us from behind the security of their cozy pensions and their steady paychecks and their healthy benefit plans. They'd expect me to come crawling on my hands and knees begging for my old job back, but they'd be wrong: I knew damn well that at my age, I'd never pass the physical. Carmine was lucky: at least he had a fallback plan.

The roads were quiet, almost deserted. I guess most people were at home, finishing up their Christmas Eve dinner and arguing over whose turn it was to do the dishes.

We crossed a major intersection. Carmine double-checked the rear-view mirror.

"That's funny," he said, "I thought the light was green when I went through it, but turns out it was red. Hope a cop didn't see us."

I craned my neck to look through the windshield behind me. The light was beaming the universal color that meant "go."

"You sure you sobered up since the Lakeside?" I asked him. "The light's still green."

"I see a red one," he answered. "Wait a minute, that's not a traffic light...it's up in the sky!"

They say you should never look back, but I did, higher this time. Sure enough, there was a bright red light approaching behind us at treetop level.

"That can only mean one of two things," I said. "Either a stray V-2 rocket is coming back to Earth for Christmas, or we've got a very shiny nose in hot pursuit."

"Shiny nose?" Carmine slapped his forehead as his brain cells put two and two together. "That means Santa! Why's he following us?"

"I doubt it's to bring us a sugarplum pudding, kid. Try to lose him."

The tires squealed as Carmine made a sharp turn to the right and headed down a one-way side street.

"How'd he know where to find us?" he asked.

"One of his elves was spying on Betty's apartment from the fire escape. I saw the little imp run away, but it was too late to try and catch him. Santa probably knows we know what we know."

"Is he still back there?"

I checked again through the rear windshield. The glowing red dot was closer.

"Yep, and gaining. Floor it!"

Carmine stepped hard on the gas, but the car sputtered in response; we were already going as fast as the old bucket could go without crumbling into a pile of rusty nuts. He hit the clutch and tried shifting down, but the engine moaned like a cat that wanted in from the rain. As he tried to get some acceleration out of the beast, it made a series of mechanical noises that belied a poorly kept maintenance schedule. I admit I hadn't been taking very good care of her lately, and cars, like women, don't reward a man for shabby treatment.

"Damn it," I said. "It's times like this when I sure wish I'd bought a faster car."

There was a "sproing" as one of the belts flew out from under the hood like a rubber band shot from a schoolboy's finger.

"There goes the fan belt!" Carmine shouted.

"Keep an inventory. We could use a list for when we get to my mechanic."

Steam started pouring out from under the hood.

"You mean *if* we get to your mechanic!" said Carmine. "It's overheating!"

"I probably should have topped up the radiator fluid last fall."

The road got bumpy all of a sudden as we hit a rough patch. We rolled over a couple of mean potholes, and sure enough, one of the tires made a loud bang. The car started shaking.

"We blew a flat!" said Carmine.

"I probably shouldn't have chintzed out on those garter-belted radials..."

Then suddenly there was a burst of machine-gun fire from behind us. Bullets thudded against the rear bodywork as the car lurched from side to side.

"He's shooting at us!"

"What's your major in night school? The Obvious?"

"I can't help it! I have acute O.E.D.!"

"What's that?"

"Obsessive Exposition Disorder!"

"Just keep driving and leave the narration to me."

There was another burst of machine-gun fire behind us as Carmine did his best to keep the car under control. Actually, the swerving was probably helping us dodge the bullets.

I realized we were sitting ducks if we didn't do something quick. "Fight or flight" is a false dichotomy: why not do both? I drew my gun, rolled down the window, and fired a few rounds in the direction of Santa's sleigh. I didn't seriously expect to hit anything––I just wanted to show that we weren't going down without a shot. Plus, I absolutely detested tailgaters, so it felt good to have a legitimate excuse to shoot at one.

Thanks to the tire blowout, the car bounced around like a tin can in a washing machine, shedding bolts and sprockets at an alarming rate.

"We've gotta bail out of this heap before it turns back into Tinkertoys!" I shouted over the din. "Turn down that alley, slow it down, and we'll jump on the count of three!"

"Jump? Are you out of your mind, boss?"

"No, but my mind is out of ideas!"

A few more bullets hit the car. The tires wailed as Carmine made a sharp turn down an alleyway and slowed down so we could bail out.

I cracked open my door. Carmine did the same on his side.

I started counting.

"One... Two..."

"Count faster!" Carmine screamed.

"ONE-TWO-THREE!"

We jumped out.

My partner and I would have hit the pavement pretty hard, but the packed snow cushioned our fall somewhat and allowed us to skid along without contracting road rash. As the car rolled away, we smacked into some stacked-up garbage cans left out in the alley, knocking them down like bowling pins (even though I got a strike, I felt more like a human gutterball).

I picked myself up from the pile of overturned cans and scattered refuse just in time to see my beloved slag heap roll straight towards a brick wall, crash into it, and burst into flames. This was a shock to me, because I'd been running on fumes.

Losing the car hurt, but not nearly as much as the scrapes and bruises from my fall.

"Ugh, would it kill anyone in this burg to throw out some nice soft pillows?" I asked Carmine. "After all, you're supposed to buy new ones every six months."

I looked around. My sidekick was nowhere to be seen.

"Carmine? Carmine, you okay?"

From a nearby pile of garbage, Carmine threw a trashcan off himself and rolled over with a moan.

"That depends," he said weakly. "How many bones are there in a human body?"

"Two hundred and six."

"Then I s'pose I still have a few left."

I ran over and helped him stand up just as a volley of gunfire slammed into the burning remains of the car, as if to ram home the point that I was going to be a pedestrian from then on.

But there was little time to mourn my "chariot afire": cast by the light of the street lamps, a shadow in the shape of Santa's sleigh and reindeer appeared on the ground in front of us, growing longer as the carriage of carnage drew near.

"Carmine, old chum, I think now is time to hit the proverbial deck."

We dove out of the way just in time as machine-gun fire tore through the mess of overturned garbage cans where we'd been standing. We were able to take shelter behind a big metal dumpster that someone must have rented for their home renovation project.

(I wish I could say that was the last time I did a "dumpster dive," but alas...)

Santa's bullets ricocheted off the thick steel sheeting of the dumpster. (I was a bit disappointed that they didn't make that "pkew" sound like they do in the movies, but never mind.) Then the unmistakable voice of Santa H. Claus boomed out, echoing in the alley.

"Come on out and get your Christmas present, Maloney!"

Man, he must have had a chest cavity the size of the Goodyear blimp.

Another burst of machine-gun fire caromed off the metal that shielded us.

"At least he's only got just the gun," said Carmine.

In response, we were sprayed by a shower of liquid flames that melted all the nearby snow.

"Okay, maybe he's got some other stuff too."

"Why would he pack a flame-thrower?" I asked.

"He's probably too lazy to shovel his driveway."

It looked like we were cornered and running out of time. I decided to try a little gunboat diplomacy, although I realized I was doing it from the wrong end of the gunboat.

"Hold your fire a sec, Claus!" I shouted. "If we're gonna die, at least let us know the reason!"

Another burst of flame roared over our heads.

"*Treason* is the reason this season!" Claus thundered.

Carmine looked at me.

"What the H-E-double-hockey-stick does that mean?" he asked.

"No idea," I said, although it was a bit of a white lie: I had a nagging suspicion that it had something to do with the elf spying on me with Betty, but that didn't make much sense. Why would Kringle go full metal jacket over it?

I drew my revolver and stuck a few bullets in the barrel to top it up. Carmine sat with his back against the dumpster, his arms wrapped around his knees.

"So what now?" he asked. "Do we just wait 'til he runs outta gas?"

There was a "clunk" of metal on metal as a heavy object landed on top of the dumpster, tumbled off the lid, and dropped right between us.

It looked like a cross between an avocado and a little green pineapple. There was a tiny red and white tag on it that read: "To: Cisco. From: Santa."

"Hit the deck, kiddo!"

We practically jumped out of our boots as we dove as far as we could and hit the ground. The grenade exploded, spraying shrapnel and scattering garbage everywhere.

(Being covered in garbage made me nostalgic for those times I'd gotten hired to rummage through people's trash to find dirt on them. Oh, how I longed for simpler cases that didn't involve getting blown up.)

We got to our feet and ended up taking cover behind a second dumpster, next to the first. Luckily for us, whoever was renovating must have been gutting the entire house.

Carmine was curled up in the fetal position, his teeth chattering away like thirty-two dice in a cookie tin.

"I don't wanna die, Cisco! I've barely even lived."

Luckily, I managed to keep hold of my pistol.

"Don't book a date for the Pearly Gates yet, kid. Like Smokey the Bear says, you've got to fight fire with fire."

I raised the gun over the edge of the dumpster, aimed it in Claus's general direction, and squeezed off a few rounds, hoping I wouldn't hit anyone innocent (fat chance in this town).

Santa immediately returned fire. It was a game of tit for rat-a-tat-tat, and I sure didn't enjoy being the tit.

Carmine plugged his ears and shut his eyes.

"I'm highly allergic to bullets," he whined.

"Let's just hope he doesn't have any more grenades," I replied, loading the gun again. "There's only so many dumpsters in this alley."

"This is why *I* should carry a gun, too!"

"Forget it, kid. You can't even use a sharp pencil without hurting yourself."

Santa fired another burst of ammo. I had no idea how long he was prepared to keep shooting at a blunt steel box, but I guess he could afford to waste bullets.

Then his voice boomed out again.

"Come on out! Time for a nice cup of lead nog!"

I tried to listen to his voice to gauge the direction it was coming from, but the gunfire started up again.

"This is getting out of hand," I muttered.

"I'll say," Carmine replied. "That was the worst pun yet."

"We need a distraction."

Carmine looked at me with wide eyes.

"Oh, no. Not again!"

Seeing how it's easier to get forgiveness than permission, I didn't hesitate: I grabbed hold of Carmine by the collar of his coat and the back of his belt, waited for a pause between Santa's machine-gun bursts, and tossed my sidekick behind a nearby group of trash cans.

He landed and rolled like a sack of 'fraidy taters. Sure enough, a trail of machine-gun fire followed him as Santa went after the bait.

I stood up fast as a jack-in-the-box, steadied my elbows on the dumpster lid, and took aim. It was hard to see through the smoke from the grenade and the burning refuse, but about thirty yards away was Santa's sleigh, hovering a few feet in the air and bearing the unmistakably obese outline of the Man in Red, topped with that ridiculous hat with the white pom-pom, which provided a perfect target to aim for.

Santa's Gatling gun was spitting bullets in Carmine's direction. I knew I'd only have this one chance, so I said a prayer to Wyatt Earp (patron saint of steady aim), squeezed the trigger, and fired until every chamber of the gun was empty.

There was a crash, then everything went silent, except for my gun going "click-click, click-click-click."

"Did you get him?" asked Carmine from his shelter.

I peered ahead through the smoke. Santa's sleigh was on the ground.

I'd got him, all right. When I was a kid, we used to shoot at cardboard Santas on people's lawns for target practice.

"I think so. Let's go check."

"I ain't going nowhere!"

"Come on!"

I dragged Carmine out from behind the trash cans and gave him a thorough dusting.

We cautiously crept towards Santa's sleigh. Reindeer scattered and ran off into the streets. I put another bullet in my gun.

"You sure this is safe?" Carmine asked. His knocking knees sounded like an over-caffeinated woodpecker.

A reindeer approached us, its nose glowing bright red. We braced ourselves. Was there going to be a fight?

As it got closer, I noticed something funny about its face. It had a pocket flashlight taped to its snout, with a red gel in front to give it color. The beast trotted right on past us and bounded off to join its kin, presumably to go play some reindeer games (whatever the heck those were). It was a bit anticlimactic to meet the ersatz understudy of the once-proud, if slightly mutated, leader of Santa's cervine entourage, but what can you do? Evidently the original Rudolph had either retired or bought the farm.

We approached Santa's sleigh, which was in bad shape from the fall, its bodywork dented and scraped. Tiny presents in colorful gift wrap and neatly tied bows lay scattered on the pavement around it.

Slumped over the dashboard was old Saint Nick, still clutching his smoking Gatling gun.

For a second, we froze.

"Make sure he's not playing possum," I said. "I got him covered."

While I aimed my gun at the Fat Man in case he made a sudden move, Carmine approached Santa and held a small pocket mirror to his lips.

"He's still breathing!"

"You sure?"

"The mirror's fogging up."

"Maybe it's a false positive."

Carmine leaned in close and sniffed.

"Nope, I'm sure of it. His breath is minty, even. At least he uses mouthwash."

"Where was he hit?" I asked.

Carmine checked him over.

"Can't tell. The whole suit's red."

I took a few steps closer. Claus was an imposing figure, even with his corpus slumped over the dash of his blizzard buggy. I pried the machine gun from his cold, not-quite-dead fingers and tossed it aside.

"Ro...Rosebud," he moaned.

"What's that supposed to be," I wondered aloud, "the name of his sleigh?"

"I think it's these chocolates he's got in his pocket," Carmine replied.

He took his tiny hand out of Santa's pocket, pulled out a small box, and shook it. Inside, chocolate candies rattled around.

"You could at least wait 'til he's dead before you start ransacking his clothes for treats."

"But then it'd be disrespectful."

I facepalmed so hard, it loosened my wisdom teeth.

Carmine popped a couple of the chocolates into his mouth.

"Maybe he wants one?"

Santa made a sudden grab for his throat.

"Shut up, you damned monkey," he growled.

Luckily for Carmine, his pencil-neck was a small target, and Santa missed. Carmine backed away as the momentum from Santa's lunge carried him off the dashboard and through the open side of the sleigh, where he hit the pavement with a dull, heavy thud. He groaned, but stopped moving after that.

Carmine looked at me.

"Guess that's a 'no'."

I pushed up Santa's sleeve and checked his tattooed wrist for a pulse. Nothing.

"At least he doesn't have to worry about cavities," I said. "Or writing us a check."

Obviously Santa's untimely demise didn't put my sidekick off his appetite; he dumped the rest of the chocolates into his mouth and rolled his eyes back from the rush. There was no point trying to stop him, but I felt a pang from my old chocolate addiction, followed by an adverse Pavlovian reaction as memories of the shock therapy kicked in.

"So what are we going to do?" Carmine fretted once the cocoa-buzz subsided. "We killed Saint Nick!"

Police sirens wailed in the distance, getting closer. Someone had probably complained that we'd scratched up their brand new dumpsters.

"We hoof it," I replied, "or you're going to learn the hard way what I meant about soap on a rope."

Chapter 19: The Squat

We hustled away as quickly as we could while the police sirens wailed behind us.

Our discretion wasn't just the better part of valor: although *I* knew I'd shot Santa Claus in self-defense, I wasn't exactly keen to stand up and prove it in front of a judge and twelve of my peers. If my experience with the legal system has taught me anything, it's that a prosecutor can come up with a thousand different ways to paint you guilty, and you can never predict what a dozen yokels who are too dumb to get out of jury duty are going to conclude, especially when celebrity is a factor. Plenty of mooks in this town might sympathize with the White and Red—I wasn't going to take any chances with the courts and risk getting jailed for manslaughter. I'd be sharing prison-space with a bunch of felons who knew I was an ex-cop, which is a sure way to get oneself shanked. Not to mention being forced to shower with all those beady eyes staring at me.

"Where are we going?" wheezed Carmine, already out of breath.

"Shush so I can get my bearings," I replied.

I looked around for landmarks, but didn't recognize anything familiar; there was just a Ferris wheel done up in neon lights, a memorial featuring a WWI-era fighter plane mounted on a plinth, and a quarter-scale replica of the Eiffel Tower that was part of an advertising stunt to promote gourmet French cigarettes.

We could have been anywhere.

My city map was in the glove box of my car, surely reduced to ashes by that point, so I had to try and navigate by following the Earth's magnetic field—lucky thing I'd had a lot of bridgework done, thanks to my wartime chocolate binge.

We finally made our way to an industrial district on the waterfront, not too far from the Easter Bunny's warehouse in Bricktown (though nowhere near as gentrified). There we reached the chained up doors of an abandoned factory building, our destination. I took out my key ring, found the right key, and unlocked the padlock holding the chains.

Carmine moaned as I opened the doors.

"Really, boss? Don't tell me we've hit rock bottom."

"The bottom doesn't get any rockier than this, kid—unless you're Jacques Cousteau."

Back when I enlisted in the Army as a fresh-faced recruit, the war had been in full swing and there was a shortage of training personnel, so we were sent to the Boy Scouts as a stopgap solution. There I earned just about every badge except Reading, First Aid, and Harmonica, and I was instilled with the motto "Be prepared." It might not have helped me much in my career, but it inspired me to keep a squat near the docks in case I ever needed to lie low.

And boy, did I need to lie low.

Even if I escaped the long arm of the law, Santa's elf crew would probably be looking for me, and Plotzky's snowgoons were still at large. I figured it was best that I hole up and drop out of sight for the remainder of the Christmas season, possibly until the New Year. The *next* New Year.

Once we passed through the factory doors, I locked the chains behind me. The place was dusty, dingy and dirty, but those who live in glass houses shouldn't cast the first pearls before swine, right?

We found the makeshift sleeping quarters I had set up after I'd first bought the building a few years back.

That was back in my salad days, just after I'd worked on a big case that netted me a bumper crop of bullion. I was hired to spy on Harvey Mollbanger, a liquor tycoon from Prohibition days who'd gone legit after the Temperance laws had been repealed. His wife suspected him of cheating on her, so she pawned her pearls to pad my pockets, hiring me to do surveillance on him.

It took me months to dig up any dirt on poor old, rich old Harvey, whose day-to-day life was about as spontaneous and exciting as a stamp-collecting conference. I eventually caught him with another woman, which would have been innocent enough if said woman hadn't been an airline stewardess whose undergarments had lost a lot of altitude.

I felt guilty in a sense, because I later found out that Harvey's wife was just looking for an excuse to divorce him so she could take half his money and marry her Calabrese lover—all the while, she'd deliberately neglected her husband's "needs" to ensure that I would eventually catch him committing an indiscretion.

To make a short story long, she got her divorce and paid me handsomely for all those billable hours, using her half of Harvey's fortune. I was worried that Harvey would discover my role in his undoing and come looking for payback, so I used some of the cash to buy the decrepit old factory, intending to use it as a safe house where I could hole up in case of trouble, and maybe flip it once property values went up. Of course I didn't realize that I'd picked it up so cheap because the place was heavily contaminated with industrial pollutants, and only found this out when the city did an assessment of the area and condemned most of the buildings. Property values plummeted, to the point where the factory wasn't worth selling, so I was left holding the hot potato. Oh well; at least the place was finally paying dividends in the form of a place to hide out.

The room I'd set up was furnished with two old cots. Carmine and I each sat on one, causing the springs to squeak. The kid patted down his bedding.

"You sure there's no mice in here, Cisco?"

I shook my head.

"Nah. They all took off when the rats moved in."

He shuddered.

I was bushed. I fluffed my old pillow, which kicked up a cloud of asbestos dust, and then climbed under the blankets of my cot and pulled them over me. Carmine did the same.

"Might as well get some sleep and hope all this blows over soon," I said. "Merry Christmas, kiddo."

"Merry Christmas, boss," he answered, clearly bummed out.

I was an insomniac and didn't normally enjoy the experience of going to sleep at night. There was something disturbing about waiting alone in the quiet darkness for unconsciousness to slip over me—I always thought of sleep as "Death Junior." But after a day of being chased around by elves and snowmen and reindeer, not to mention the gunfights and grenades and flames and imminent danger of getting killed to death, it was almost enough to make me wish for the sweet serenity of the hereafter, a.k.a. good old oblivion. Sleep sounded just dandy at that point, and maybe after a bit of shuteye, things would start to look better in the morning.

Something in my pocket was poking into my leg: I reached in and realized it was the syringe with Plotzky's remains inside. *A lot of good this'll do me now*, I thought. I put the syringe back in my pocket, tucked my gun under the covers beside me, then sank into a deep slumber within seconds of my head kissing the pillow...

I had a machete held tightly in my right hand, while the other hand was holding a meringue pie...or maybe it was a soufflé. My old schoolteacher walked into the room and asked me if I'd done my homework. All my classmates turned in my direction, and I realized I wasn't wearing any pants. I had my socks on, so I tried to pull them up over me, but they were made of denim and wouldn't stretch far enough, so I ran out of the classroom. In the hall, I was met by an Algerian Cossack who wanted to tell me that his real name was Grygoriy Yussef Rodriguez von Tamerlane the Fourth of Bavaria, which was impossible, since he could barely get the words out. He presented me with a horse and told me to deliver a paradiddle to the King of Flams, who was having his drawbridge re-shingled. Once I arrived at the castle and inspected the bridgework, I felt my teeth coming loose and flicked at the dangling cuspids with the tip of my tongue. I was disturbed to think I'd never be able to chew my way out of the leather harness I was wearing, but a smack from a riding crop wielded by the mistress of the dungeon quickly took my mind off mastication. She smacked the backs of my thighs and shouted: "The note, Cisco! The note! THE NOTE!"

Man, I always get weird dreams when I go to sleep dead tired. I woke up in a groggy daze, still hearing the mistress's voice in my head as the dream faded away.

Carmine was sawing logs. I sat up with a strong impression that someone was in the room with us. There was a folded piece of paper on my pillow with a little spot of my drool on it. I wiped my mouth with a corner of the bed sheet, lit my trusty Zippo™ lighter so I could see better, and unfolded it.

In the flickering light of the Zippo™, I read the fancy cursive handwriting:

"Wake up, sleepyhead! Look under your pillow."

The note was signed with a lipstick kiss mark, and smelled like it had been dipped in breath-mint perfume.

I reached under my pillow, found a stack of twenty-dollar bills wrapped in a silver ribbon, and wondered how they could have gotten there. How could someone manage to break in? Had I forgotten to lock the doors? Was all this still part of the dream?

I searched the dark room but saw no one, so I grabbed my gun, pulled the blankets off me, and stood up out of the cot, the sleep glue still stuck in my watery eyes.

I could just make out a shadowy figure standing in the corner. I took aim with the revolver, but gradually lowered it as my eyes adjusted and I recognized her.

I holstered the peacemaker.

"How did you get in?" I asked.

Betty stepped out of the shadows, dressed in her gown and tiara and holding her sparkly wand. She waved the wand and vanished in a puff of pixie dust, and then reappeared right next to me. Needless to say, I had a bit of a shock: in my experience, when a woman disappears, it's usually for good.

"I'm the Tooth Fairy, remember?" she said with a smirk that dimpled her cheeks. "I don't have to go down sooty smokestacks like that corpulent Kris Kringle. He probably had to butter his giant butt to squeeze it down all those chimneys."

I noticed she referred to Santa in the past tense.

"So you know what happened to Claus?"

Stupid question.

She planted a kiss on my forehead that sent shockwaves of pleasure around my skull.

"Of course," she cooed. "I know all about my big, brave hero. Thanks to you, I don't have to live in fear of that monstrous lardbag anymore."

Carmine stirred in his cot and wheezed. It sounded like his adenoids were acting up again.

"Looks like you don't have to leave town after all," I muttered.

She gave me a squeeze on the cheeks that forced my lips apart, and inspected my front teeth.

"Not without you, I'm not. I mean, look at those marvelous incisors. Now come on, let's get away from this dump."

She grabbed me by the arm and tried to drag me off, but I held back.

"Hold on a minute. I can't leave Carmine alone like this."

She pouted.

"But you have no problem leaving *me* all alone?"

"Somehow, I think you'll do just fine."

She waved her wand, which shimmered in an arc of dust. A suitcase appeared on the floor in front of us.

"I'll need a bodyguard, Mister Maloney. And I think you'll find the compensation quite agreeable."

She waved the wand again, but nothing happened. She tapped it on her palm a couple of times.

"Batteries must be getting low."

With another wave of the wand, the suitcase snapped open to reveal stacks of bills inside, wrapped neatly in bundles with silver bows around them. It was the most massive mound of money I'd ever seen.

"Great gallopin' goat herds!" I exclaimed. "Where'd you get that kind of cabbage?"

"Never mind that," she replied. "Why don't we take a well-deserved vacation, you and me? There's plenty here for us to have a grand old time somewhere warm and sunny. Tahiti, maybe?"

She put her arms around me and drew me close. Before I could react, she planted a kiss square on my lips.

I could hear romantic string music swelling up again, only this time I wasn't sure if it was real, or just my smitten imagination.

Carmine sat up in his cot.

"Where's that music coming from?" he asked.

Then he saw me and Betty boxing tonsils.

"Gadzooks, Cisco! How did *she* get in here?"

Then he took a look at the suitcase full of greenbacks.

"Stacks a'mighty, who brought the mint?"

Mint?

I unlipped the girl and held her back at arm's length.

"Wait a second! Carmine, you said Santa's breath smelled like mouthwash, right?"

"Yup. Wintermint, I think."

I shook a finger at Betty.

"You, sister, have been kissing Santa Claus!"

There was a musical stinger played by the shabby brass band, which was huddled together in a dark corner at the other side of the room. (Good gravy, was there no respect for private property anymore?) They were immediately set upon and attacked by the string quartet, which had been playing the romantic music. An all-out brawl ensued.

Betty chuckled and brushed my pointing finger aside like she'd just been offered the wrong brand of caviar.

"Me, smootching Santa? How does that follow?" she asked. "Maybe we use the same brand of mouthwash."

I tried to contain myself, but it all came gushing out like ketchup from the bottle.

"You had your claws in Claus, too! One of his elves saw us kissing through your bedroom window. That's why he came after us: it was jealousy!"

She put a soft hand to my forehead.

"Darling, don't be delirious. Are you running a fever or something?"

It's true that I was getting hot under more than just the collar, and her Florence Nightingale routine didn't help stop my temperature from rising. I did my best to resist the soft, tender touch of her hands—she must have spent a fortune on moisturizer and manicures.

"You set it up so Santa would find out we were snogging on the sly," I said. "You wanted to make him jealous on purpose."

"Now why would I do a thing like that?"

She pouted and started playing Rummoli with my coat buttons.

"To make him come after me," I said. "Then I was forced to shoot him in self-defense. You wanted him out of the way, didn't you? Unless you expected him to finish me off? In which case, I'm even *more* ticked."

I admit I was clutching at straws a bit, but sometimes you have to go out on a limb if you want to pick the fruit.

She laughed gaily, then flashed a wicked, polished smile, her teeth gleaming like the reflectors on a kid's bicycle

"You're a keeper, Cisco. I'd never put you in any kind of danger...outside my boudoir, that is."

"You planned it all along," I stammered. "Starting with Plotzky..."

My brain tried its best to fit all the puzzle pieces into place, though it had to swim against the tide of hormones flooding it like a testosterone tsunami. Her hand was still on my sweating brow—I probably shouldn't tell you what her other hand was doing, so just imagine the most pleasant medical examination you've ever had, and you're pretty darn close.

"I was wondering how you got into Plotzky's apartment," I continued. "He let you in because you two were having an affair! Then after you killed him, you shot the Easter Bunny with a crossbow from your store; another lover crossed off the list! You ran out of the warehouse and used your wand to disappear, leaving the jingle bell strap to convince me it was Claus, the last leg of your paramour tripod. And for the final act, you lured me into your web like a black widow does a fly, only to use me to bait Santa Claus himself for the grand finale. And now all three of them are dead!"

She purred into my ear, close enough to tickle the hairs I'd neglected to pluck.

"Oh my, that leaves a power vacuum, doesn't it?" she whispered. "Maybe this town could use a woman's touch in running things."

I pushed her away.

"You had me do your dirty work, and I didn't even bill for it! Of all the quadruple-crossin', deceitful dames I ever met..."

She whipped out her wand and waved it menacingly.

"Mind your manners, Fauntleroy!" she cackled. "Like you've seen, I can make problems disappear mighty quick."

Carmine and I backed away from her, but she advanced on us like a tigress on her prey. Having seen her twinkle-stick in action, I knew there was no point reaching for my gun.

"So what do you say, loverboy?" she asked. "Are you coming with me, or are you staying with Runty Wilt-skin, here?"

I looked down at Carmine, then back at Betty.

"I'm staying here," I heard myself say. "Someone has to tell the cops what you did."

"In that case," she replied, "I'm starting to think maybe you've outlived your usefulness."

I remembered reading in the papers a few years before about the government debating a law banning magic wands. At the time I thought it was just a frivolous infringement on our rights, but now I could see the point, even if the entire issue was as crazy as a rabid wombat tea party.

The wand sparked in Betty's hand as she aimed it at us. We prepared for the worst...

Just then there was a commotion outside, like the sound of dozens of wolves all trying to hork up a massive loogie, followed by a crash. The front doors of the building were smashed open by a mob of snowmen using a giant Christmas tree as a battering ram (jumpin' jack-in-the-box: they didn't even have the patience to take the decorations off it first).

Once inside, they immediately spotted us.

"There they is!" one of them shouted.

From the gaudy scarf, I recognized him as the leader of the gang that had cornered us in the alley behind Cupid's. Before we knew it, we were surrounded by angry-looking blobs of snow and ice.

"Well looky what we gots here," said the leader. "Cisco Maloney, his pet monkey, and little miss Tooth Fairy. Seems like we got our Christmas wish, after all."

Betty drew closer to us, keeping the wand clutched in her hand.

"Do you expect us to confess?" I asked.

"We're not that sophisticated, really," he answered. "Mostly, we expect you to pay."

"Uh, I'm a little short right now. How about I get back to you Tuesday?"

"Not *that* kind of pay," he growled. "I mean pay, as in *dearly*. And this time, I don't see any bags of salt lying around."

The rest of the gang chuckled and grunted with approval. They drew their well-honed icicles and closed in.

I unholstered my gun and aimed at the leader, doing my best to sound assertive yet nonchalant (you had to get the cadence just right or it all fell apart).

"Maybe you should cast your coal peepers on this, slushy boy," I said. "I'd step back if I were you."

The leader laughed. His gang followed suit with a volley of guffaws.

"You think we're scared of your little pipsqueak peashooter? Why don't you try it? Go on, shoot me."

He inched a bit closer. Did he think I was bluffing? I pointed the pistol at his big, round head, but the snowman ringleader didn't seem the slightest bit concerned, and kept his advance, icicle in hand. I'd never shot a snowman before. *Would a shot even hurt him?* I wondered. *A red-hot bullet would probably just...*

BANG!

Betty whacked me in the arm, which made my finger squeeze the trigger.

Everything went silent for a second.

A tiny hole appeared in the middle of the snowman leader's forehead. His eyes crossed as he looked up at it.

"Ouchy," he said. Then he smiled a crooked grin.

His gang hooted with derision. They even high-fived each other, which I thought was a bit sophomoric.

I stared hard at Betty.

"I had the situation under control, you know."

"Aw, our first fight," she replied. "But you'd better let me handle this one, big boy. You're in way over your head."

It was time for a little emergency diplomacy.

"C'mon, fellas," I said to the snowmen as I held my hands up and dangled the gun on my thumb. "I thought revenge was a dish best served cold. Why don't you all check back in with us in February sometime? My schedule's clear."

None of them answered. Instead, they closed in with their sharps. So much for negotiations...

Then there was a clicking sound. I thought maybe it was Carmine's teeth chattering again, but realized it was coming from outside. The snowmen blinked and turned around to face the door where the noise was coming from. It got louder and louder, like a swarm of alarm clocks. The chains on the doors rattled...the building shook...the snowmen hollered:

"ELVES!"

Sure enough, a blurry swarm of mechanical elves rushed into the building.

"Re-venge...re-venge...re-venge..." they droned in their high-pitched robotic voices.

As they came within fighting range, the snowmen quickly turned their attention away from us and locked in combat with their mortal enemies.

"Hands off!" shouted the snowman leader at the robotic intruders. "They's ours!"

There was an avalanche of uppercuts, right and left crosses and haymakers as the snowman gang defended themselves against the onslaught. Also, I heard a couple of swear words that were completely new to me.

The elves, meanwhile, weren't just a bunch of wind-up pushovers. They had obviously trained in the ancient art of tae-kno-shih-tsu (I guess they were all made in Japan?), and served it back to the snowmen with karate chops, kung-fu steaks, and judo cold cuts.

The battle was low-down and dirty: snow and metal parts went flying everywhere as the snowmen and elves fought each other for the right to be the first to tear us limb from limb. I saw plenty of moves that would have been considered unsportsmanlike in an Ultimate Fighting Championship match: the eye-gouge, the Bronx basketweave, the Tijuana tamale, and even the dreaded Siamese screwpull.

With the unsavory melee raging between us and the only exit, Betty, Carmine and I could do nothing but stand back and watch.

"Pathetic losers," Betty snorted. "We can just sit back and let them fight it out. Too easy."

But not all of them ignored us. An elf broke through the line of snowmen and ran up to Betty, brandishing a shiv made of candy cane. I pistol-whipped it with the butt of my gun, smashing its head in. Gears and cogs fell out of its brain case as it tumbled to the floor.

"Don't count on it," I said. "It's us they're after!"

A few more elves followed, rushing at me. Carmine tripped up the first one, and the rest came tumbling after. A few hard stomps of the boot cleaned their clocks, but then two snowmen came at us with sharpened icicles.

I picked up an old chair and used it like a lion tamer to keep them at bay, but unfortunately I didn't have a whip. They swiped at me with their icy daggers, but I managed to break off the tips with a couple swings of the furniture, and then with a final heave, knocked them down like bowling pins. We wouldn't be able to stand our ground forever, though, and there were still plenty of them left.

"Carmine?!" I hollered. "I could use a little help over here!"

I looked to my right and saw Carmine pinned to the floor by a snowman and an elf, who both traded punches and slaps as they fought over which one would get to punch and slap him.

"He's mine!" growled the snowman.

"Ne-ga-tive!" droned the elf.

I ran over and with a "flying leap" move that I'd learned from watching carny wrestling matches as a kid, knocked them off my sidekick and into the general melee, where they were caught up in the battle between snowman and machine.

I pulled Carmine up from the ground.

"You okay?"

"Probably not for long."

Betty twirled her wand.

"That's enough fooling around, then," she said as she concentrated on the brawling mob, lining them up in her sightline. "Go on, boys, huddle together and make this easier."

Carmine and I hugged each other.

"Not you, you dolts!"

She gave the wand a majestic wave and—POOF!—every last one of the elves and snowmen disappeared into thin air.

And it was over, just like that.

The room fell silent as it filled with fairy dust, no doubt the toxic byproduct of teleportation.

"Holy vanishing ink, they're gone!" Carmine exclaimed, displaying his mastery of the self-evident.

"Yeah," I said, "but guess who's not?"

Betty blew some dust off her wand, then twirled it in our direction. Despite how ridiculous that sounds, it was actually pretty threatening.

"Where did you send them?" I asked, stalling for time.

"I believe they're floating around somewhere in the South Pacific, maybe off the coast of Borneo or Java," she said as she tossed her hair back. "In any case, the fat flakes have probably melted into soup by now, and the salt water is sure to bring a rusty end to those walking cuckoo clocks."

She took a step closer.

"Now, as for you two little nuisances, what do you say we send you to the South Pole, hmm? I hear it's a two-thousand-mile hike to the beach. You might reach it just in time to starve to death."

She raised the wand. Carmine and I cringed and braced ourselves to be teleported, coach class...

And then uniformed police officers stormed in through the breached door, guns drawn.

"Police! Nobody move!"

"More distraction," said Betty with a frown as she turned to face the fuzz. "Let's hope there's enough juice to send these pigs back to Hogtown."

The wand sparked.

To my astonishment, Carmine ran up behind her and snatched it right out of her hand.

"Gotcha!" he shouted. Then he dashed back and hid behind me.

Betty spun around.

"Argh! You little weasel!"

She stomped her heel as her eyes flung daggers through my pelvis at Carmine.

"Freeze! Hands in the air!" shouted the boys in blue.

She slowly put her hands up.

Man, was I ever glad to see them. (The cops I mean, not her hands. Although they really were nicely manicured and clean, in contrast to how dirty they were in the metaphorical department).

"I said freeze!" shouted an officer, who glared at me and Carmine. "You two need a hearing aid?"

Whoops, forgot they also meant us. We put our hands up as the police moved in, their guns aimed at our heads.

"Nice work, buddy," I whispered to Carmine. The words of praise sounded strange without the usual sarcasm.

The cops put Betty in handcuffs and dragged her away. They cuffed us, too, as they were all too young to recognize me—it was mostly juniors and rookies who got stuck with the Christmas Eve shifts, while the old salts with seniority got to stay home with their wives, children, and leather-bound whiskey flasks.

We were escorted outside to a waiting paddy wagon. I couldn't really complain about getting the perp treatment, seeing how we'd just had our bacon snatched from the frying pan. Considering that a) my car was now a pile of charred scrap, b) I was facing eviction from my apartment, c) would probably lose my office, d) I'd fallen hard for a girl who then tried to kill me, and e) my prospects of seeing any profit for all my trouble were quickly galloping off into the sunset, getting arrested was an improvement.

Heck, I'd have liked to see things try to get any worse.

Chapter 20: The Wrap

After a silent ride in the back of the paddy wagon, two young officers hauled Carmine and yours truly into the police station.

Chief Murray was waiting for us.

"Well, well, well," he crowed, "if it ain't the man who shot Santa Claus!"

It was the first time I'd seen him happy in years. It sure looked like he'd been saving it up: the Cheshire Cat could take lessons from this guy on how to look smug. Talk about *Schadenfreude*.

"It was self-defense, Murray. I swear."

Carmine pitched in.

"He tried to kill us first!"

Murray snorted and shook his head.

"Who could blame him? But I'm not half as interested in Santa Claus as I am in meeting the saucy little spitfire I've heard so much about."

There was a commotion behind us, which quickly upgraded to a scuffle: Dutch Blinsky and a few other uniformed cops walked in through the doors escorting Betty by the arms, her wrists handcuffed in front of her. Anger was plastered all over her face; she looked like a caged wild animal that was getting poked at with a stick.

Murray's eyes opened wide when he spotted her in person for what I presumed was the first time. He licked his thumb and ran it across his eyebrows.

I knew exactly what was on his mind: back when we were partners, he would always put the moves on every good-looking gal we met, just when I'd finally decided to gather up the courage to contemplate the thought of possibly asking them out on a date. Under that hard-nosed exterior he was an incorrigible bird-dog, and it was obvious that Betty's charms didn't fail to make an impression on the old lecher.

Dutch was carrying her suitcase in one hand, and in the other he held her sparkly wand wrapped in a piece of cloth. He passed these to Murray with a nod, then went back and planted himself next to Betty like a big, dumb tree.

She threw the temper tantrum into reverse when she saw me, and shifted to a full-on damsel-in-distress act.

"Cisco, honey! Tell them how Santa tried to kill us."

Murray looked at me sidewise.

"*Honey*? Don't tell me she's got her hooks in you, too?"

I avoided looking him in the eye.

"I don't know what you're talking about."

"The black widow over there. My men have been watching her for months."

"Perverts!" shouted Betty. "You've been spying on me without just cause. I haven't done anything wrong!"

"Well, that's funny," Murray shot back. "We happened to be running surveillance on Plotzky, the Easter Bunny, and Santa Claus, and couldn't help noticing that you were spending lots of time with all three of them. So we got a warrant to keep tabs on you too, and found out all about your little liaisons."

Carmine knitted his brow.

"Liaisons?"

"It's something French people do," I explained. Then I turned to Murray.

"What did you dig up on her?"

"Nothing at first. She didn't have a record, not even a traffic ticket. But after Plotzky was killed, we watched her round-the-clock. She was seen taking a crossbow off the shelf in her store. Then the next thing you know, the Easter Bunny winds up with a hole in his back."

He held out his palm.

"I'll take the bolt, if you don't mind."

There was no point trying to cover up the fact that I'd snatched a key piece of evidence from a murder scene. I took out the crossbow bolt, still wrapped in the bloody handkerchief, and handed it to him. Like I said earlier, taking it hadn't been the brightest idea; I guess hindsight is 20/20 after all.

Murray stepped up to me and breathed his coffee-and-chaw halitosis right in my face.

"I should charge you right now for tampering with evidence, but I don't need the extra paperwork. So scram, and don't let me see you for at least another year."

He turned to the young officers who'd brought us in.

"Let these schmucks go. We've got enough on our hands as it is."

They unlocked our handcuffs. Carmine yelped as the metal pinched his wrist.

"Yowz! That ouches!"

A stone-faced rookie handed me back my revolver. I looked in his eyes and saw nothing of the ambitious, plays-by-his-own-rules spirit that I remembered having when I first put on that uniform. Where was the derring-do in the kids these days? The moxie? The gumption? The other synonyms? I suddenly felt really old.

I holstered the pistol, glad to have it back.

"I guess I owe you a thanks, Murray. You don't even want to ask me about Santa Claus?"

"We've been trying to pin something on him for years, but nothing stuck" he said. "You just saved us a lot of trouble. That's the only reason I'm turning a blind eye to the bolt business."

So that was that. I took the strap of jingle-bells from my coat pocket and handed it to Betty.

"Here," I said, "you might want these back."

Murray snatched them out of my open mitt.

"I'll take those, too."

He gave them a playful shake, and then remembered he was supposed to be in charge.

"Uh, it's evidence. Plus, they'll be good for our Christmas party tonight."

He hastily grabbed Betty's suitcase, put it on top of his desk, and opened it. The stacks of bills were still stuffed inside. I froze at the sight of all that money, a fraction of which would have solved all my problems (and then created some new ones, which it would keep on solving in a vicious cycle until I was broke again).

"Bring her here and take her prints," ordered Murray.

The recruits dragged Betty before him and started inking the details of her digits while Murray sifted through the banknotes.

I looked at the fallen fairy, trying to make eye contact and come up with some poignant parting words.

"Heat packs and crossbows, huh? Guess you like 'em silent but deadly."

She and the others started snickering.

"What? What'd I say?"

She wiped her eyes.

"I like a man who makes me laugh, Cisco, but it helps when it's intentional."

I pointed at her cuffs, changing the subject.

"Guess there won't be anyone around to take care of your old man now."

Murray butted in.

"Oh, Sketchley wasn't her real father. She was dating him."

"*Dating* him?"

He checked a file on his desk.

"Sorry, I mean she was *se*dating him: keeping the poor guy doped up so she could control his store. Let's just say Sketchley was a few jokers short of a full deck."

"He did seem a few clubs shy of a flush," said Carmine.

Betty rolled her eyes.

"You men and your stupid poker metaphors."

To my surprise, my feet brought me a few steps closer to her until we were face-to-face.

"It's really a shame, Betty," I said. "If circumstances were different, like maybe if you weren't a deceptive, psychopathic, murderous, obsessive molar hoarder..."

Before Dutch could stop her, she grabbed me by the lapels, permanently staining them with the ink on her fingers.

"We could have had something special, Cisco."

She pulled me close and jammed her lips against mine, bringing back the fleeting sensation of vertigo mixed with cardiac arrhythmia. The romantic string music cued up again, not played very well this time; the bruised and bandaged string quartet was over in the corner, trying its best to get through the tune without falling to pieces. I guess the brass band must have given them a run for their pesos, but I was too dizzy to pay attention.

"All right, all right," interrupted Murray. "Enough with the lip wrestling. Get her out of here, Dutch."

Dutch grabbed Betty by the shoulders and pulled her away.

"Come on, lady," he said.

I snapped out of it.

"How long do you suppose she'll be on the inside?" I asked Murray.

"I've already talked to the prosecutor. He's going to push for a combined sentence of 247 years. Of course, thanks to these soft-on-crime politicians, she'll probably only serve half of it."

We all stared as Dutch hauled her off toward the detention block.

"Who'd have thought?" I muttered, mostly to myself. "She almost took over the city's entire underworld. That would have brought in enough dough to buy every molar and cuspid in town."

Carmine whistled.

"Talk about platinum-blonde ambition."

Betty wriggled as she fought against Dutch's butcher-hook grip.

"You haven't won, Chief!" she spat. "If I go to the big house, someone else will take my place!"

"Who the hell would want to be a tooth fairy?" asked Murray.

Betty drew a revolver from under the folds of her gown, pointed it at Dutch's head, and cocked it.

"Oh, I know a dentist or two who might be keen."

Where the hell did she get a gun?

The pistol looked familiar. I patted the holster under my coat: it was empty.

"Much obliged, sugar-slacks," she said to me. Then she turned to Murray. "Now I'll take my wand, if you don't mind, or your overgrown mule here gets it."

Making a face like a bowl of sour milk, Murray slowly unwrapped the cloth from the wand.

"*And* the suitcase!" she added.

He stood up, shut the suitcase, and carried them over. I have to admit, it was almost worth having my gun stolen to see that smug look on his puss deflate and wrinkle up like a drying prune.

"On the floor, copper," she snapped at him as she snatched the wand with her free hand. "Then back off nice and slow."

Murray put the suitcase down on the floor in front of her and slowly backed towards his desk.

Betty twirled the wand and the cuffs vanished. She shoved Dutch away, tossed me the gun, and picked up the suitcase.

"Catch, loverboy! And sayonara, suckers..."

She waved the wand. Her body flickered in and out of sight for a few seconds, but she failed to vanish. Surprised, she tapped the wand against the suitcase.

"Damn it! Why did I buy those off-brand batteries?"

There were a dozen hammer clicks from a dozen police specials as the officers in the room drew their guns and took aim.

"Looks like you've run out of power," I said, trying not to collapse from my own gravitas.

She shrugged.

"Looks like you're not the only dead weight I'm going to have to ditch, Cisco," she said.

She dropped the suitcase, waved the wand again, and vanished completely this time, leaving a puff of fairy dust behind.

Murray rushed over to the spot where Betty had been standing, but the old lug was way too late.

"Drat and tarnation!" he spat. "We had her!"

He turned to me and shook an accusing fist.

"It's all your fault! You let her take your gun! What a time to go all soft in the head over some little piece of fluff!"

He stamped his feet.

"Looks like you got a bit soft yourself," I shot back. "She was *your* prisoner."

Murray erupted like a constipated Krakatoa.

"That's the last time I let you carry a loaded weapon in this precinct!"

Loaded? I popped open the cylinder of my six-gun. Every single chamber was empty. I stifled a laugh.

"This'll put a smile back on your face, Murray," I said. "Would you believe I forgot to put bullets in it?"

I thought Murray was going to yank out every last remaining strand of his hair, starting with what was left at the top of his crown and working his way down to the toe-knuckles.

"Aaaaaaarrrrgh!"

That was all I could make out. The rest was drowned out by BLEEPs.

Chapter 21: The Epilogue

Murray stormed off to go punch things in frustration. There was no point in hanging around, so Carmine and I headed for the exit. I wasn't sure where we were going to go: my car was totaled, my landlady was ticked, and my reputation was toast.

It seemed like every time a good-lookin' moll gave me the time of day, she turned out to be a first-degree murderer who would trick me into shooting someone. Sometimes a humble private eye just can't get a break, even at Christmas.

Usually, when I'm feeling down in the dumps, I think of others who've had it worse than me, so I gave it a try.

I thought about Plotzky, the displaced snowman who overcame the odds and won the hearts of children everywhere with nothing but his raw talent. So he sold a few snowballs on the side...so what? There are worse things kids could be messing around with. He didn't deserve what he got.

I thought about the snowmen Betty had whisked away. It was a relief to know they wouldn't be coming after me anymore (or so I hoped), but could they be blamed for wanting to avenge one of their own? There was something admirable about their doggedness: at least they shared a sense of loyalty that you don't see too often in regular folks.

I thought about the Easter Bunny, who'd seemed like a pretty decent guy; whatever his vices might have been, he didn't deserve to get framed, shot, and made into a call girl's Christmas present to herself.

And then I thought about Santa. Claus had the world at his fingertips: money, fame, women, his own underworld empire, complete with theme park...and ended up paying the ultimate price, all over a jealous fit of imagined rivalry, orchestrated by the one girl he wanted but couldn't have. It just goes to show that the bigger, fatter and jollier they are, the harder they fall.

Thinking about the Fat Man gave me a pang of conscience. I never felt good about myself after I shot someone, especially if they bought the Big Ticket to Restville. You'd think I'd have gotten used to it after serving in the war and on the police force, but it always gnawed away at me like mice on telephone wires.

Thankfully, Carmine derailed my morbid train of thought.

"What are we gonna do now, boss?"

"Might as well go back to the office and make some horrible eggnog before they repossess my eggbeater."

"You keep eggs there?"

"No. There's plenty enough on my face."

As we reached the doors of the station, we heard the brass band playing Dixieland-style Christmas carols. Obviously, the precinct party was getting into swing.

Carmine and I walked through the station doors. The air was still, and the snow had finally stopped falling. The city was as calm as a Japanese tea garden in the eye of a hurricane.

A snowball whacked me in the side of the head, knocking off my fedora. Laughter burst forth from a gang of teenage misfits across the street. "Merry Christmas, loser!" one of them hollered.

"Hey!" shouted Carmine. "That's my buddy you just hit!"

To my surprise, he took off after the juvenile delinquent who'd lobbed the snowball, caught him by the scruff, and gave him a thrashing fit for Dennis the Menace. The rest of them scurried away into the night.

Shaking the fluffy stuff from my head, I picked my hat up from the sidewalk. At least the snowball didn't have a rock in it, which was one upside to the riddance of Plotzky's gang. I reached into my pocket for a handkerchief to wipe myself off and poked my pinkie on something sharp. Ouch!

It was the syringe I'd filled with Plotzky's remains. I took it out of my pocket and had another look at the liquid inside.

"What's that?" Carmine asked as he trotted back, having sent the little scamp running back to juvie headquarters with freshly tanned hindquarters.

"Plotzky's corpse-juice. I sucked it from the bucket just before you up-chucked in it."

He peered at the syringe.

"What are you gonna do with it?"

"Not much we can use it for, except maybe to pay our last respects. You want to say something?"

"I'm not one for speeches, but I'll try."

He cleared his throat.

"Plotzky was a talented performer who touched children everywhere (wait, that didn't sound right). Through the miracle of radio and television broadcasting, he gave us all the gifts of laughter, wonder, and product placement. He will be missed by anyone who is young at heart and soft of head. Amen."

To my surprise, he made the sign of the cross, followed by a military salute.

Not one to stand on ceremony, I squirted the syringe into a nearby snow bank, and then tossed it into a garbage can that had "Keep Wurstburg Clean" stenciled on it.

Carmine put his arm down.

"Not much of a funeral, was it, boss?"

"We can't all have the luxury, kid. Doesn't matter anyway...it's not like he's going to come back and rate it."

There was a crackling sound coming from the snow bank.

Carmine and I turned to look, and saw crystals of snow rising up in a lattice structure, which took the form of three stacked balls that rose and expanded until they reached my height.

The structure was a no-frills snowman, without all the usual accessories. It twitched a little, flopped over onto the ground, and then sprang back up again, this time with two rocks in the top snowball where the eyes would normally be, and two twigs for arms stuck into either side of the middle.

The figure turned to us. A mouth opened up below the eyes as it spoke.

"Whěre am I?" it asked in a Slavic accent. "Whât day it is?"

Stunned, I could barely get the answer out.

"It's Christmas Eve," I said. "You're at police headquarters."

It looked around, then gave me the once-over.

"Poliče? You not poliče, are yóu?"

"No. I was just leaving."

"Whât háppen in the łast twenty-fóur hóurs?"

"Not much...other than Plotzky, Santa Claus and the Easter Bunny getting killed."

"Is that źó? You haven't heard anything about a wóman with płâtinum-błónde hair, hâve yóu?"

"The Tooth Fairy? She was arrested, but she used her wand to get away."

The snowman looked at me funny, then flashed a broad grin.

"I cán live vith that. Thânks a lót, chump!"

The snowman shook my hand vigorously, gave me a friendly smack on the shoulder, and slipped his other stick hand in my coat pocket.

"By the vay, pal, gót a smóke? Maybe a little míckey of vódka?"

I took a step back to stop him rummaging around. Good thing my wallet was in my pants.

"Sorry, I'm tapped out at the moment. Say, are you really..."

He put a twiggy finger to my lips.

"Tút-tút-tút, Little Jack Hórner. Let's nót give the game avay. Just act like yóu never saw."

And with that, he turned around and tap-danced off into the night, chuckling to himself and singing a filthy sea shanty about two sailors and a bilge pump.

"That was him!" said Carmine, snapping out of his state of shock. "I'd know that voice anywhere. But how could he be back?"

"I guess snowmen have nine lives."

Just then, Dutch walked out through the station doors. He was covered in tinsel and wearing a Santa hat, and held the strap of jingle bells in one hand and a big glass of punch in the other. The punch smelled like a mixed-berry aftershave.

"Hey there, Cisco," he said. "That was sure some hard luck you got tonight."

"Tell me about it," I replied. "Although you'd think I'd be getting used to it by now."

"Sorry things didn't turn out in your favor. The girl mighta got away, but it's not a total loss."

I guess he was half right: we still had a good chunk of the hundred dollars Santa had given us, but that would barely cover my bar tab at the Lakeside, let alone rent, food, and other frivolities.

"Maybe for you, Dutch," I said, "but it's the end of the line for me. I'm finished now. No more detective business, no more freelancing. I'll probably have to get a job doing security at a department store."

He cut me off (which was a first: normally, Dutch needed a few seconds to catch up).

"Well, you never know what might come your way. You should try to keep *abreast* of the situation."

He tapped his fist against his chest, shaking the jingle bells.

I stood there, gape-mouthed.

"What?"

The big galoot gave me a not-so-subtle nudge with his elbow.

"You know, the grass is always greener in the other *pocket*."

"I'm afraid I don't quite follow."

He undid the top button of his jacket.

"Sometimes you've gotta push the *envelope*."

From inside his jacket, there was something white poking out.

"Dutch, is there something you're trying to..."

He clapped his hand over my mouth.

"Shhhh. If you can't take the hint, then I guess I'm gonna have to serve it to you."

He took a thick white envelope out of his breast pocket and stuck it in my hand.

"Aw, come on...you're giving me a fine? I thought Murray said I was off the hook!"

Dutch winked and shook his head.

"You are. I don't think Murray needs all the evidence in that girl's suitcase."

Was I hearing him right?

I tore open the envelope.

My eyes bulged out of their sockets.

Carmine got on his tippy-toes to try and look.

"What is it? Lemme see!"

Lo and behold, the envelope was filled with my favorite denominations of sweet legal tender. There was enough in there to pay our bills, get a new car—okay, a used one—and still have a bit left over for a traditional Maloney Christmas dinner: turkey sandwiches at Schlmozzle's Deli.

"The Chief hasn't counted it all yet," said Dutch. "He won't notice anything missing."

"Wow, Dutch...I mean, thanks. But why are you doing this?"

"Murray gave me a written warning just for taking a bathroom break. He's turning into a real control freak."

"I get that, but I still don't see why you're sticking your neck out for me like this."

Dutch smiled broadly.

"Murray's ego won't be so puffed up as long as you're still a thorn in his backside."

It was a bit of a backsided compliment, I guess, but I wasn't going to look it in the mouth.

"Shucks, pal. I...I don't know what to say."

Dutch hiccupped and took a gulp from his punch glass.

"Just shut up and get out of here before I run out of Christmas spirits."

He raised his glass as he headed back to the party, jingling the bells and singing along to the brass band's tune. Not in key, mind you, but anyways...

I stuffed the envelope into my pocket. Carmine stared up at me with an expectant look in his eyes.

"Boss, how much is in there?"

"Unfortunately, not enough to save Cisco Maloney Investigative Services, Inc. I'm going to have to shut it down."

"Shut it down? How come?"

"Change of name. From now on it's 'Maloney & Appelbaum.' Or maybe we can call it 'Maloney-Appel' for short? Naw, that sounds too fruity. 'Maloney & Appelbaum' it is."

"You mean it? Gee, that's swell of you, boss!"

"I'm not your boss anymore. Looks like we're in business, *partner*."

I grabbed his hand to shake on it.

"Partner?" he asked. "As in, fifty-fifty?"

"Fifty-fifty, Mister Appelbaum, and to all a good night. Now come on: let's go see if we can find that crazy old lady's cat."

THE END

ABOUT THE AUTHOR

David Ray Pauwels has one wife, two parents, three children, and four goals in life: 1) keep the wife happy, 2) make the parents proud, 3) raise the children right, and 4) find time for other goals. One of these is writing farfetched stories that have absolutely nothing to do with the human condition, current events, or popular appeal. He lives in Canada and his hobbies include listening to music and tasting food. He also enjoys deveining tangerines and scolding his imaginary butler. He has no pets but plans to hold auditions in the near future (Anopheles mosquitoes need not apply).

Made in the USA
Middletown, DE
13 February 2022